GOIN

C000264056

To Mum and Jack Davis —
both of whom encouraged my
writing in the difficult early years

GOING HOME

STORIES

Archie Weller

ALLEN & UNWIN

Cover painting: *Warlugulong* by Clifford Possum Tjapaltjarri,
in part assisted by his brother Tim Lorra Tjapaltjarri,
Anmetjera Tribe,
Acrylic on canvas, 168.5 × 170.5
Aboriginal Arts Board, Australia Council 1981
Art Gallery of New South Wales

First published in 1986
This edition published in 1990
Allen & Unwin Pty Ltd
9 Atchison Street, St Leonards, NSW 2065
Phone: (61 2) 9901 4088
Fax: (61 2) 9906 2218
E-mail: frontdesk@allen-unwin.com.au
Web: http://www.allen-unwin.com.au

National Library of Australia
Cataloguing-in-Publication entry:

Weller, Archie
Going Home
ISBN 0 04 442316 0
I. Title
A823.3

Set in 9/11pt Century Schoolbook by Eurasia Press, Singapore
Printed by Australian Print Group, Maryborough, Victoria

11 12 13 14 15 16 17 18 19 20

CONTENTS

ACKNOWLEDGEMENTS

'GOING Home' was first published in the *Canberra Times*; 'Pension Day' first appeared in *Artlook* magazine; 'Fish & Chips' first appeared in *Paper Children* from Darling Downs Press and 'Herbie' was first published in *Simply Living* 1984.

GOING HOME

I want to go home.
I want to go home.
Oh, Lord, I want to go home.

Charlie Pride moans from a cassette, and his voice slips out of the crack the window makes. Out into the world of magpies' soothing carols, and parrots' cheeky whistles, of descending darkness and spirits.

The man doesn't know that world. His is the world of the sleek new Kingswood that speeds down the never-ending highway.

At last he can walk this earth with pride, as his ancestors did many years before him. He had his first exhibition of paintings a month ago. They sold well, and with the proceeds he bought the car.

The slender **black** hands swing the shiny black wheel around a corner. Blackness forms a unison of power.

For five years he has worked hard and saved and sacrificed. Now, on his twenty-first birthday, he is going home.

New car, new clothes, new life.

He plucks a cigarette from the packet beside him, and lights up.

His movements are elegant and delicate. His hair is well-groomed, and his clothes are clean.

Billy Woodward is coming home in all his might, in his shining armour.

Sixteen years old. Last year at school.

His little brother Carlton and his cousin Rennie Davis, down beside the river, on that last night before he went to the college in Perth, when all three had had a goodbye drink, with their girls beside them.

Frogs croaking into the silent hot air and some animal blundering in the bullrushes on the other side of the gentle river. Moonlight on the ruffled water. Nasal voices whispering and giggling. The clink of beer bottles.

That year at college, with all its schoolwork, and learning, and discipline, and uniformity, he stood out alone in the football carnival.

Black hands grab the ball. Black feet kick the ball. Black hopes go soaring with the ball to the pasty white sky.

No one can stop him now. He forgets about the river of his Dreaming and the people of his blood and the girl in his heart.

The year when he was eighteen, he was picked by a top city team as a rover. This was the year that he played for the state, where he was voted best and fairest on the field.

That was a year to remember.

He never went out to the park at Guildford, so he never saw his people: his dark, silent staring people, his rowdy, brawling, drunk people.

He was white now.

Once, in the middle of the night, one of his uncles had crept around to the house he rented and fallen asleep on the verandah. A dirty pitiful carcase, encased in a black greatcoat that had smelt of stale drink and lonely, violent places. A withered black hand had clutched an almost-empty metho bottle.

In the morning, Billy had shouted at the old man and pushed him down the steps, where he stumbled and fell without pride. The old man had limped out of the creaking gate, not understanding.

The white neighbours, wakened by the noise, had peered out of their windows at the staggering old man stumbling down the street and the glowering youth muttering on the verandah. They had smirked in self-righteous knowledge.

Billy had moved on the next day.

William Jacob Woodward passed fifth year with flying colours. All the teachers were proud of him. He went to the West Australian Institute of Technology to further improve his painting, to gain fame that way as well.

He bought clean, bright clothes and cut off his long hair that all the camp girls had loved.

Billy Woodward was a handsome youth, with the features of his white grandfather and the quietness of his Aboriginal forebears. He stood tall and proud, with the sensitive lips of a dreamer and a faraway look in his serene amber eyes.

He went to the nightclubs regularly and lost his soul in the throbbing, writhing electrical music as the white tribe danced their corroboree to the good life.

He would sit alone at a darkened corner table, or with a painted-up white girl—but mostly alone. He would drink wine and look around the room at all the happy or desperate people.

He was walking home one night from a nightclub when a middle-aged Aboriginal woman stumbled out of a lane.

She grinned up at him like the Gorgon and her hands clutched at his body, like the lights from the nightclub.

'Billy! Ya Billy Woodward, unna?'

'Yes. What of it?' he snapped.

'Ya dunno me? I'm ya Auntie Rose, from down Koodup.'

She cackled then. Ugly, oh, so ugly. Yellow and red eyes and broken teeth and a long, crooked, white scar across her temple. Dirty grey hair all awry.

His people.

His eyes clouded over in revulsion. He shoved her away and walked off quickly.

He remembered her face for many days afterwards whenever he tried to paint a picture. He felt ashamed to be related to a thing like that. He was bitter that she was of his blood.

That was his life: painting pictures and playing football and pretending. But his people knew. They always knew.

In his latest game of football he had a young part-Aboriginal opponent who stared at him the whole game with large, scornful black eyes seeing right through him.

After the game, the boy's family picked him up in an old battered station wagon.

Billy, surrounded by all his white friends, saw them from afar off. He saw the children kicking an old football about with yells and shouts of laughter and two lanky boys slumping against the door yarning to their hero, and a buxom girl leaning out the window and an old couple in the back. The three boys, glancing up, spotted debonair Billy. Their smiles faded for an instant and they speared him with their proud black eyes.

So Billy was going home, because he had been reminded of home (with all its carefree joys) at that last match.

It is raining now. The shafts slant down from the sky, in the glare of the headlights. Night-time, when woodarchis come out to kill, leaving no tracks: as though they are cloud shadows passing over the sun.

Grotesque trees twist in the half-light. Black tortured figures, with shaggy heads and pleading arms. Ancestors crying for remembrance. Voices shriek or whisper in tired chants: tired from the countless warnings that have not been heeded.

They twirl around the man, like the lights of the city he knows. But he cannot understand these trees. They drag him onwards, even when he thinks of turning back and not going on to where he vowed he would never go again.

A shape, immovable and impassive as the tree it is under, steps into the road on the Koodup turnoff.

An Aboriginal man.

Billy slews to a halt, or he will run the man over.

Door opens.

Wind and rain and coloured man get in.

'Ta, mate. It's bloody cold 'ere,' the coloured man grates, then stares quizically at Billy, with sharp black eyes. 'Nyoongah, are ya, mate?'

'Yes.'

The man sniffs noisily, and rubs a sleeve across his nose.

'Well, I'm Darcy Goodrich, any rate, bud.'

He holds out a calloused hand. Yellow-brown, blunt scarred fingers, dirty nails. A lifetime of sorrow is held between the fingers.

Billy takes it limply.

'I'm William Woodward.'

'Yeah?' Fathomless eyes scrutinise him again from behind the scraggly black hair that falls over his face.

'Ya goin' anywheres near Koodup, William?'

'Yes.'

'Goodoh. This is a nice car ya got 'ere. Ya must 'ave plen'y of boya, unna?'

Silence from Billy.

He would rather not have this cold, wet man beside him, reminding him. He keeps his amber eyes on the lines of the road as they flash under his wheels.

White ... white ... white ...

'Ya got a smoke, William?'

'Certainly. Help yourself.'

Black blunt fingers flick open his expensive cigarette case.

'Ya want one too, koordah?'

'Thanks.'

'Ya wouldn't be Teddy Woodward's boy, would ya, William?'

'Yes, that's right. How are Mum and Dad—and everyone?'

Suddenly he has to know all about his family and become lost in their sea of brownness.

Darcy's craggy face flickers at him in surprise, then turns, impassive again, to the rain-streaked window. He puffs on his cigarette quietly.

'What, ya don't know?' he says softly. 'Ya Dad was drinkin' metho. 'E was blind drunk, an' in the 'orrors, ya know? Well, this truck came out of nowhere when 'e was crossin' the road on a night like this. Never seen 'im. Never stopped or nothin'. Ya brother Carl found 'im next day an' there was nothin' no one could do then. That was a couple of years back now.'

Billy would have been nineteen then, at the peak of his football triumph. On one of those bright white nights, when he had celebrated his victories with wine and white women, Billy's father had been wiped off the face of his country—all alone.

He can remember his father as a small gentle man who was the best card cheat in the camp. He could make boats out of duck feathers and he and Carlton and Billy had had races by the muddy side of the waterhole, from where his people had come long ago, in the time of the beginning.

The lights of Koodup grin at him as he swings around a bend. Pinpricks of eyes, like a pack of foxes waiting for the blundering black rabbit.

'Tell ya what, buddy. Stop off at the hotel an' buy a carton of stubbies.'

'All right, Darcy.' Billy smiles and looks closely at the man for the first time. He desperately feels that he needs a friend as he goes back into the open mouth of his previous life. Darcy gives a gap-toothed grin.

'Bet ya can't wait to see ya people again.'

His people: ugly Auntie Rose, the metho-drinking Uncle, his dead forgotten father, his wild brother and cousin. Even this silent man. They are all his people.

He can never escape.

The car creeps in beside the red brick hotel.

The two Nyoongahs scurry through the rain and shadows and into the glare of the small hotel bar.

The barman is a long time coming, although the bar is almost empty. Just a few old cockies and young larrikins, right down the other end. Arrogant grey eyes stare at Billy. No feeling there at all.

'A carton of stubbies, please.'

'Only if you bastards drink it down at the camp. Constable told me you mob are drinking in town and just causing trouble.'

'We'll drink where we bloody like, thanks, mate.'

'Will you, you cheeky bastard?' The barman looks at Billy, in surprise. 'Well then, you're not gettin' nothin' from me. You can piss off, too, before I call the cops. They'll cool you down, you smart black bastard.'

Something hits Billy deep inside with such force that it makes him want to clutch hold of the bar and spew up all his pride.

He is black and the barman is white, and nothing can ever change that.

All the time he had gulped in the wine and joy of the nightclubs and worn neat fashionable clothes and had white women admiring him, played the white man's game with more skill than most of the wadgulas and painted his country in white man colours to be gabbled over by the wadgulas: all this time he has ignored his mumbling, stumbling tribe and thought he was someone better.

Yet when it comes down to it all, he is just a black man.

Darcy sidles up to the fuming barman.

''Scuse me, Mr 'Owett, but William 'ere just come 'ome, see,' he whines like a beaten dog. 'We *will* be drinkin' in the camp, ya know.'

'Just come home, eh? What was he inside for?'

Billy bites his reply back so it stays in his stomach, hard and hurtful as a gallstone.

'Well all right, Darcy. I'll forget about it this time. Just keep your friend out of my hair.'

Good dog, Darcy. Have a bone, Darcy. Or will a carton of stubbies do?

Out into the rain again.

They drive away and turn down a track about a kilometre out of town.

Darcy tears off a bottle top, handing the bottle to Billy. He grins.

'Act stupid, buddy, an' ya go a lo—ong way in this town.'

Billy takes a long draught of the bitter golden liquid. It pours down his throat and into his mind like a shaft of amber sunlight after a gale. He lets his anger subside.

'What ya reckon, Darcy? I'm twenty-one today.'

Darcy thrusts out a hand, beaming.

'Tw'n'y-bloody-one, eh? 'Ow's it feel?"

'No different from yesterday.'

Billy clasps the offered hand firmly.

They laugh and clink bottles together in a toast, just as they reach the camp.

Dark and wet, with a howling wind. Rain beating upon the shapeless humpies. Trees thrash around the circle of the clearing in a violent rhythm of sorrow and anger, like great monsters dancing around a carcase.

Darcy indicates a hut clinging to the edge of the clearing.

'That's where ya mum lives.'

A rickety shape of nailed-down tin and sheets of iron. Two oatbags, sewn together, form a door. Floundering in a sea of tins and rags and parts of toys or cars. Mud everywhere.

Billy pulls up as close to the door as he can get. He had forgotten what his house really looked like.

'Come on, koordah. Come an' see ya ole mum. Ya might be lucky, too, an' catch ya brother.'

Billy can't say anything. He gets slowly out of the car while the dereliction looms up around him.

The rain pricks at him, feeling him over.

He is one of the brotherhood.

A mouth organ's reedy notes slip in and out between the rain. It is at once a profoundly sorrowful yet carefree tune that goes on and on.

Billy's fanfare home.

He follows Darcy, ducking under the bag door. He feels unsure and out of place and terribly alone.

There are six people: two old women, an ancient man, two youths and a young, shy, pregnant woman.

The youth nearest the door glances up with a blank yellowish face, suspicion embedded deep in his black eyes. His long black hair that falls over his shoulders in gentle curls is kept from his face by a red calico headband. Red for the desert sands whence his ancestors came, red for the blood spilt by his ancestors when the white tribe came. Red, the only bright thing in these drab surroundings.

The youth gives a faint smile at Darcy and the beer.

'G'day, Darcy. Siddown 'ere. 'Oo ya mate is?'

"Oo'd ya think, Carl, ya dopy prick? 'E's ya brother come 'ome.'

Carlton stares at Billy incredulously, then his smile widens a little and he stands up, extending a slim hand.

They shake hands and stare deep into each other's faces, smiling. Brown-black and brown-yellow. They let their happiness soak silently into each other.

Then his cousin Rennie, also tall and slender like a young boomer, with bushy red-tinged hair and eager grey eyes, shakes hands. He introduces Billy to his young woman, Phyllis, and reminds him who old China Groves and Florrie Waters (his mother's parents) are.

His mother sits silently at the scarred kitchen table. Her wrinkled brown face has been battered around, and one of her eyes is sightless. The other stares at her son with a bleak pride of her own.

From that womb I came, Billy thinks, like a flower from the ground or a fledgling from the nest. From out of the reserve I flew.

Where is beauty now?

He remembers his mother as a laughing brown woman, with long black hair in plaits, singing soft songs as she cleaned the house or cooked food. Now she is old and stupid in the mourning of her man.

'So ya come back after all. Ya couldn't come back for ya Dad's funeral, but—unna? Ya too good for us mob, I s'pose,' she whispers in a thin voice like the mouth organ before he even says hello, then turns her eyes back into her pain.

'It's my birthday, Mum. I wanted to see everybody. No one told me Dad was dead.'

Carlton looks up at Billy.

'I make out ya twenty-one, Billy.'

'Yes.'

'Well, shit, we just gotta 'ave a party.' Carlton half-smiles. 'We gotta get more drink, but,' he adds.

Carlton and Rennie drive off to town in Billy's car. When they leave, Billy feels unsure and alone. His mother just stares at him. Phyllis keeps her eyes glued on the mound of her womb and the grandparents crow to Darcy, camp talk he cannot understand.

The cousins burst through the door with a carton that Carlton drops on the table, then he turns to his brother. His smooth face holds the look of a small child who is about to show his father something he has achieved. His dark lips twitch as they try to keep from smiling.

''Appy birthday, Billy, ya ole cunt,' Carlton says, and produces a shining gold watch from the ragged pocket of his black jeans.

'It even works, Billy,' grins Rennie from beside his woman, so Darcy and China laugh.

The laughter swirls around the room like dead leaves from a tree.

They drink. They talk. Darcy goes home and the old people go to bed. His mother has not talked to Billy all night. In the morning he will buy her some pretty curtains for the windows and make a proper door and buy her the best dress in the shop.

They chew on the sweet cud of their past. The memories seep through Billy's skin so he isn't William Woodward the talented football player and artist, but Billy the wild, half-naked boy, with his shock of hair and carefree grin and a covey of girls fluttering around his honey body.

Here they are—all three together again, except now young Rennie is almost a father and Carlton has just come from three months' jail. And Billy? He is nowhere.

At last, Carlton yawns and stretches.

'I reckon I'll 'it that bed.' Punches his strong brother gently on the shoulder. 'See ya t'morrow, Billy, ole kid.' He smiles.

Billy camps beside the dying fire. He rolls himself into a bundle of ragged blankets on the floor and stares into the fire. In his mind he can hear his father droning away, telling legends that he half-remembered, and his mother softly singing hymns. Voices and memories and woodsmoke drift around him. He sleeps.

He wakes to the sound of magpies carolling in the still trees. Rolls up off the floor and rubs the sleep from his eyes. Gets up and stacks the blankets in a corner, then creeps out to the door.

Carlton's eyes peep out from the blankets on his bed.

'Where ya goin'?' he whispers.

'Just for a walk.'

'Catch ya up, Billy,' he smiles sleepily. With his headband off, his long hair falls every way.

Billy gives a salutation and ducks outside.

A watery sun struggles up over the hills and reflects in the orange puddles that dot the camp. Broken glass winks white, like the bones of dead animals. Several children play with a drum, rolling it at each other and trying to balance on it. Several young men stand around looking at Billy's car. He nods at them and they nod back. Billy stumbles over to the ablution block: three bent and rusty showers and a toilet each for men and women. Names and slogans are scribbled on every available space. After washing away the staleness of the beer he heads for the waterhole, where memories of his father linger. He wants—a lot—to remember his father.

He squats there, watching the ripples the light rain makes on the serene green surface. The bird calls from the jumble of green-brown-black bush are sharp and clear, like the echoes of spirits calling to him.

He gets up and wanders back to the humpy. Smoke from fires wisps up into the grey sky.

Just as he slouches to the edge of the clearing, a police van noses its way through the mud and water and rubbish. A pale, hard, supercilious face peers out at him. The van stops.

'Hey, you! Come here!'

The people at the fires watch, from the corner of their eyes, as he idles over.

'That your car?'

Billy nods, staring at the heavy, blue-clothed sergeant. The driver growls, 'What's your name, and where'd you get the car?'

'I just told you it's my car. My name's William Jacob Woodward, if it's any business of yours,' Billy flares.

The sergeant's door opens with an ominous crack as he slowly gets out. He glances down at black Billy, who suddenly feels small and naked.

'You any relation to Carlton?'

'If you want to know—'

'I want to know, you black prick. I want to know everything about you.'

'Yeah, like where you were last night when the store was broken into, as soon as you come home causing trouble in the pub,' the driver snarls.

'I wasn't causing trouble, and I wasn't in any robbery. I like the way you come straight down here when there's trouble—'

'If you weren't in the robbery, what's this watch?' the sergeant rumbles triumphantly, and he grabs hold of Billy's hand that has marked so many beautiful marks and painted so many beautiful pictures for the wadgula people. He twists it up behind Billy's back and slams him against the blank blue side of the van. The golden watch dangles between the pink fingers, mocking the stunned man.

'Listen. I was here. You can ask my grandparents or Darcy Goodrich, even,' he moans. But inside he knows it is no good.

'Don't give me that, Woodward. You bastards stick together like flies on a dunny wall,' the driver sneers.

Nothing matters any more. Not the trees, flinging their scraggly arms wide in freedom. Not the peoople around their warm fires. Not the drizzle that drips down the back of his shirt onto his skin. Just this thickset, glowering man and the sleek oiled machine with POLICE stencilled on the sides neatly and indestructibly.

'You mongrel black bastard, I'm going to make you—and your fucking brother—jump. You could have killed old Peters last night,' the huge man hisses dangerously. Then the driver is beside him, glaring from behind his sunglasses.

'You Woodwards are all the same, thieving boongs. If you think you're such a fighter, beating up old men, you can have a go at the sarge here when we get back to the station.'

'Let's get the other one now, Morgan. Mrs Riley said there were two of them.'

He is shoved into the back, with a few jabs to hurry him on his way. Hunches miserably in the jolting iron belly as the van revs over to the humpy. Catches a glimpse of his new Kingswood standing in the filth. Darcy, a frightened Rennie and several others lean against it, watching with lifeless eyes. Billy returns their gaze with the look of a cornered dingo who does not understand how he was trapped yet who knows he is about to die. Catches a glimpse of his brother being pulled from the humpy, sad yet sullen, eyes downcast staring into the mud of his life—mud that no one can ever escape.

He is thrown into the back of the van.

The van starts up with a satisfied roar.

Carlton gives Billy a tired look as though he isn't even there, then gives his strange, faint smile.

'Welcome 'ome, brother,' he mutters.

THE BOXER

THE scruffy tents were littered around the overgrown clearing; gaudy canvas facades. At night, the music blared and the coloured lights fluttered in the deep sky, enticing the townspeople to spend their money. As moths are attracted to a candle and burned to death, so ordinary people who hid from the harsh truths of life were shrivelled into nothing when they tried to penetrate the show people's little world.

This was just a small sideshow company, travelling the circuit of hundreds of country towns; putting up for a night here, two nights there, taking in all the agricultural shows, and once a year the biggest of them all, the Royal Show in Perth.

There was a shooting gallery, a darts competition, a laughing clowns stand, a merry-go-round, drag cars—and the star turn of the small company, the boxers.

It was these three who kept the show going, because there were always big country boys willing to win or have a go at winning the $40 offered for knocking out the champion and plenty of their friends willing to pay to see them try.

Young Jimmy Green was blonde haired and confident, with a cheeky smile playing over his smooth brown face and twinkling black eyes peeping from behind his tangled fringe. He was small and slight and seventeen.

Hector Nikel was slowing down and growing a bit fat. His black hair was going grey and his pugnacious face was wrinkling. Soon he would be finished as a boxer and would fade away. But right now, he still fought wildly, trying to stay on longer.

The last member of the troupe was the one who brought in all the money. He stood supreme and silent, staring out across the crowd, letting the waves of noise wash over him. He even had a show name.

'Come up an' fight Baby Clay ... If you last three rounds, you can earn forty dollars! (Or $60 or $100—Mal varied the amount according to the size of the town.) 'Come up and try yourself.'

Mally's metallic voice would writhe among the crowd of spectators and the tentacles always dragged up a would-be champion.

The name had been Mally's idea, too. The boxer's proper name was Clayton Little, hence Baby Clay.

He would stand, confident in his prime, and wait.

From where he stood, on the shaky, creaky platform outside the tent, he could see the merry-go-round. He liked the merry-go-round, with its tinny music and happy children. It reminded him of life. The horses in a fixed unmoving stance, bright paint hiding the real ugliness underneath, glassy eyes staring ahead, going round and round, yet going nowhere. And always the laughter.

He had never had much reason to laugh as a child on the reserve, with his mostly-out-of-work father and his thin, dried-up, whining mother. Yet laughter had always been a part of their existence and, even now, a smile flitted across his squat, unreadable face as he remembered those early years.

The Littles had ten children. Clayton was the third eldest and the oldest boy, and, as such, the leader of the clan. Under his guidance they would wander through the town, gathering bottles and other discarded valuables. The town dump was a favourite source of supply. It was amazing what toys one could find in a rubbish dump. Once Clayton had found a twisted, tyreless bike, the victim of a smash. With the help of his two brothers he straightened it out and for months they used it to race, bumping down the bare brown hill, followed by the younger children in a hill trolley, also a product of the rubbish dump. Shrieking and laughing, they would all arrive at the bottom of the hill. Sometimes the trolley tipped over, spilling Littles all over the ground like a handful of grain. Then they would all trail up the hill for another go.

Sometimes Clayton and his young clan would press their faces flat against the glass of the town's toyshop and their expressive dark eyes would light up at the glory they beheld. But they knew such treasure was not for them and agreed that the toys they made from scraps were more fun—and free.

As Clayton grew older, he and his friends would wander through the bush around the town. Swarming up tall trees, swinging from branch to branch like ragged little monkeys, playing in the sand quarry by leaping off the top into the soft sand six metres below. They all owned shanghais and were expert shots, taking home parrots, rabbits or wild ducks for the family meal around the open fire.

Jack Little did not believe in drink, and he made sure his family realised its danger, too. So Clayton wasn't there when his two mates robbed the hotel and were caught. They were sent to a reform school to begin the long, cruel, well-worn and inevitable path that most of their people trod. Clayton was sad when Willie Cole and Harry Casey were sent away. He became restless and his mother feared he would do something to join them. So his father bought an old ute, and the family moved off; Jack sullen and grey-haired at the wheel, Reenie and the two babies beside him, and all the others stuck at odd points among the junky furniture piled in the back. The whole family left except Nancy, who was seventeen and intended marrying Wongi Cole when he came out of jail.

That was their style of life for the next few years. Rumbling along on the lumpy back of the rusted-red and white ute, a slow, cantankerous animal travelling the highways, being stared at by people passing, the people who were safe behind the shiny windows of their smooth new cars.

After grade seven, Clayton hadn't had much education. It wasn't his fault, nor his father's; it was just life, having to move every six weeks or so. And, being the eldest son, he began work, helping his dad on the farms they stayed on. But he had learned to read, and enjoyed it.

'Why does that boy waste 'is time readin' them books?' Reenie would want to know, and Jack would reply, 'Aah leave him, honey. 'E's real clever, Clayton. Pity 'e was born a Nyoongah, but. Them wadgulas won't give 'im a chance.'

The Little children enjoyed a carefree, easy life that seemed to consist mainly of playing and sleeping and playing again. At weekends the two younger brothers would help Clayton and his dad pick up roots or rocks, muster sheep, do fencing or any little odd jobs. But they still found time for fun. Out in the paddocks they were always surprising snakes, goannas or rabbits. Then Clayton would show off his prowess with a shanghai, and teach Arley and Lennard how to use it.

Sometimes at night Jack would take out the ute and hunt for a kangaroo or two. They would charge across rolling paddocks, the three older boys shouting with laughter and the sheer joy of living. Then Clayton would bring the bounding form skidding bloodily to earth. Lennard and Arley would leap out of the ute, often while it was still going, and dance around the dead kangaroo like blood-thirsty dogs. Jack would smile briefly, and pat Clayton's thin shoulder.

'Good shootin', kid. You'll git somewhere with that skill.'

His father rarely spoke and hardly ever smiled. But on nights like this he was once again a member of the Wile man people. He was hunting, as his ancestors had done before being shattered and scattered by the white man's lust.

Sometimes he let Clayton drive the precious ute—precious because it was the only valuable item the Littles owned. It had cost all their savings and, more important, it was the only way Jack could move around getting work, so that he could keep his pride and not have to accept handouts and scorn—or pity, which is worse. Clayton understood this honour of being driver, and was proud of being a man in his father's eyes. Although there were some nervous moments when he nearly crashed the ute, he soon became quite skilled. On these occasions the boys were treated to the sight of their father's amazing shooting. He could put a bullet through the head of a leaping kangaroo from the back of the swaying ute almost every time.

Afterwards they would head back home with the loose, slack bodies bouncing in the back. They would skin them and keep what meat they wanted, then feed the rest to the pigs or dogs next day. The two younger boys would burst in, bright and bloody, to tell the family what they had done. Old Jack and thin Clayton would smile quietly and listen. Then perhaps Jack would play his guitar for them and sing before they went to bed.

So the Littles remained a happy, close-knit family. Clayton's second eldest sister peeled off in Katanning and married Michael Hall. Then the family moved off again, leaving her behind.

But they were Aborigines, bound to find trouble sooner or later. Even if they didn't look for it, they were the scapegoats of society, so the police pounced on Jack Little.

Clayton was seventeen then, tall and thin as a young tree being tossed in the winds of uncertainty. He was just reaching tender fingers out to feel life when the three policemen trod brutally upon them.

There had been signs of a thunderstorm. The heaviness of the air and laziness of the flies told the Aborigines this, while a dull grey curtain of cloud kept the sun and sky and spirits out.

Jack had parked the ute under some stringy white gums, their cool, smooth, white trunks marred by scars of grey, with bright green leaves offering shade to their dark, dusty brothers. Long strips of bark hung like torn dresses off the pale, virginal skin.

The youngsters were playing a game with the iron-brown pebbles by the side of the road, laughing and chattering. Arley and Lennard, both teenagers now—believing they were above the standard of baby games—played 'stretch' with an old vegetable knife. This was a game chiefly involving hurling a knife as close to your opponent's foot as possible. Clayton and Jack were burrowing into the engine, fixing it up for the thousandth time. Old Jack might not have been well educated, but when it came to a car engine he could keep it going when most people would have put the wreck on the dump.

Suddenly, Reenie cried out anxiously, 'Jack! Jack! Police comin' here, look!'

The small man looked up uneasily and wiped his oily hands on his faded trousers.

'What them bloody munadj want, well?' he mouthed.

The sleek blue car pulled up with menacing slowness, and the only sound was the crunch of gravel. Then the three policemen got out and looked around. People going past on the highway stared scornfully out the window at yet another boong family being caught. Only once a carload of colourful surfies in a battered old Holden whistled, catcalled and shouted, 'Leave 'em alone, you fuckin' pigs!'

But the police had their victims now, so ignored them. The surfies probably forgot about the incident the next day, anyway. After all, it is common knowledge that if a darky's not on the dole he's in jail, isn't he?

The three policemen circled the now silent camp, studying and looking. One, a thick-set, beefy sergeant with a broom-like black moustache, sauntered over to Jack and Clayton. He deliberately ignored them and looked into the engine.

'Not much of a car we have here, is it? I hope you don't expect to drive it on the road.'

''Ow else you reckon we goin' to get to work? 'Ow you reckon we got 'ere, well?' Clayton said before Jack could answer.

The policeman clicked his tongue and called over his shoulder,

'We've got a right little bugger here, Joe. Got all the answers ready on his hot little lips.'

Then he sauntered around to join the policeman who was rummaging in the back of the ute. Jack hissed angrily at his oldest son.

'You keep your mouth shut, boy. Wanta go to jail, or somphin'? Just let 'em be boss for awhile, then we can go.'

Clayton was surprised and hurt as well. He had thought a lot of his dad. Now the old man was crawling and cringing from these three who, after all, were just men, the same as he and his dad.

'Come here, you! Do you have a licence for this gun?'

Jack shook his head. 'No, I never 'ad time to. We're always movin', see.'

'Right, Joe, unlicensed gun, red sticker on the car. I think we ought to check this whole outfit out.'

'Yeah,' said Joe, staring coldly at Jack with his unblinking, pale eyes. 'Never know what these Abos have collected.'

'What's your name?' the sergeant said to Jack.

'Jack Little.' He murmured and anticipating the question that always followed, 'I only been in trouble when I was a young bloke.'

The third man wandered over to Lennard, Arley and Clayton. He was thin and sallow, with a cynical smile playing about his lips. He seemed a little kinder than the other two, although Clayton sensed danger lurking behind his face.

'Righto, son, let's have your names.'

Lennard gave a cheeky grin.

'My name's Jimmi 'Endrix, look. Shall I play my guitar for you?'

'Very funny son, but if you don't give me your real name now I'll book you,' the thin man snapped.

Clayton didn't even look up from the smoke he was rolling. It was about time these cops got some of their own treatment.

''Is name is Lennard Bracken Little an' that's Arley George, 'is brother. Lennard's fifteen, Arley's thirteen, an' they never bin in trouble before. Anythin' else you wanta know, well?'

'Quite a bundle of information, young one. Now suppose you tell me what you're smoking?'

'Drum, like it says on the packet,' Clayton smiled, full of cheek.

'Let me check it out, shall I?'

The policeman took the packet and thoroughly searched it. Clayton ignored him and lit his cigarette. He gave Lennard a drag, then the brothers' dark eyes swivelled on the policeman again.

'That's all right, son. We never know what young people of today are getting up to.'

'Where am I goin' to get the money to buy dope, eh?"

Clayton could see the man was getting angry and smiled at him again. He would show anyone he wasn't to be pushed around.

The thin man stared at him coldly and silently, then beckoned the boy away from the other two. He almost hissed, so the boy was suddenly scared, sensing he had gone too far.

'What did you say your name was?'

'Clayton Little.' '

'Ever been in trouble with the police?'

'Nuh.'

'Well, let's keep it that way, shall we? What I could have done, you cheeky little smartarse, isn't worth thinking about.'

This last sentence was said so quietly that only Clayton heard it. He was frozen with hate and frustration.

Meanwhile, the other two policemen had thrown the Littles' scanty, ragged belongings all over the dusty ground. Now the sergeant held aloft a wet oatbag containing a cut-up sheep.

'Well, where'd you get this?'

'Mr Wilson gave it to me for work I done,' Jack mumbled.

'We'll ask him when we take you to the station.'

'Hey, what? Why for should I go to jail? I done nothin',' Jack protested. Lennard, the wildest of the Little sons, shouted, 'Leave 'im alone, you shitty ole pigs!'

The thin policeman seized him by the shirt and dragged him over to the sergeant. Clayton was about to spring at him, but Jack yelled, 'Don't you dare try, Clayton. It's orright,' he added softly, seeing the destruction of his family and not being able to do a thing about it.

The cold blonde constable, Joe, feeling a hardness in Lennard's back pocket, pulled out the old blunt vegetable knife.

'What have we here, sarge? A dangerous weapon?'

'Rightio, then. We're taking you two in,' the sergeant said, then jabbed a heavy finger at the sulking Clayton. 'And just be thankful you didn't get included, son. I hate people who annoy the police.'

What had the Littles done to annoy them? Clayton thought. In one hour the Littles had turned from a happy family into a headless snake, twisting and writhing in agony, now that the leader of the family had gone.

Jack and his son, were bundled into the back seat with Joe.

They drove off, small, black and alone, not looking back at their destroyed family.

As soon as they were gone, Clayton savagely kicked a battered brown case. Then he began loading up the ute, ignoring Reenie, who was crying and trying to comfort the young children. He worked in a world of his own, angry and puzzled. Then Arley's timid voice broke through his barrier.

'What we doin', Clayton?'

'We're goin' to go into the reserve there, in town, and find a place to stay, and wait till Dad gets out. Might be we can get some money to pay for bail or a fine or somphin'.'

'You reckon Dad'll go to jail, well?'

Clayton didn't answer that question. He was too upset to think what life would be like without his silent dad.

Suddenly Reenie cried, 'What you think you doin', Clayton? 'Ow you think we goin' to drive, with no one 'avin' a licence?'

'I can drive,' Clayton said over his shoulder, then jumped, when his mother sprang for him and held him against the ute. She was still full of life and could give out a good hiding if she wanted to.

'You listen to me, boy,' she cried as the others gathered around. 'I aren't havin' any more of my kids sent away. They took Dad and young Lennard, but they not takin' you! 'Ow you think we'll live if you go to reform school, Clayton? We goin' to stay here and send Arley to town to git someone to pick us up.'

'What good'll that do?' Clayton flared. 'You ask them kids if any of them wanna go off walkin' in the dark. I'm drivin' us to town and fuck the pigs, I reckon.'

For a moment Reenie stared angrily at her oldest boy, then dropped her eyes and turned away. Her floral cotton dress hung from her thin frame, and a holey, brown cardigan tried to keep out the cold. She looked more like a woman of sixty than forty. A lined, wrinkled, sad old woman, with her eyes red with tears and her hair messed up by the wind; her round, brown face blank and bewildered. Clayton felt sorry for her.

'Clayton, you changed today. I 'ope you goin' to learn to stop that anger, like your dad done, before it's too late,' she said quietly, remembering.

'Yeah, orright. But we just goin' to get wet 'ere. Let's go into town,' Clayton said.

So they set off along the road; Clayton, Reenie, baby Howard, and young Vera crowded in the front. The rest huddled up on the back, getting wet.

The rain drummed with regularity on the rusted cab roof. The trees were being whipped to and fro like feather dusters tickling the dormant grey belly of the sky.

The police were waiting two kilometres off, hidden among some low, bushy shrubs. Arley's twin sister saw them coming up behind and banged on the roof. Arley himself, to prove he was as good a man as Clayton, gave the occupants in the car the up sign and swore. Then the car was pulling up beside Clayton, who had stopped and was now sullenly looking out of the window. His dark, angry eyes watched as the sergeant strode over, confident and supreme.

The big man pushed his face through the window.

'This ute's got a red sticker on it.'

'You oughta know. You put it on, unna?' scowled Clayton, ignoring his mother's hand on his leg. He remained staring into the blue, angry eyes, refusing to be beaten· by this man who had demolished his family.

'Have you got a licence, son?' the sergeant spat.

'Nuh.'

'Then get out, you little bastard!' the policeman suddenly shouted and his face, contorted in rage, scared the thin dark youth. He was pulled out by his patched shirt and pushed against the policeman's car. The door was opened, and he was pushed in next to his father and brother. Jack gave him a sad, dejected look, all life gone out of his round, brown eyes.

'I told you, Clayton. You gone too far, young 'un.'

'Fuckin' pigs,' Clayton mouthed and beside him Joe the policeman looked at him coldly yet triumphantly.

'What did you say, Clayton?'

'Nothin',' and the boy cringed away. Now he was scared as well, and, because of this, he was angrier than ever.

The following day Jack Little was sentenced to nine months for possession of an unlicensed firearm and stealing a sheep, despite his protestation that the carcase had been a gift. Mr Wilson, the supposed donor, had left for a holiday on the coast and an impatient magistrate was not prepared to allow an adjournment. After all, everyone knew Aborigines were liars as well as thieves.

From that day, Clayton changed. The Littles moved out in the same week that Jack went to Fremantle. Their uncle, who lived in the town, drove them to the next town and said he would let Jack know where they were. The lived on the Social Service—or whatever Lennard found. He had become quite a wild youth now and, in the first three months that his father was away, he blundered on down the road of destruction. He fought and drank and stole. Then in the end he knifed a man.

One day, Lennard and Clayton were out in the bush hunting when they came upon their little brother and sister, Darryl and June, crying.

'These two cryin', look. Whaffor you cryin', well?' Clayton squatted down and pulled the slight, small bodies to him. His hard eyes softened and his smile wiped away their tears. He hated to see his family cry, especially these two who only had their happiness and laughter to protect them; they would lose those soon enough as they grew older.

'Mr Douglas shot Flannagan and tole us never to come there no more,' Darryl said.

Clayton stiffened in anger. Old Flannagan was the Littles' hunting dog. No one knew what breed he was—all they knew was that he was as fast as a flick of the fingers and could bring down a kangaroo of any size. Flannagan had been happy and gentle, and loved all the children—especially Darryl and June, whose dog he had been. Besides, Flannagan had been more than a dog to the Littles. How often had he brought down their next meal with his big, bloody, white teeth? Whenever the children had needed comfort, the kind that only silence brings, they would bury their heads in Flannagan's matted, tattered, wiry coat, and their worries would go away. Now Flannagan was dead, murdered by a man who could buy a dozen dogs if he wanted to, who had no understanding of the calamity he had caused the Littles and wouldn't have cared anyway.

That night at tea Lennard was moody and afterwards he disappeared. He came back late at night but wouldn't tell anyone where he had been, not even Arley or Clayton, who shared a room with him.

But the family found out soon enough. The local policeman came down to the reserve, asking for Lennard. With him was a white-faced Mr Douglas. Clayton was reading in the sun, Lennard sitting propped against a tree near him, when the shadows fell upon him. Lennard opened his eyes. His face grew frightened when he saw who was there, then it settled into the blank hostility it had worn since his father had gone to jail.

'Where were you last night?' the policeman fired at him.

'I was 'ere, unna, Clayton?'

'Yeah, we was playin' cards with Arley, just muckin' round,' Clayton agreed.

'I'm afraid you weren't, son. I know this knife is yours.' The policeman held up Lennard's new Bowie knife.

Lennard shrugged and grinned.

'Orright, I done it. You goin' to tell me brother what I did so 'e can tell Mum?'

The night before, Lennard had gone over to the Douglases' farm. He had killed every one of the farmer's dogs, two of which were champions. However, Mr Douglas had been aroused by the noise the dogs made, and caught Lennard just as the boy was leaving. Then Lennard had attacked him with his knife and, after slashing his arm, had run away.

Lennard was sent to Riverbank for two years. Clayton's mind moved even further away from this white society that could allow such injustice, for nothing happened to the murderer of harmless Flannagan.

It was in this year of turmoil that Clayton started boxing. He would buy books on famous boxers and read and read. He got old Harry Bennett, a scarred refugee from a boxing troupe, to teach him. Then every Sunday the kids would set up a ring in the bush and have competitions. That had been fun; dancing with hard, bare feet on the dusty ground, ducking, weaving, and darting out, short sharp punches, like the bite of a snake. With the trees' shadows boxing each other as well, and playing on the boys' supple brown backs.

'Look 'ere! They don't call me Lionel Rose for nothin',' the winner would shout, and laughter would ripple from the crowd of youths. Sometimes one boy would talk like the spruiker at the local show.

''Old it, 'old it, 'old it! Now 'oo we got 'ere, well? 'Oo wants to fight young Clarry Lawson, lightweight champion of Australia, look? Fifty dollars if ya knock 'im out, bugger all if ya don't, 'cept a boot up the bum.'

Clayton filled an old oatbag with sawdust from the mill and hung it on a tree. Then he would pummel it until sweat ran down his back, oblivious of the admiring crowd that stood silently around him. Soon he knew just where to place his punches to get the best effect, when to block or duck, all on that old bag.

Harry Bennett said, 'Ya could go a long way, Clayton, or ya could fail, it's up to you. I seen plenty o' young blokes go down 'cos they give up early. Even though they got promise, look.'

But Clayton hadn't given up. When the next show came along, he was there, amongst the crowd; sizing up the boxers on the bare, narrow stage. He had gone to shows ever since he was a young, skinny, shy little boy. Like every Aboriginal, he was attracted by the noise and colour and bustle. As he grew older, Willy Cole and Harry Casey had taught him how to pick pockets. With the money they had gone on rides or tried out the shooting gallery or the darts.

They had never gone into the boxing tent, however. But this time, a lanky, lithe youth stood alone in the seething crowd, staring at the boxers and guessing their weak points. Then he had advanced, out of the ordinary crowd, onto the platform of truth, and life and reality.

'Well, and what's your name, young 'un?'

'Clayton Little.'

'Ever done any fighting before, Clayton?'

'Aah, you know, just muckin' around down the camp,' Clayton had muttered, feeling shy and unsure.

'Who do you want to fight, Clayton?'

'The bloke in the red shorts,' Clayton said quietly.

'Hang on, son, he's the champion. What about one of these other—'

'No,' Clayton had said decisively. 'I wanna fight the champion.'

The man had tried to persuade him, but Clayton had been insistent. He had seen Arley staring stupidly up at him from the crowd, then run off, slipping in and out between legs. Off to tell their mother. 'Mum, Mum! Clayton's goin' to get killed by th' boxin' champ, look,' and he thought of all the fuss there would be.

From the back of the crowd, Harry Bennett called, 'The young bloke's good, mate. Give 'im a go, and if 'e loses then 'e learns, don't 'e?'

So Clayton had fought the champion. In the first round he rushed and forgot all he had learned. The champion had knocked him down easily, but the boy had risen before the count of ten and in the second round everything became clear. He moved so fast the champion couldn't touch him. Clayton sent a volley of blows about the man's flat stomach, then two sneaky, short jabs to the jaw, and the champion reeled. He finished up with another blow to the jaw and the champion was knocked out. Clayton's mother, who had just burst through the flaps and witnessed her son's success, didn't know whether to cry, laugh or scold.

Clayton earned much praise and $60.

After the show, Mally Price had come down to the dusty reserve. He had spoken of riches, fame and glory, standing amongst the dirt, discarded objects and the little gathering of Aboriginal people.

'Come with me, boy, and I'll make you a real champion no one can beat.'

So he had gone, the second son to be peeled away from the tight-knit family. But he was going to be someone and make everyone respect the Little name. Then there would be no more pushing or bullying of his family he loved so much. Instead, there would be awe and praise and pride for his poor old beaten parents. He kissed his mum, and told Arley to behave himself because he was the man of the family now. Arley was all right, anyway. Wasn't he the quiet one of the family and clever, too? He would look after his mum better than sullen Clayton or wild Lennard or unlucky Jack.

So Clayton had gone off with the show and for eight years had been boxing and beating. For that was life, really—keep on fighting and you come out tops; give up and you are kicked to the canvas and forgotten or just given a black eye. Boxers had come and gone but Baby Clay had stayed on; ever dominant, ever powerful. People would flock to see his thin frame weave and duck and jab out those vicious punches. If an Aboriginal came to try his luck, Clayton would be gentle with him. But, with any white person he fought angrily, remembering the shame of his father and the cruelty dealt out to his brothers, sisters and friends.

When he was young, he had been alone and afraid, shy and silent. But now he was part of the show life's gaudy, canvas body. Now he would grin down on the crowd of upturned mostly white faces, which reminded him of clumps of toadstools or fungus, and enjoy his grandeur.

Whenever he passed the town he visited his mum and dad and grown-up brothers and sisters. Arley was working in a bank up in Perth, Boo had a little son and was pregnant again. Darryl and June were the same as most other teenagers, just discovering life. Clayton would look at Darryl and hope the youth, who still found a joke in everything, would never turn out like him—he who had to use his fists because that was all he could do. Lennard was lost somewhere in the restless bowels of the naked city, probably in trouble again. His mum and dad, going grey and sterile, still lived in the old tin shack he had helped build. Only Howard and Vera kept them company now, playing in the sunny sand outside and sometimes going to school.

The young man would talk and smile and shyly show off his prowess to the reserve youths. Then he would leave his parents some money and return to his impatient pursuit of power.

The barren, well-worn notes of the bell clanged over the lights and illuminated air and was lost in the crowd. The insistent booming of the drum hammered out a song of war.

'Hold it, hold it, hold it! Right! Now, ladies an' gentlemen, we have time for one last fight before we stop for the night. Have we a fighter in the crowd? Let me just tell you about these boys. Over on the left we have young Jimmy Green, only seventeen and out of ten fights he has only lost one. Put up your hand there, Jimmy!'

Up went the boy's thin hand, eagerly showing everyone who he was. He grinned over the faces to a group of giggling Nyoongah girls up the back.

'Then we have Hector Nikel, named after Hector Thompson, or is it the other way around?' Mally got his usual trickle of laughter at this old joke that he made in every town. 'He weighs eleven stone five, and will fight any man in the crowd. If you beat him you win forty dollars; if you knock him out, you win sixty. Put your hand up, Hector, so the boys can see.'

Clayton had heard this speech so many times that it ran automatically through his head. He had seen the same crowd so many times as well, watching, waiting and finally daring. So he looked out over the showground to the whispering darkness of the trees and wished he was home with his parents.

'Finally, we are honoured with the presence of our champion, Baby Clay.' Clayton showed his strong, white teeth in a smile and danced a few steps on the platform, flexing his muscles.

'Now, is anyone here game to take him on for three one-minute rounds? All you have to do is last three minutes and you can earn one hundred dollars! So let's see you up here!'

As usual, there were some hotbloods in the audience. The first to come up was a stocky white boy, with long, tangled, blonde hair, a black ragged shirt, and tattoos up his arms. Clayton guessed he had a girl down there to whom he had probably promised that he would 'beat up one of those boongs'. But Clayton didn't care what they thought, just so long as they came up so he could punch them down. The youth elected to fight Hector and boasted he was the best street fighter in the district. A solid, fat man, with small eyes and greased black hair lumbered up onto the stage. He boomed out that he was a shearer and would take on the champ. Clayton grinned inwardly; there was one in every crowd, and on the whole they were better off wrestling sheep or pulling their axes in their big, knobbly hands.

Then, from the depths of the clamouring horde, there rose a giant, gleaming in the light like a blue mackerel shining in all its splendour in the sun. He was as elegant as one of those awesome fish. He stood well over six feet tall although he was only young. His brown skin was covered with fine, golden hairs, and his muscles bulged beneath the shirt he wore. His deep blue eyes stared out calmly from his smooth brown face.

'I'll fight the bloke in the blue shorts,' he rumbled.

Clayton glanced at Mally, expecting him to say that the fight was unfair. But the hawk-nosed little man took no notice as he called out, urging people to come in while the Aborigines with their victims went below to put on their gloves and to loosen up.

Soon the tent became filled with gaping spectators looking for a bit of blood and excitement, people who could live in a dream for a few false minutes, pointing out how they would have fought the fight when, if the truth were to be known, they would have run at the first clenched fist. So they gaped and cheered and lied and boasted, as do most spectators, for it wasn't *their* blood being spilled. Some people have to drink a lot to become someone while others have to lie, but it's all the same—liquor or lies. They stared at the champion and made comments about him as though he were a prize dog. Clayton sat against the post, serene and solemn, staring into space with his sour, sad brown eyes. He ran his fingers through his short, curly hair then looked anxiously at Jimmy's huge opponent, who was grinning and muttering to some of his pals. Jimmy himself gave Clayton a big smile and waved from across the tent, where he sat with the Aboriginal girls all around him like dark bees around a rare, sweet flower. Clayton smiled faintly in return.

Then Kenny Clench, the fat, bespectacled referee, called Hector and the stocky boy together for the first fight. He warned them, then blew the whistle and the fight began. Hector displayed some of his flagging skills, but the youth was young and fast. Suddenly in the second round, he rabbit-chopped Hector to the ground and sunk a boot in before Kenny got to him. The wild youth swung a blow at Kenny, who ducked and smashed him across the face.

Then Hector got up and pulled the dazed youth to his feet, only to send him sprawling into the shouting assemblage with a terrific haymaker.

Kenny declared Hector the winner, and some of the youth's mates, in the corner, booed and hissed and declared that the referee was unfair. 'One boong hangs around another. They're like bloody flies.'

Then Hector had gone for them as well, clouting one under the ear before they slunk off. That was Hector, moody and glowering, holding a grudge behind his smouldering eyes.

The champion got up then.

'Righto, you two—no dirty fightin'—fight clean and fair; no 'ittin' below the belt or bitin', kickin', so on. Make it a good fight,' Kenny mouthed like a human tape recorder. He had said the same thing so many times before that he scarcely realised he was talking. Words without meaning, yet meant to convey meaning. Like the paintings flapping outside, in the wind; or Mally's mouth flapping outside in the sun. But only the sun and the wind really meant something.

The gross, greasy shearer came swinging blindly at the thin, agile Aboriginal, thinking eagerly of all the beer $100 would win. The air whistled where Clayton's head had been, then the shearer grunted in astonishment as two hard fists found his heavy gut. It was David against Goliath, sheer strength against skill. It was always the same, and always the heavies would topple and smash like empty beer bottles, to be swept into the gutter.

It was the end of round one, and the two moved to their corners for a rest. The shearer was already sweating and unsure. He had depended on an early knockout, but now he would have to last two more rounds.

Clayton hissed to Jimmy, who was winking at the Nyoongah girls. 'Hey, koordah. See that big bastard? You watch 'is left, look. Keep blockin' and you'll be right, brother.'

'Yeah, Clayton,' Jimmy smiled, then the whistle went for the second round.

This round, Clayton didn't waste time. He ducked a few round-house swings, then closed in. Before the shearer could get in a clinch, Clayton sent a punch that cracked on the big, fat man's dirty stubbled jaw. Three more in the same place toppled him over to the canvas, where he stayed for the count. This was Clayton's trademark, and it always worked.

It was Jimmy's fight now and Clayton warned him again.

'You look out, koordah. No muckin' round with *this* bloke.'

'Orright, Uncle Clayton,' the youngster beamed at his joke.

The giant came out fighting and left the boy no hope at all. The white man's first lightning punch wiped Jimmy's smile off his face and sent him tumbling. He stood up gamely though groggily and was knocked down again. Up he sprang, angry and bewildered, almost in tears because of his shame in front of his women. The giant idly brushed him away with a superior smile. It seemed so easily done that the crowd laughed as Jimmy crashed to the canvas and stayed there. Sadly Ken counted ten then went to hold the towering winner's arm up. The man pulled his arm away and held it up himself, ignoring the embarrassed Kenny. He relished the laughter of the mediocre mob. Over against the wall, Clayton's blazing eyes flared.

The people filed out, having seen their violence for the day. They ignored thin Jimmy, who was being supported out the back by his two pals. Yet if he had won they would have been swarming around him, anxious to get a glimpse of the young hero.

Out of the stuffy tent, smelling of man and manmade feelings, Hector and Clayton laid the boy down gently. Lights from the shooting gallery flashed green, blue, red and white on the three.

'Geeze, 'e took a beatin', look. Done 'is nose in, I reckon,' Hector growled, and his heavy, dark face looked more incensed than usual.

'What's bloody Mally playin' at, well? Even a kid could see Jim was no match for the big gorilla. Shit, not even I could beat 'im properly, unna?' Clayton raged.

Then Kenny came out with cold water and a towel. He was expert at fixing up broken wrecks, so went about his job in silence, watched by the boy's only two mates, with faces as blank as the canvas walls that hemmed them in.

They didn't see the little boss until later that night. By then Jimmy had recovered, although his snubbed nose that all the girls thought was so spunky was crooked and red. It was a trophy of defeat he could have done without. They sat inside the caravan they shared, playing cards. They used matchsticks, every stick representing 5c. On these occasions, when they were alone, even sour old Hector would raise a laugh or two. They were happier in their small group, with some of Jimmy's women beside them sometimes, giggling and whispering and laughing at Jimmy Green's antics. The boxers would sit in their dirty caravan, with the pictures of other boxers, footballers and nude women gathered around like the audiences in the boxing tent, grasping any spare wall space they could find. That was their world in the small crowded caravan, private, warm and safe from the white, milling, unfeeling mass outside.

The door flew open and Mally Price burst in unceremoniously. His round, pink head gleamed in the white light and his small eyes swept over the boxers.

Clayton roared, 'Hey, you white prick! What you reckon you doin', makin' Jimmy fight that big cunt today?'

For a moment fear crept into the little man's eyes, then indignation flared blackly across his pale face.

'Never mind about that, Clayton. You just listen here. You can worry about other people's fights when you perfect your own.'

'Hey, what? Where did I go wrong today? Well? You never even come down to watch, so 'ow'd *you* know, you skinny weed?'

The other two stared down at their cards, trying to ignore the argument.

Mally Price stared into the angry black eyes and a look of cunning covered his sallow, yellow face. He hissed through his crooked, brown teeth:

'I've just about had enough of your cheek, Clayton. Now listen, on Saturday night, the bloke who fought Jimmy is going to fight you. He's the champion of the district, so you had better've paid attention to his moves. But it will draw a big crowd all right!'

'You used Jimmy for a punchin' bag, you weak creep. I oughta bust you one,' snarled Clayton.

'When did you last seriously train? When did you get Ken to give you a workout? Let's see your guts, boy.'

The questions hit Clayton more powerfully than any punches. Price knew the young man had not done any proper training for months and was getting slow. Clayton could see that Price almost wished he *would* lose, so he would have to grovel in his own blood and start up the weary, hard ladder all over again.

The little man leapt around the table and began jabbing Clayton in the stomach. The Aboriginal, taken by surprise, had no time to cover up, and backed off.

'Huh,' the man sneered. 'Baby Clay really is a baby.'

He turned and pushed his way to the door. Then he spun around with a triumphant look on his thin, foxy, face.

'Yes, Clayton, boy. You got no time to be rude or cheeky no more. You're just the same as the rest, you see? You *can* be beaten; and if you *are* beaten on Saturday night, you can say goodbye to this tent, because I won't want you. I really have got a team of boxers here, haven't I,' he jeered. 'A skinny little starter-off, who couldn't stop a fly if it wasn't for his mate the ref; an old has-been —'

'I can still box,' Hector growled. 'You oughta be careful what you say, else we might walk out on you.'

'Sure, walk off, Hec. Don't expect to get another job as a boxer, though.' Price dismissed Hector's anger. The old man rubbed a sleeve across his broken, bulbous nose, knowing Price had spoken the truth.

'But I haven't mentioned the prize of my show yet.' His eyes swirled across to the fuming Clayton. 'Our champion—Baby Clay!'

The way he said the name was not a compliment but a mockery. Perhaps it had always been that way. While Clayton had thought he was getting somewhere in life, he had, in reality, been going nowhere. Worse, he had been a puppet in the hands of Price, jerking and smiling and knocking men out. All the time he had thought he was someone—Baby Clay, the champion boxer—and all the people had stared and laughed to see him act the fool. He should have remained Clayton Little, sleeping in the sun under a tree, getting the odd job. He had thought he had found truth but had found only false glory. The boxing tent was an open wound and he was one of the maggots feeding off the poison. One day he would turn into a disgusting fly whom no one liked, not into the beautiful butterfly he had dreamed of becoming. Then he would fly off and live among the rubbish he thought he had left behind him when he became famous.

Price sneered again. 'I want to see you training tomorrow, boy,' he ordered, then went out.

There did not seem much point in playing cards any more, since all the fun had gone out of the evening. Not even Jimmy, who could double up in laughter at the sight of a yawning cat or a dog scratching fleas, made a joke before he went to bed. Hector patted the glum youth on the back.

'Hey, look 'ere, koordah, don't you get worried. Clayton's the one to worry, look. 'E's goin' to fight that big cunt and 'e's *gotta* win.'

Later, Clayton lay sleepless in his creaking bed. He heard Hector snore and the wind playing around the dark caravan. He could hear the noise of the show faintly through the fibreglass walls. Once a young couple came scuffling into the dark secrecy behind the empty boxing tent. They kissed and squeaked and giggled. Over in Jimmy's bed, Clayton heard the youth giggle, too. The boy had already forgotten Mally Price's scathing words—but Clayton hadn't. The soft velvet lips of the night kissed his soul but he would not be quietened. He tossed and turned, finding comfort in the squeaky noises the bed made. Then, at last, he fell into a restless sleep.

The next day huge mountain ranges of clouds towered in the sky, heaving and rolling and creating an ever-changing panorama in shades of turquoise blue and black and faded grey. Clayton squinted up into the sky and was awed by the grandeur of it all. To think that wind and clouds had formed all that beauty and all those colours.

Jimmy was chewing a piece of sourgrass, meditating. He grinned at Clayton through his bruises and suddenly, for an instant, Clayton was reminded of a day in his youth when Lennard had grinned down at him as he had woken up.

'Lookit the champ. 'Oo ya goin' to beat up today?'

'The bastard who laid into you yesterday.'

'Goin' to win today, koordah?'

'Nuh,' Clayton smiled and punched at the boy playfully. The next minute they were both rolling around on the dew-stained grass, clowning like children. Hector gave a faint smile from where he sat in the shade and wished he were young again.

'Don't 'it me, don't 'it me, Mr Champ! I gotta look pretty for all me womans, you know,' Jimmy giggled.

'Any rate, time you got Ken to fix your muscles up. Big fight t'night,' Hector rumbled from the flapping shadows.

Clayton grinned over at the old man. His eyes became quiet and still.

'I thought I might go walkabout, 'Ec. Pick up a woman, 'ave a drink, 'ave some fun, for once.'

'But the fight—'

'Fuck the fight! Clayton snarled. 'Yeah, fuck everybody. I'm goin' to town and that's that.'

He spun around and wandered off, alone, as he always had been.

The showground was dead at that time of the day.

The tinny music from the merry-go-round drifted hand-in-hand with the wind. Pieces of paper were kicked into the air by the wind's idle feet and cartwheeled away. Magpies carolled as they swooped round and round in the sky on their own merry-go-round.

The garishly painted figures of famous boxers on the canvas writhed in the hands of the wind as they sparred. That was all the fighting they would ever do now. Clayton stared into the fixed, bland eyes of his own image and knew in his heart that that was the most he could expect from life. To be pinned forever on Mally's canvas; picked up, painted over, every few years, by Mally's thin fingers—in his power at last.

Clayton shambled away.

The town was only small, mainly a depot for the farmers. A church, a co-op, a few shops and houses, a garage-cum-petrol depot and the hotel.

A few old cars and trucks dozed by the side of the one gravel road as Clayton stumbled over the railway line towards them. He whistled a song and forgot about the show.

'Hey, mister! Hey, mister!'

Around the corner of the hotel slunk four scraggly figures. The oldest child, a boy about twelve years old, cried again, from behind his cigarette, 'Hey, mister, you that boxer, unna?'

'We seen ya last night, any rate, didn't we, Johnny?' piped the other skinny boy. The two girls stood silently, staring shyly at the man.

'Ya give old Bobby Hornton buggeries, unna,' Johnny grinned. "E thought 'e was good, too,' and the boy laughed.

All the children were dressed in patchy clothes too big for them, except for the older girl, whom the mother tried to keep pretty. She was the only one to wear shoes, but they were laceless and cracked and two sizes too big.

'Yeah, man. Me and Micky snuck under the tent and seen ya fight.'

'Pretty good, eh?' Clayton smiled.

'Me and Johnny gonna be boxers one day, unna, Johnny?' little blonde Micky cried, and skipped with the shadows.

Clayton's mind cried, 'No, no, don't become like me. Look at me, look into me. Stay as you are, dancing with the grey dappled shadows.'

Johnny spat, ignoring his brother.

"Ere, koord, 'ave a smoke.'

Clayton accepted one: the first he had smoked for a long time. He drew the blue fumes back deep inside him.

'Eh, mate, ya got a spare twenty cents on ya?' Micky pleaded.

Clayton looked down with vague eyes. He looked at eager Micky and the shy girls and thin Johnny, who was already almost a man. He was once again back home with his brothers and sisters, the leader of his clan.

He dug a hand deep into his pocket and pulled out $20.

'Go and 'ave some fun, you fellahs. Remember Baby Clay give ya that, orright?'

He watched, sadly, as the children swooped and whooped away. Only dust left now. All his children, all his people.

He made his way across the street to the hotel, whose blackened brick walls frowned down at him, daring him to come in.

No one was there. Only the publican, who warned him, 'Now, look, you—I don't want any trouble, all right? Any of your mates comin' 'ere?'

'Just me,' Clayton said sullenly, and moved off to a corner table, out of the way. It was the same wherever he went. He was a hero in the regions of the boxing tent, but once he was free of its stifling hold for even half a day, he was just another darky.

When he returned to the showground, Mally Price was waiting for him.

'All right, Clayton, I warned you. Now you wander off, getting drunk, and not caring about training for this important fight. What's the matter with you? If you beat him tonight he'll want to have another go before the end of the show, and that means more money. Doesn't that mean anything to you?'

The Aboriginal stared down at the twisted little crook quietly and impassively. But he was no longer the king, for the jester had found out his secret.

'Well, watch your guts, Clayton. You go over to Ken and get him to work you over.' Mally strode off, muttering to himself.

Clayton picked up a book and lay reading in the shade. He watched Hector playing two-up by himself and thought of the fight. Six rounds. If the challenger won, he got $200. If he was knocked out, he got nothing. If he lasted all the rounds but lost on points, he got $100.

He stayed there the rest of that afternoon, alone and meditating, undisturbed. The soft dusk drove the harsh reality of the day away. The sun turned the clouds into a rosy pink or bloody red. The colour was darker on the bottom of the cloud layers so it looked as though a giant animal had ripped its claws cruelly across the pulsating belly of the sky, and the blood dripped into the horizon, while night hid the agonizing beauty of the sun's death.

He could hear Mally raving on, behind the canvas walls.

'Come on, don't go past. This is the fight of the show! Your champion and the tent's champion in a six-round fight. The prize

33 /

is two hundred dollars, so come right in and for a few bob see a fight you'll never forget.'

Clayton stared up at the stars. They made him think of people; some in organised groups, others like himself, alone in their own space.

Hector came along and stared down at the young man sadly.

'Geeze, Clayton. You done no trainin' all day, look, and you been drinkin', too. Ya never even got Kenny to give you a massage. 'Ow you think you goin' to win that fight now?'

'Use me fists, Hec,' Clayton smiled, then stood up languidly. 'S'pose I better get ready, unna?'

'It's on in fifteen minutes, big boy. 'Ere, let me give you a rubdown.'

They went into the caravan and Clayton pulled on his maroon silk shorts, crumpled and meaningless now. How often had someone cried out, 'I'll fight the champion, the bloke in the red shorts?' And how many people had he knocked out? Then he stood calmly while the older man pummelled at his body, loosening up the muscles. Hector's hands came to his stomach, where his muscles yielded more—soft and weak. Dark smouldering eyes stared sadly at him.

'You watch your guts, koordah. Keep 'em covered, orright?'

Then he smiled and took out a 20c piece.

'Toss you, Clayton. Double or nothin'.'

The coin spun crazily in the stuffy air, and Clayton said disinterestedly, 'Heads.'

It tinkled to the floor and Hector looked up. 'Tails, koordah.'

Clayton shrugged and took out 40c. Then the door burst open and Mally Price came in.

'What a crowd we've got, Clayton! You'd better give them a good go for their money—and no dirty fighting.'

'Do I ever fight dirty, you white bastard?' Clayton said sullenly, then stood up to go.

Outside, the noise was deafening and sickening. Up on the platform, coloured lights played upon the young champion's dark body. He stood apart from the shouting show, yet he needed the coloured non-conformity to hide in. Without the show he was naked, lost and vulnerable. He stared, immobile and undemonstrative, over the seething people. He looked at the merry-go-round, but its monotony made his head spin like that coin of Hector's so instead he stared up at the stars, so far away from the earth's troubles. They reached out cool hands to take their brother away, but he remained on the rickety stage, being exhibited by a rickety little man in front of all these stupid, gawking people.

'Now, ladies and gentlemen, here is the challenger—David Howard.'

The hulking blonde giant mounted the steps and stood beside the slight Aboriginal, ignoring him.

'Now, let's see your money as you step this way to see the big fight. Jimmy, ring that bell; Hector, go and help Ken sell tickets.'

Jimmy Green rang the bell and the noise went round and round in Clayton's head. Then he had to go below into the packed tent, the tent that bulged with farmers and farm labourers, shearers and townsfolk—all white, so he lost sight of all the stars and trees and grass. He was terribly alone, bounced along by the hubbub of spectators.

Ken sat the young man down and rubbed him over. His dark eyes ran expertly over the champ. He patted Clayton on the back reassuringly.

'Just keep at him, Clayton. The big bastard can't last six rounds.—A minute's a long time, unna?'

'Yeah.' Suddenly Clayton felt weary. He wished it was all over, so he could go away from this throbbing ulcer that was his life.

Mally Price was going to referee this fight himself and grab a mouthful of glory. He held up his hands and the two boxers came together: David Howard wary, with a cynical smile on his big face, Baby Clay, dead inside. Then the whistle blew.

For the first round, both men sparred, checking each other out and trying to find weak spots. Clayton was too slow and was hit a stunning blow to the face, but he came nowhere near the nimble giant. In the second and third rounds he began to fight better, getting in some good punches, which nevertheless failed to make an impression on the white man. Instead, the giant closed in with a right cross to Clayton's forehead, opening up a cut above the eye. Clayton reeled and David Howard attacked his stomach. Clayton tried to cover up, but the white man kept on slogging and slogging, driving him back to the edge of the canvas. Mercifully, the whistle blew and Clayton staggered to his corner, feeling sick.

"Alfway over, Clayton,' Ken hissed. 'Geeze, that's a mean cut you got there, look. Time to bust 'im now, old kid, before 'e gets too cocky.'

Clayton nodded his sweating head and struggled to his feet as the whistle blew. David Howard came out, fresh and fast, brushing aside the slight young man's defence and belting into the soft stomach again. He had discovered the champion's weakness and stuck at it. This time, Clayton gritted his teeth and gave the big man a jarring left to the jaw, followed by a right hook. He closed up and sent a volley of punches raining over the white man's body. He tried to hit the man's solid jaw again, but David Howard kept ducking. At least his stomach was given a reprieve.

In the fifth round, both men were getting tired. The wiry Aboriginal danced and ducked while the white man followed him doggedly, trying to get some good blows in. At the end of the round, Clayton wheezed to Ken and Hector, 'If I don't get him this round, I've lost on points.'

'You'll get 'im, Clayton. That fellah's about done, look,' Hector said.

He nearly did get the huge hulk when they began again. He punched him twice on the jaw and Howard fell to his knees. Then the white man got up and fell into a silent, violent tempo of punching. There was nothing Clayton could do except take it, punch for punch, while the crowd yelled for his blood. He felt sick and shaky, yet refused to fall down. His legs were rubber, and hate and the sour taste of that day's beer welled up in his throat. Now he knew what losing was like and having to lose to such a man in front of such a crowd was the worst of all. He wanted to end it all and fall onto the floor. His head spun round and round like the mad merry-go-round.

He scarcely heard the whistle blow for the end of the fight.

He almost didn't feel Price hold up his limp hand and announce him the winner.

Brash David Howard had been parading around the ring with his hands in the air. Now he looked amazed—as did many other people—at Mally's decision. The crowd began shouting and threatened to tear the tent down. Hector, Jimmy and Ken moved forward, ready for trouble.

'Gentlemen. Gentlemen, please. I think I know more about boxing than anyone here. I've been a referee for twenty-odd years, and a boxer for another twenty. Sure, the challenger was going strong in the first three rounds, but Baby Clay came back in the last three.' Mally Price could talk his way back to life if he wanted to, and his words reassured and quietened the crowd. 'But, just to show what a sport I am and how I appreciate your challenger's courage, I'll add another fifty dollars to the original purse. Now, let's have a round of applause for the Aboriginal—come on!'

There was a half-hearted spattering of clapping then Clayton was let go. He staggered through the hostile white crowd and out into the friendly darkness. He fell to his knees, vomiting blood and pride. He had *not* won that fight, and Price knew he hadn't: everyone knew. The little white man owned him now for saving his reputation. He would never be free again, but go on boxing until Price thought it was time for him to go.

He made up his mind then. He would go away, and live out his destroyed life. All along, he had been no one. Not like Lennard who was feared, or Arley who was respected. They had something concrete to hold on to. All his life, while he had believed he was getting somewhere, he had really been meandering meaninglessly nowhere. Perhaps, one day, his name—and painted picture— would have flapped lifelessly in the laughing wind. That would have been his reward for being Baby Clay.

He packed his battered, dusty, cracked case with his few belongings. At the bottom of the case he came across an old newspaper clipping, yellowed with age. He looked at it curiously. He remembered it now; it was his first mention in a newspaper! 'Baby Clayton defies all". There was a photo of him punching a bag and a bit about his successes. It had been important to him; the first step towards a better life—or false life? He crumpled it into his pocket. He slipped quietly away into the eerie blue night. His shadow danced jerkily on the flat, grassy ground as he walked into the glare of an occasional light; yellow bravado daring the truth to hide its cruel glow. How many mothlike believers smashed themselves against the light of fantasy because they were afraid of the dark of reality outside?

He felt in his coat pocket and pulled out the yellowed paper clipping.

He turned back. Over the trees he could see the glow of the show that had held him for so long. He gave a queer little smile then tore up the clipping and watched the pieces of paper blow away in the wind.

JOHNNY BLUE

No one liked Johnny Blue much. They reckoned he was a larrikin, a rebel and a lout.

But I liked Johnny all the time he was here, because he was the Nyoongah's mate, and mine especially. The only person who ever understood me and the only white bloke to notice me as a human instead of just a hunk of meat who could run fast.

You see, when me old man went to jail, Mum and me moved down the country because now me old man was a crim like, us Maguires had got a bad name. So we moved to Quarranocking.

There wasn't much at Quarra: only a school, a pub, a store, and a few houses settled in the yellow dust like a flock of tired cockatoos. We went and lived down the camp, near the river with the other Nyoongahs, and Mum sent me to school.

All the other kids there, most of them off farms, was older then me, and brainier and bigger too, so, being coloured as well, I got smacked up first day out. That's what the kids down these little towns is like.

There was these two big blokes pushing me around when, out of the shadows where I hadn't seen him stepped this cruel big bloke and says, quiet like,

'Youse buggers let the kid alone and fight me.'

Well, I see the big bloke's got a name about, because the two bullies let go of me like I was a tiger snake, and scooted off. Then the big bloke said, 'What's ya name, skinny ribs?'

So I says back me name, which is Jesse Maguire, then he said, 'Well my name's Johnny Blue, but I got others what people call me, whenever they find sumpin's missin'.' Then he laughed. An' I reckon he sounded like a kookaburra.

Then he tells me to come and sit in the shade and have a fag, so I do. He was me mate from that very day and us two stuck together like feathers on a bird.

He was the only white bloke ever to show any real kindness to me, except perhaps me dad. Most white blokes have always pushed me round until sports days or footie seasons come around, then they lay off and even suck up because I'm a good runner.

But in Quarranocking no one touched me while I was Johnny's mate. Once Eddie Callanan tried to fight me when he reckoned Johnny wasn't around. But he was, and he came in like a cornered boomer. He gave a right that lifted Callanan off his feet, then a haymaker to the Irish kid's belly that laid him stiff as a board.

That was one of the things I admired about me cobber. He could fight like a bunch of wildcats and he was as game as a dozen Ned Kellys.

Like the time he jumped off Dogger's Ledge, sixty feet into the waterhole, just for something to do, or when he fought five chicken kids who reckoned they would have a chance of beating him in a mob. But he laid them flat, every one of them, on his own. Or when he kicked the priest's gate down because the father had abused his mum.

No one else would have touched the priest because most of them was Catholics anyhow. Besides, the priest would go straight to the town cop, who was another mick, if anyone even gave him so much as a dirty look. But this didn't stop Johnny after he come home and found his mum howling.

Johnny really loved his old mum, but he never liked his dad, who was always drunk, fat, dirty and vicious. He was bigger and stronger than Johnny, too, so the kid got hell. Once when he come to school with a real beaut black eye he swore to me he'd get his old man one day.

Johnny was kind to all us Nyoongahs. He was a real good carpenter and made ripper toys for us, like the hill trolley he made for the Innitts, which lasted until Riley Johns smashed it into a rock and nearly brained himself. He was a good carver too and made tons of bonzer carved things for the kids down the river. He made me a horse out of red gum on a wandoo stand. Struth, it looked good—real muritch, you know—all red and shiny and all.

He loved making us kids laugh, though he never laughed much himself. He'd get us up by the dump and dress up as Miss

Raymond, our teacher for maths. He'd stick an old pillow in his shorts, put a wig of mattress stuffing on his head and, speaking in a high voice, 'teach' us maths. By Jeeze he was funny, and he had us rolling around in stitches. Sometimes he'd stick a tin on his head and put on a pair of broken glasses and, with an old piece of piping, creep stealthily among the rubbish acting like the town cop.

He was funny allright, a real good actor, and I felt pretty proud that such a clever bloke was my mate.

And I admired him because he never treated us any different. When we was all laughing and fooling around together at the dump, we was all equal and all mates. And at school or in town, in front of the other white folk, he was just the same. And that's really something. A lot of white folk are friendly if no one's looking, but when there's a crowd around, they don't want to know you if your skin's black.

Johnny Blue never had a girlfriend, but he wasn't queer.

He was handsome enough in a rugged sort of way. His eyes were black like the backs of beetles and were often hidden behind a fringe of his curly black hair that grew thick and long enough to hang over his broad brown shoulders. Sometimes his eyes squinted up with laughter but mostly they were as cold as the middle of a dam in winter, them eyes of Johnny's. His nose was flat and broken like Billy Keith the boxer's, who smacked up the shearers every year in the local show. Except when he was fooling around with us kids, his mouth was always drawn back in a half-snarl, like one of them dingoes in the South Perth zoo. But his teeth was big and white and he had a ripper whistle—better than anyone else.

Another thing about Johnny Blue, he could fight, chuck boondis, spears or boomerangs, spit and run better than anyone, but he never bragged or boasted. He let other kids think they could beat him in everything, except fighting.

Winter came and the dust turned to mud around the town. The kids had mud fights instead of using boondi or conky nuts, and the old man was due out of jail soon.

Johnny and me was sharing a fag under the tank stand when Micky Rooselett came and told me Acky wanted to see me. Acky was our nickname for Mr Ackland, the headmaster. I gave a grin to Johnny and says, 'Silly bugger'll probably cane me for not doing me maths.'

Johnny gave a snarl. There was no love lost between him and

40 /

old Acky, they were always getting into yikes together like a pair of male dingoes fighting over a bitch. Acky didn't like us Nyoongahs either so, since I was the only one in his class, I got the lot, too.

I got into his room and it was dark with only a bit of light shining through the cobwebby, dusty, flyspotted window panes. Acky was in a shirty mood that day, and he grabs me shoulder and yanks it around so me neck fair gets twisted. I could smell the beer on him, so I reckons, 'Look out, Jesse, this bloke's as drunk as Johnny's old man.' I was buggered if I was going to get caned by him in such a temper, 'cos I reckoned he'd half-kill me. I was scared—so I done a silly thing.

I sticks me hand in me pockets and says, 'If you hit me, I'm gonna get my old man onto you when he comes 'ome next week.'

Well, that gets him as wild as a dog in a cat's home. He pulls me about and drags me hands out and tries to lay six across them. The thing is, only one of them hit me hand and, since me fist was clenched, it only hit me knuckles but it still felt like me fingers was cut off.

Another hit me face and fair near took me eye out, and the rest got me around the shoulders, and when he'd finished he chucked me out the door.

Me arm was numb right up to me elbow and the mark on me face starts to hurt like the time Mickey Redgum, a stockman on a station where the old man was working one time, sent his stock-whip across me face accidentally. I had to bite back the tears: it would never do for a Nyoongah to cry in front of our number one enemies, by whom I mean our loving white brothers. But when I got to Johnny I couldn't keep the tears back. He wouldn't tell, and besides he was me mate.

When he saw me hand and face, he up and goes for the head's office before I can say 'struth' and, by the time I can get after him, it's too late. I hear a cry, then Acky yelling out something about ringing up Johnny's dad and Johnny shouting out that he can do what he likes but no one is going to push his little cobber around. Then Acky tells him not to come back to school, and Johnny says he won't come back for a million quid.

So Johnny was expelled. But he didn't care.

That night me life was changed. I aren't no scholar and I don't know any big words, but I guess after that night I was never really a kid any more.

I was lying in me bag and newspaper bed, watching the lightning flash like spears across the black sky. I loved the rain pelting onto the tin roof of our home-made house, though when it came through the cracks in the rusty walls and all the old nailholes in the roof, it wasn't so good.

Suddenly, I hears a thudding on me window that's not hail, so I up and opens it and in hops Johnny, looking like the bunyip coming up out of a muddy creek. I says, surprised like, 'What's up, Johnny mate?'

And he says, in a dull voice, 'I killed me dad and you've gotta help me.'

Now Johnny never lied, and anyhow, what sort of a galah would swim through all that mud to bull to a kid? Not Johnny Blue, I can tell you. So I asks him what he wants me to do and he tells me.

What happened was, after he got home from school after the stoush with Acky, the silly old coot *had* rung up like he said he would. Johnny's dad was angrier than a wounded grizzly and told the boy all sorts of things, like he had to quit fighting, to stop going around with the Nyoongahs, and that he was going to belt Johnny good for being such a fool. Then he pulls off his belt and starts to lay into him, but Johnny's mum steps in. Now old man Blue was in a cruel, wild mood, so he pushes Missus Blue out of the way and lashes her across the face with his belt.

Then Johnny went mad, because, you see, he loved his mum. He grabbed the bread knife and stuck it into his Dad's fat belly. Johnny stuck old man Blue so full of holes he was looking like a sieve, then he took off, because he didn't want to go to jail. So he came to our place, to his only mate—to me.

And he'd worked out a bit of a plan, and it was a pretty smart idea.

He reckoned they'd be looking for him pretty soon, and they'd know, with the river in flood, he couldn't swim over, and the bridge was fifteen miles down. But us Nyoongahs had made a raft out of old four-gallon kerosene drums and bits of wood, and his plan was that we both cross over then I would bring the raft back and tie it up again and hop into bed, and don't know about anything. See, if he just took the raft they'd know straight away that he'd got over. But this way, they'd spend all day tomorrow looking on this side and by then he'd be up in East Perth with his Mum's family, and they'd hide him until maybe he could go over east or something.

Well I got out of bed and into me trousers and we went off down to where the raft was. The river was all white foam, and brown, and green; and rushing and twisting like a giant koodgeeda, dashing itself against rocks and snags. It was the only way Johnny could hide from the fuzz, else I wouldn't have even gone near it, let alone try and cross it. But Johnny was the only bloke I'd have done it for, no sweat.

So we got on and pushed off from the bank with the two poles, then we're off like a flaming rodeo steer, bucking and tossing, pigrooting and rearing. But we was getting across.

We was in the middle when it happened.

I was using the pole to keep the raft off a dirty big boulder, sticking its head above the water like a water spirit. Suddenly the pole broke and the raft rammed full pelt into the rock, smashing into a thousand pieces.

Well, I wouldn't know how many pieces, really. All I know is that there was water instead of wood under me feet, and I was being dragged along like a bleeding racing car driver. I never been so fast in me life.

I couldn't swim, and I reckoned I was done. Not a nice way to croak, thinks I, so I yell for nothing in particular. Then I feel a strong arm under me and Johnny soothing me down. He used his body to protect mine, so it was him that bumped into most of the rocks and snags, but I didn't realise that at the time. Only a horrid roaring in me ears and brain, and being tossed along by the Quarra's green-brown hands.

Then we hit the bank. I felt Johnny give me an almighty push, and that's all I remember, until morning came and there I was lying flat as a tack among the reeds, like a drowned possum.

Johnny was gone and at first I thought he'd got away, but not for long. Actually, they found him before they found me. When morning came and they found me and the raft missing too, they drove down the river and over the bridge and started to come up the other side, and they found his body wrapped around a tree about half a mile down river.

Well that was the end of Johnny Blue, the Abos' mate.

He was kind to us, he fought our battles, he made us laugh and stopped our crying, he made toys for us and shared what little he had in life with us. And for all those things I admired him.

But most of all I admired him because he really *did* treat us as equals, not just people to be kind to.

You see he was a strong swimmer, he could have made it to the opposite bank alone.

I was only a skinny little Nyoongah, a quarter-caste, a nothing. But to him I was a person and an equal and his mate, and he gave his life for me.

SATURDAY NIGHT AND SUNDAY MORNING

T HEY burst into the service station just before closing time.
The leader is tall and stooped, thin and black and very
worried. A faint moustache clings to his upper lip, desperate
to prove he is older than he is.

He cries dramatically, 'Don't nobody move, else I'll shoot ya!'

Mouth very pink in his darkness. As dark as a drooping, dying
flower. His neat, straight, black hair caresses his clean, gay-
flowered shirt, sitting lumpily on his shoulders. Flared jeans and
muddy stockman boots. So different from his shabby dirty companion by the door.

The old man, greasy and white, fat and frightened, hears him.

The tall boy's gun points unerringly at the fat white man, who
stares in shocked silence at the two dancing shadows and the
swinging guns.

'Orright, ole man. Give us ya monies, quick way!' the leader
shouts nervously. He is scared and uncertain of the plan his
younger cousin has suggested only minutes before. 'Next place
we'll 'old up, Elvis,' Perry had grinned from the back seat. Driving
along on the grey ribbon of road, leading them to tomorrow's
life—if they got there.

There is fear as well as anger in the old man's pale eyes so the
boy feels powerful. This is his big chance to become someone. All
his life he has been kicked into the dust of his dirty existence and
made to eat the leftovers. But now he is in control.

Going to be rich and famous.

' 'Urry up, Elvis. Stop clownin' around. Ya want the munadj to come, or what?' hisses the second youngster by the door. He is small and dark, with a deadpan face and blank brown eyes. There is a hardness about him as his lips draw back in a vicious snarl. He caresses his shotgun in knobbly brown hands as his eyes flicker warily around the room. His heavy black mane curls back from his forehead and cascades down over his shoulders.

He huddles into his flapping old greatcoat and sneers at the old man. A silver-painted skull grins from the ragged black T-shirt stretching across his wide chest. Flat brown feet are planted on the dusty floor. No boots for him.

Both youths wear blue denim caps. But Perry's is faded and patched, like his denim trousers.

The only new thing about the boy· is the shotgun.

'Now, don't try nothin' smart, ole man, else Wolf 'ere will blow out ya guts, understand?' Elvis says, confident again.

He knows where he stands now. Just a scared old mechanic here. Useless rusted nuts and bolts. A half-naked car, looking ugly in the garage.

Elvis strides over to the till and wrenches it open.

Perry glides softly over to the cool drink vendor and puts two cans in his coat pockets. Grins slowly at his older cousin who is lifting out handfuls of money. It flashes and tinkles in the naked glare of the yellow, swinging light. He is lucky, for the man hasn't been to the bank all week so all the takings nestle there. A smile lights up gangling Elvis's flat face. A happy gleam shines in his worried eyes, for a brief second.

'Come *on,* fuck ya, Elvis. What, ya growin' the bloody stuff, or somphin'?'

Elvis swings around grinning to join his anxious companion, and it is then that he sees the girl squeezed into a cobwebby space between the two shelves holding odd parts of engines. She is slim and small with long brown hair. Her round blue eyes are full of fear.

Elvis jabs a blunt finger at her. 'She's comin' with us, just so's ya don't tell the p'lice too soon,' and he drags her roughly from her hiding place.

The old man awakens from his stupor.

'Leave her alone, you little black larrikin!'

He grabs a spanner. But the smaller youth is beside him in a second. Smash the shotgun butt across the white-grey face. Slam him down to the floor. Mad eyes alight with a viciousness that shakes his small body.

45 /

'Ya know 'oo I am, old man? Perry bloody Dogler, and I'll fuckin' shoot ya straight out if ya try anythin'.'

Send a foot crashing into the fat man's side while the man stares up, bleeding and groaning on the ground like a rabbit in the grip of a cruel trap.

The whole of the south-west knows about Perry Dogler by now. He has been roaming around the countryside for two months: robbing stores, stealing cars, causing terror. One farmer cornered him in the woolshed, stealing a sheep for food. The angry little Nyoongah stabbed him in the stomach three times. He beat a storekeeper senseless in one of his hold-ups just because the man was too slow in obeyiing instructions. Oh, yes, there is reason to fear Perry Dogler.

Now the youth stands over the shocked man, ready to blow his brains out and take his daughter away, to harm her at his pleasure.

Elvis touches his cousin gently on the shoulder, whispering softly, 'Leave 'im, Wolf. 'E's nothin' to us boys 'ere. We rich, look. Got monies—and a woman.'

Wolf kicks the man again. He turns away and shrugs.

'Yeah. I'll kill the cunt next time. S'pose the demons come too soon, 'e won't never see 'is girl again.' And golden eyes glare down at the silent, beaten man.

Run out of the garage. Leap into the battered old Ford, tattooed in many colours. The boys huddle in their coat of many colours, like Joseph. But none of *them* would be emperors.

The girl is shoved into a corner and hot, musky bodies press beside her. She shakes with fright and her agonised eyes watch as the lonely service station that is her life vanishes into the blackness of the bush. Half an hour ago she was getting ready for the big night out in her isolated life, preparing to go to the disco held in the town every Saturday night and meet her few friends in the warm atmosphere of the hall. That is another world away now.

Only a set of violent black skid marks and a sobbing old man remain to show that the boys have been.

There is another youth. A white boy, the driver. His eyes sweep over the silent girl.

'What yer bring her for, Elvis, yer simple nigger? We'll be in enough trouble without her, too,' the thin driver shouts in a raspy voice, over the noise of the escaping car.

'Shut ya 'ole, Willy. You was too gutless to come in, even,' snarls Perry from where he sulks, still feeling angry. He growls at his cousin, 'What ya stop me for, Elvis, from gettin' that white bastard? 'E'd of killed ya with that spanner, true as God.'

Elvis wraps an arm around Wolf. His face loses its worried look and collapses into its happy-go-lucky lines now they have, once again, successfully pulled off an escapade—with lots of money this time. He grins, 'Cos I'll tell ya why, ya little black wolf. Munadj would 'ave ripped open ya big black lovely 'ole, then. They'd 'ang ya up, down in Central, an' split ya right apart.'

Willy sneers at the road.

'Jesus, don't tell me our hero went berserk *again*. One day yer might shoot *yerself*, with luck.'

Perry stiffens but Elvis's hand pushes him back into the seat, as he asks, ''Ere, koordah, what about them cans ya got?'

So he pulls out two cans and gives one to his lanky cousin lolling happily against the door, the flourbag full of money at his feet.

'Hey, what about me, Perry? Don't I score?' Willy drones nasally.

'Ya want a drink, get it yaself, shithead,' snarls Perry.

''Ere y'are, Willy, share mine,' Elvis says.

He hands over his can. His worried eyes glance into his cousin's hot cruel gaze.

'Fuckin' 'ell, Elvis, ya love that white bloke, or what? Ya give 'im everything,' Perry spits.

'Say I love a man again, Perry, and I'll kill ya, straight out, cousin or no cousin. Try them jokes when *you* been in jail,' Elvis says quietly, then looks out the window.

Perry grunts and glances down at the girl beside him. She looks at him with fearful eyes, then at her feet.

But Elvis is rich. He can't stay angry for long. He grabs Wolf around the shoulders and punches him softly.

They smile a secret smile.

'Hey, look 'ere, Willy, koordah. Us mob are really rich now,' Elvis sparkles.

'Yeah.' Willy grunts unenthusiastically.

The car's insides roll as it lurches around a wet slippery corner. It groans and clanks and bangs like an old man coughing his life out in jerky harsh gasps.

Empty beer bottles and cans and a wine flagon. Old rags and screwed-up cigarette cartons and an old shoe. A bottle of water and a length of hose for stealing petrol. Used-up things from the used-up boys.

Perry finishes his drink and leans across the girl to wind down the window. She cringes away from that muscular arm, pushing herself into the hard, unyielding seat. He stares at her again and a little smile flutters across his solemn lips. But the wind, rushing into the car, wipes it away, and he is hard and cold, like the red Coca-Cola can bouncing across the road. It rolls into the bush. Something else successfully stolen, gone and forgotten.

Willy drives. The cousins laugh and joke about their latest victory. The girl is alone.

She is only about seventeen. She cannot bring herself to look at her laughing dark captors, so she stares unseeing at her purple, crumpled lap. She wonders how her father is. Thinking of him, she lets a tear slip out of her eye and roll down her pale cheek. Catch it with the tip of her tongue and hold the other tears back. Must not let these thieving and vicious people see her cry and so gain satisfaction from their power.

The rain covers the dark world with a soft mist. In front of the probing spotlights, writhing forms of rain men leap in the joy of being free. Tears roll down the window when they look inside at all the trapped, lonely people.

Willy's white, thin, finger flicks on the radio. Tinny music darts madly and loudly around the car's stuffy cold interior.

Willy leers at the girl in the rear vision mirror that is dirty and spotted like his pasty face. There is lust in the cold black depths of eyes set too close together, separated only by a pointed nose. He looks a little like a rat.

Outside in the night, trees, ghostly white or shadowy dark, stamp out a wild dance, throwing their heaving bodies into strange and beautiful shapes. Perhaps imprisoned in each one is an Aboriginal soul, moaning to be let out to float up to the sky. Every one of them is an ancestor of cruel Perry Dogler and laughing Elvis Pinnell. But they do not know these two, who wear white man's clothes and use white man's weapons and dream white man's dreams.

'Hey, Willy. This time tomorrow we'll be out of the state, unna?' Elvis says. 'Soon's we get to Melbourne I'm going to drink a brewery dry, boy, an' that's no lie.' He chuckles softly to himself.

'*I'm* buyin' one big knife; sharp as all buggeries. With a golden 'andle, same way as we seen in that film,' Perry mutters.

His slender fingers gently stroke the cold, gleaming barrel of his gun as he slumps back in the seat and purses his lips in thought.

'Roll us a smoke, Elvis,' Willy grates as he spins the battered vehicle around a corner. Perry is pushed against the girl. She is enveloped in his warmth and muskiness before she tries to move away. The boy's gun, that smashed her father's face open like a watermelon, presses into her soft thigh. Hard and truthful, it reminds the girl of what this boy is. As unfeeling as the shotgun he uses so callously.

'Listen, Willy, we'll buy a whole carton of tailors, now. I'm gunna drown meself in tailors, I reckon. Stuff rollies, unna?' Elvis says as he rolls them all smokes.

Perry's eyes, vacant of all feeling, take in the girl.

'Ya wanna smoke, 'oney?' he asks quietly.

From the front, Willy's dry cackling mingles with the raucous music from the radio. Just a noise to hide the silence from these boys. In silence there is time for thought and these three have no time at all.

'Perry, do yer fancy that woman, do yer? A little bitch for a crazy wolf, eh? Where yer going to set up kennel?'

'Shut ya 'ole, Willy, ya white cunt, or I'll stuff me gun up it,' Wolf yells, and the girl is sickened by his violence.

'As long as it's not ya big black gun.' Elvis says genially, trying to break the tense atmosphere. Perry's face breaks into a strained smile as he quietens down again. He always does when Elvis cracks a joke.

Suddenly Elvis hisses, 'Car comin', Perry,' 'Slide onto the floor,' he growls at the girl, tense and worried but trying to sound tough. But he is not the dangerous one, she knows.

'Sit where yer are an' don't try nothin', woman, else ya guts'll mess up Willy's car an' 'e wouldn't like that at all.'

Perry points his gun at the girl's stomach and she stares in mute horror at his black unfeeling face and golden eyes.

She wonders dimly if she will be dead in the next minute. Everything has to be a dream and she will wake up all right in the morning and go to church.

She looks into Wolf's eyes and thinks she sees a silent plea, asking her not to make him pull the trigger and send noise and pellets bursting through her purple dress.

The car creeps up beside them with a rustling whispering noise. Headlights bathe the wrecked, ragged, interior, and the four bodies with a soft yellow-white light. Some little children wave to her from the back seat. She almost weeps when she thinks how close to safety she is.

The car leaps past. Oily blackness grins grimly in at her again.

"Ow much further till this 'ut, Willy? I forgot where it is,' Elvis asks as he untangles himself from the clinking bottles on the floor. Yet he never will be rid of the empty bottles and discarded rubbish that litter his life.

'Nearly there, Elvis. But there's something wrong with this engine.'

'Yaaaaahh!' spits Perry. 'Just like a bloody wadgula's car. No bloody good at all.'

A kangaroo hops across the road. Such a delicate, exquisitely formed animal. Perfect in all its movements. Surely a queen of the bush.

The girl wishes she was out there with the kangaroo. Two soft bodies fading into the mysterious peace of the lonely bush.

But she is here. Wedged between the boy who almost murdered her father tonight and the car door that can do nothing for her.

She screams silently and bites her lip to stop her tears.

The moon is happy, running and leaping through the clouds, just as the carload of boys is happy, running and leaping through the bush. But the moon lives forever.

Blue smoke from the cigarettes mingle with the music from the radio and Elvis's rolling laughter. All joining together in a close, safe world.

Willy spins off the highway onto a rutted track. It sprawls on the yellow-black sandy soil like a prostitute. Bare and stripped of all her virtues in the form of gracious trees and small, flowering bush plants. Lying back, waiting to be raped by the rain that tears into her, or being felt by sensuous shadows in the warm sunshine.

They arrive at a small stone house, part of which has fallen down. It is hidden in the swirling green mists of the bush, only reached by twisting, dubious paths.

Elvis leaps out of the still moving car and his cousin leaps on top of him. They laugh and shout in the mud and rain. Wrestle like two wiry, sinewy mongrel dogs. That is all they are really— mongrels. They belong to no race, spawned by lust. Elvis's father never saw his son, nor does he want to know that he exists. Even Elvis's name is a dream. A deserted, skinny woman named him after a dashing singer whom she fantasised as his father.

'Hooo-eee! We 'ome and safe forever, look! Easy as winkin', unna, Wolf?' cried Elvis. The two Nyoongahs do a wild dance of joy. Their own corroboree to thank their God for making them rich. Like the trees, they fling their bodies around in gratitude and send their youthful laughter up to the lonely sky so far away.

The moon comes out of hiding to see what there is to laugh about on the ugly earth. She sees it is just two of her disinherited sons glowing, temporarily, in false grandeur. So she hurries back into the cloud bank and the world is black once more.

The cousins cling together, punching each other gently and laughing softly.

'"ow much we get, cousin?' grins Wolf.

'A lot, any rate.'

'Plenty o' fun for us boys now, unna, Elvis?'

'Yeah, Wolf, brother. Ya just watch! Jenny Narlier'll be all over me now I got monies.'

Over by the car, Willy watches impassively as the Nyoongahs celebrate. He gets out of the car and opens the girl's door.

Gentle rain wets her bare legs coldly and wets Willy's long tangled hair.

His thin fingers roll a thin smoke.

She looks up at him then glances warily over at the merry Aborigines.

A match rasps and flares into brief life. The boy flicks it away, dead. Just as he will flick her away when he has finished with her.

'Yer should of gone out tonight, sweetheart. Listen, when Elvis Pinnell and Perry Dogler start something, they never stop.'

Black eyes stare out from his drained face. He is the oldest and cleverest of the three. He is the most dangerous.

When Elvis grabbed her in the store, her dress was torn, laying bare part of one breast. The smooth mound, like the moon, burrows into the cloth. But while the moon provokes meditation, she provokes only lust.

'Yeah. Elvis is not *too* bad—for an Abo. But that mean little Wolf. He's mental, you know. I really would hate to be you tonight, sweetie.'

He looks down at her before she covers her nakedness.

'Of course I'll do me best to protect you.'

She can read neither hate nor compassion upon his pale, pinched, pimply face—just nothing.

'I don't know how I got mixed up with them; money, probably. I've been in trouble before. That's how come I know Elvis. But nothing like this. Listen, Elvis broke outta jail. Now he's wanted everywhere, I reckon, for stealing cars and such. He doesn't care what he does; what's he got to lose? But the Wolf? Well, he murdered a man up in Perth—in cold blood. Jesus, the pigs will kill him when they catch him, then throw the remains in jail for life. There's nothing more dangerous than a dangerous boong on the run, believe me. Yer saw him tonight, trying to get me into a fight. Yer just watch out for them.'

He puts an arm around her and squeezes her. Cold, clumsy fingers slither down her dress and probe at her breasts.

'Just stick close to me, yer unnerstand, sweetheart. We don't want those two around,' he breathes.

It has begun. The girl has been expecting it at any time. Yet she cannot scream or run or plead.

She sits, frozen, and lets the crooked fingers crawl all over her breasts and legs and thighs as he lifts her purple dress off her lap.

Thin white spiders becoming fat from her innocence.

'Hey, look 'ere, Wolf. Willy tryin' to con up our yorga 'ere.'

Willy stands back. The girl is safe for the moment.

She slides away and whimpers to herself. What does it matter, anyway? White boy or black boy, or all three, will rape her soon enough—and maybe even kill her, in this lonely, deserted house.

'What ya reckon, cous? Big 'andsome Willy, or 'oo?' laughs Perry, coming up behind Elvis. He is happy, standing in the chuckling silver rain—his rain—getting wet. Tomorrow he will be in a new life and able to start all over again. Even his eyes sparkle in delight as he clings to Elvis's shoulder and laughs helplessly.

He looks beautiful, as he must have been as a child long ago, before reality strangled the love in his heart and the laughter of his eyes.

Willy explodes as his manliness is shattered by the Nyoongahs' bubbling laughter.

'Yeah, laugh away, yer simple crazy nigger! All yer *can* do is laugh. Yer can't drive cars without smashing them up—and yer mates; that's why I'm here. Yer can't even fight unless you've got a knife or picket or broken bottle, yer gutless wonder.'

Perry's laughter cuts off suddenly. He springs forward, hard and cruel in the headlights of the car and in this second he could kill Willy as easily as he killed his last white man.

'I'll give ya broken bottle, ya white cunt!' he shrieks as his skin goes yellow in rage.

Then Elvis has a tight hold of him, glaring at Willy, who glowers back.

Elvis is rarely angry, but when he is everyone takes notice. He is angry now. 'Settle down, Perry, an' get ya fuckin' temper under control. Geeze, ya always fightin', youse two! What, we 'aven't got enough problems without fightin' goin' on too?' he shouts.

'Ya deaf or what, Elvis? Ya didn't 'ear what that white cunt said about me smashin' the ute, when Johnny and Malcolm was 'urt?' Perry snarls, and he struggles to get free and crush this white boy with his too truthful words.

Thin Willy clenches his fists. For a month the fight has been building up. Now the time is right. He will smash the dark youth to the ground. Squash him under his boot as he would a redback spider.

Perry gives up trying to struggle from the older, stronger boy's grip. He goes limp against Elvis's panting chest and glares viciously into Willy's sneering eyes. Willy gleams triumphantly back at him because he knows he has touched a weak spot in the boy's angry soul.

John and Mal Pinnell were two other cousins in the gang before Willy came. One night, while escaping from the police, Perry spun off the road into a tree. Johnny was badly battered around and Mal (poor gangly big-eyed Mal, who couldn't do anything much, except tell jokes and make people happy) had permanent brain damage.

'Piss off, Willy, and get this car fixed up, orright? We gotta get across the Nullarbor tomorrow, an' that battery's flat an' them tyres too bald,' Elvis says.

'Where's my money, Elvis? I'm not going without my money.'

Elvis's round, worried eyes become wooden. He lets go of Wolf, holding his hands high in the air and staring into Willy's suddenly frightened face with quiet, deadly eyes.

'What, ya don't trust me, Willy? Yer old koordah from Fremantle'?'

Willy senses little Wolf closing up behind him, a piece of rusty pipe in his clenched hand, shaking for vengeance.

'I don't trust yer cousin Elvis, if it comes to that. I don't know him like I know you.'

'Hey, listen, budda, us Nyoongahs stick together, like this.' He crosses his fingers.

'Any rate, ya stupid git, 'ow ya reckon we goin' to get out of 'ere without yaself drivin'? Fly, or what?' Wolf snarls.

'All right.' Willy is resigned, and besides he no longer feels safe with Perry just behind. 'Give us some money in case I can't nick this stuff,' he shrugs.

Evis's fingers dig into the lumpy heavy flourbag. Pull out a pile of crumpled notes.

Willy smiles as he takes the notes.

"Ere y'are, koordah. Oughta do ya for a bit. Buy some beer if ya can, or gabba. We'll 'ave one big party, when ya come back, unna, Wolf?'

He smiles, happy that once more he has made peace in his gang. It was better when there were just the four cousins. All Nyoongahs together, sharing laughter and jokes and admiring girls every day and night.

But Willy is cleverer than all four of them put together. It is *his* plan to go over east, out of Western Australia. Even overseas to New Guinea, or New Zealand. Besides, no one would stop a white boy driving his own car and there would be less chance of them being picked up.

All this time, the slim white girl has been ignored.

Now Wolf steps forward to drag her from the dubious safety of the car so that she, too, is wet and cold. One of them.

'We'll take the woman, but. Just so's ya come back with th' car,' snaps Wolf.

His temper burns behind his sombre eyes while his teeth are a white slash across his dark face. Just like the Milky Way slashing across the sky, showing where his God has trodden in glory, even before white man was thought of. That is how old his people are. Timeless and never dying, like the land they are buried under. Then their bones became the trees and dancing rivers and folding mountains and their souls became the stars. They float to the end of time, yet are the beginning.

Except now his God is the steel and wooden shotgun he points at the girl. He worships it with his whole hating spirit.

Willy slides onto the faded vinyl seat. Takes one last look at the girl before the car coughs into unsteady life in the mournful twilight. It jerks back down the track.

There are just the girl, the Nyoongahs, the night and the rain.

'Orright, 'oney, ya'll be looked after by us two real good, unna, Wolf?' Elvis winks and the Wolf laughs cruelly.

'Please. Don't hurt me,' the girl whispers, speaking for the first time. She gazes beseechingly up into the boy's flat faces.

'Why don't you let me go now?' Just a whisper. Sick with fear.

Suddenly everything that has happened that night descends on her. The robbery, the destruction of her father, and so of herself. He loved her and is all the family she has. To see him battered onto the ground has horrified her.

Now she has experienced the horror of frigid white fingers all over her solitary body, and soon, black ones—like the night creeping coldly over a sunny happy day that will never happen again.

She has tried to be brave but now her courage breaks. It melts, drippping down her face in hot tears.

'Oh, please let me go. You don't want me any more, and I want to go home.' She sobs and stares at the muddy ground. No help there.

A gentle arm steals around her cringing body and soft words are spoken.

'It's goin' to rain harder d'rectly an' ya don't wanna get wet an' die of cold, unna? Any rate ya'd only get lost in the bush, look,' Wolf says. 'Dry ya tears, girl, we aren't goin' to 'urt ya.'

Wet eyes gaze into shadowy eyes, surprised at this sign of gentleness from the boy who has shown only uncontrolled anger up to now.

Elvis has loped up the shaky wooden steps, oblivious of her tears. A light flicks on.

'Electricity an' all!' He grins back at them.

The house is like the two boys. Long dirty strands of lichen and creepers, like hair, falling down its sides. Blank dusty eyes hide everything from everyone.

All around in the grey muddy earth, old rags and pieces of car lie where they have fallen.

No mansion for the outcasts. Only a house that, like their race, is being pulled down into the rubble. Once it was a fine proud house; now it is a mere skeleton of its former beauty.

Two rooms are left standing. The bigger one is where the three runaways live. The smaller room is where they sleep, on three formless beds of grey blankets and rags.

From out of the ragged nests the ragged fledglings are born.

From the bare tin ceiling a dusty fly-spotted eye swings in meticulous arcs, surveying its kingdom and its subjects.

Shapeless armchairs sprawl all over the floor. A sofa slumped against the damp-stained wall vomits out its insides from a dozen different places. A picture of a deep brown surfer on the peak of a huge curling green wave clings desperately to the wall with yellow sticky-taped fingers.

And over all these, the shadows creep out of the corners where the spiders and dead flies are towards the lonely girl. But they scurry back if she or the Wolf turns.

'Siddown somewheres, youse two, an' I'll make a cuppa tea,' says Elvis's hoarse voice.

'No beer, unna, Elvis, cous. Beer makes us wild fellahs.'

'Makes *you* wild, ya little street fighter. Only makes me sleep,' grins Elvis. They cackle together.

"Ow much we get, Elvis?" Wolf asks once again. To drink the sweet essence of glory that is so rare for him.

'Dunno, find out d'rectly,' the big Aboriginal shrugs.

Elvis slouches over to the other side of the room and begins stoking up the old wood stove. He softly sings a pop song, twitching his lithe body in rhythm.

Wolf drops down onto the other end of the sofa so the girl cringes away. She is still unsure and still a prisoner of these two. She is an attractive girl and they are boys with nothing more to lose. So she huddles into the lumpy softness of the sofa.

Her anxious eyes flicker over towards the boy and he is staring at her with his deadpan eyes. Gloomy, like a cemetery. All the bones of his failures are buried under them.

'Don't be scared, 'oney. I told ya we wouldn't 'urt ya. You our passport, look. With you an' Willy sittin' in the front and us two 'idden in the back we got no worries. Munadj wouldn't stop wadgulas—only Nyoongahs, see,' he smiles, to comfort her.

'You beat up my father, a defenceless old man,' she cries, temporarily forgetting her fear. 'The white boy was right. You *are* a dirty fighter.'

Wolf's smile fades. His eyes flare in anger, so the girl is afraid again.

'Willy?' Wolf shouts, while Elvis turns anxiously from the stove. 'Willy fuckin' Jones? Listen, ya simple bitch, Willy Jones got no brains at all! 'E was goin' to rape ya, like that.' Fingers make a circle into which he jabs his thumb. He glares at the girl, who is shocked at his crudity. 'Don't talk to me about Willy Jones, the big white poofter. What, ya didn't see 'im tonight?'

He stands up abruptly.

For a long time he stands there, looking at no one, then turns and snarls at the girl—but without the anger he had for Willy.

'Any rate, ya ole man shoulda used 'is brains. 'E was goin' to kill Elvis, but, with that spanner. What, ya want me to kiss 'im, or shake 'is 'and, or what?'

He moves over to his cousin for comfort and calm. The girl can hear them talking softly, then comes a low gentle chuckle. All is at peace once more.

She can see that these two love each other dearly. Their blood is mixed together and they share the hard knocks, so their troubles do not seem so bad. She understands now why Perry beat her father. She realises how easy it would have been for the angry boy to shoot him. He has already killed once, according to the cynical Willy. So she understands and is almost able to forgive.

But she is still afraid of her strange little captor whose moods are as erratic as the forked lightning spat out of the sky during a thunderstorm—and often just as violent. Not like his cousin, who is older and quieter, happy with his stolen money. There is a restlessness in Perry Dogler's soul that wrenches him left and right, like a rudderless boat in a storm.

The two Nyoongahs come over with stale bread and jam and cups of tea. To her frightened eyes they seem to circle around her with hungry stares. They glide silently, like crows or vultures, she thinks, waiting until she dies with her courage. Then they will fly in and claw out her virginity with thoughtless talons.

"'Ere's our tea then,' Wolf smiles quietly at her.

He hands the girl a cup. She mutters, 'Thank you', and stares deep into the boy's dark face. Suddenly she sees him properly for the first time that night.

Youth, sorrow, uncertainty.

A feeling begins to emerge from her muddled mind; a lessening of her fears.

'Might as well 'ave a feed too, 'oney, cos we won't be stoppin' for breakfast,' Wolf says.

'Across the Nullarbor, eh, Perry? Dunno why *we* never thought of that.'

'We was too busy doin' this 'ere.' Wolf makes seductive love to an imaginary woman as the two laugh.

'Hey, look 'ere, you watch them girls come runnin' when they 'ear us two in town. The big EP and Wolf 'ere. You know what EP stands for? Elephant Piss. Ya know why? Cos that's 'ow my big cous makes love—long and slow, unna, Elvis?' and he smiles at the girl, giving a cheeky wink.

The cousins laugh, hugging each other in happiness. They are so different from the unruly violent pair who held up the store that night. They look so young and cheerful that the girl involuntarily smiles too. A small strained smile, but Wolf sees it. His round eyes widen in feigned surprise and he nudges Elvis.

'Hey Elvis, she can smile. True's God, I nearly died when I seen 'er. No, true, I thought 'er face 'ad cracked in two.'

Then the two roll around on the dirty floor, punching each other, just as they did as little boys on the mission down home, howling with unbounded joy at being alive.

Always laughing with their pink mouths.

The girl stares down into her cup, smiling properly. And she is beautiful.

The rain drives steely grey stakes into the quivering body of the earth that sweats watery mud. Finally it can no longer keep back its agony and its screams thunder across the whole sky. It is heard even above the noise of the deluge drumming down upon the roof. The trees moan for mercy and shake their wet heads wildly as their gleaming bodies squirm. But there is no forgiveness from the black oppressive sky.

The only light is the one globe hanging, dead and dull yellow, in the boys' hideout.

The house stands, stolid and alone. Noah's ark on the sea. Except that only the sinners are saved and only Ham's children survive.

The Universe is so black; so cold; so evil, with all the spinning galaxies hidden by the heaving billowing bile spewed up across the sky.

Amidst all the noise, everything from the rolling growling clouds to the drooping light is waiting tensely for something to happen. For this is just the night for a happening.

'Well, I'm goin' to count our money out, then 'ave a sleep till Willy comes back,' Elvis says. He flops into an old faded armchair with his lumpy bag of power and life and every good thing.

The girl glances furtively towards the Wolf. He is once again staring at her, but this time she looks back at him. Her honest blue-grey eyes sweep over his tortured face and caress his soul, so his eyes flicker away and then back again.

'Why do they call you Wolf?' she asks, hushed and hesitant. But she has nothing to fear, for Wolf welcomes a chance to talk to her.

'Might be 'cos of me name, Dogler. Wolf's like a dog, unna?'

'Willy Jones told me you killed a man,' she whispers.

In the armchair, Elvis watches to see how his cousin will react to this taboo subject.

Slowly, Wolf's dark eyes swivel from the safety of the vacant fireplace into which he had been gazing.

Tugs off his denim cap. Black hair falls about his hurt, yet angry face.

Twists the cap around in his nervous hands as he remembers.

'Willy, eh? Big mouth, little brain, they reckon. 'Course I killed a man. It was easy, too; just like this.' He snaps his fingers. The sound seems louder than the rain, even louder than the thunder.

He gives a savage snarl and crashes his knobbly fist down on the sofa. 'Yeah, fuckin' detective. The simple cunt thought he'd found just another boong to beat up, but I bashed the shits out of 'im with an iron bar. I wisht I'd killed 'is mate too, but I never,' Perry shouts, and the girl is afraid of the hate she has unleashed.

'I give 'im *this,* an' *this,* an' *this!*' he howls and smashes his fist again and again into the worn-out cloth to pummel away the memory of the dead white face.

He leaps up. 'Oh, Jesus bloody *Christ!*'

He stands by himself, shivering like a cornered kangaroo, reliving the episode. When he had been dragged from the noisy joy of the poolroom up into the sinister silent alley, when, pushed against the wall by the man's big hand and goaded by the flat, cruel laughter and mocking voice, he had suddenly gone berserk. He picked up the first thing he found, slammed the iron bar into the surprised detective's face. Across the stomach. Across the head. Across the neck. Heard the triumphant sound of cracking white bones. From the man's head and mouth and nose oozed bubbling, bright red blood—and something else. He left him lying there like a broken egg. Then ran. Ran! Out of the alley. Smashed the bar through the detective's car where the other two waited and escaped in the confusion.

He swings around, and his anger is gone. There is just a cold quiet calm now, like the flat grey sea before a cyclone comes.

'*That's* whaffor they call me the Wolf. But it's a good name, unna, cos it all belongs to me, an' is all I got left.'

He sits down beside her again. She wants to crawl away from this violent youth. Yet when she looks deep into his eyes, she can see another part of him that no one has ever discovered. And when white society finishes throwing spiteful stones into the pond, when he can get away for a little while and let the pool become still, there is a reflection that is a most precious thing.

He looks at her and pushes his hair back from his face. Such fine, black, thick hair.

'What ya reckon, 'oney? Am I dangerous?' he says softly.

'I—I don't—know.'

She wants to say, 'No. No, of course not. You're beautiful.' But that would only be half-true, and people who say half things are only half people. She so much wants to be a whole person with Perry Dogler, the first boy she has ever really known in her lonely life, for he has a power and magic that draw her to him.

'Jesus, Perry, it's cold. I wisht we 'ad a proper fire 'ere. Freeze an

Eskimo's balls off, this weather would,' Elvis mutters from the chair.

He laughs softly at his joke, trying to bring his cousin back to him.

'It'll be good when we get outa 'ere, Wolf. Look 'ere, we'll go to Kellerberrin an' pick up Jenny, then take off over east. Drop the *wadgula* girl off at Ceduna an' be gone, unna.'

'Yeah,' Wolf says uncertainly. He looks at the girl beside him, catching her beseeching stare before she turns away. Into his own deep eyes puzzlement drifts slowly. He studies his brown feet, chewing on his bottom lip, thoughtfully.

'Yeah,' he mutters again.

Then his eyes look up and he smiles at her reassuringly.

'Hey, 'oney, ya wanna listen to some music?'

''E just wants to show ya 'is radio 'e pinched, look,' Elvis grins. 'Keep away from 'im, 'oney, 'e's the biggest thief out, ya know.'

'It's more better than anythin' *you* ever stole, any rate,' Wolf retorts.

'Why steal at all?' the girl wants to know.

Elvis stares at her and giggles nervously. Dark Perry gazes at her. He tries to express something, but cannot. He shrugs his powerful shoulders and gives a half-smile. 'Dunno, really.'

He would like to tell her how once everyone shared everything and no one was poor. How could anyone be poor with the silver songs of birds raining down from the cool leaves, and honeyed flowers for jewels, and diamond-eyed children with hearts of gold? Now their hearts are stone and they are cracking up, with moss dragging them down into gentle destruction. He would like to tell her how the white man stole his soul and filled the empty husk with white man's thoughts and hate instead of the love of his people. He would have told her how they stole him away from his mother when he was only young and adopted him to an ugly white brick mother called a reformatory. There he learned a new type of kinship. He could have told her all these things because she understands him, as no one has done for a long time. She has peered behind the curtain of his eyes and seen his scarred, distorted soul. It is more hurtful and terrible than anything she knows. His pain becomes her pain. She forgets her fright as his desolation swamps over her.

But he doesn't know how to tell her.

'Ya know what, 'oney?' he says. 'I dunno ya name yet. We can't keep on callin' ya '"oney" all the time.'

'It's Melanie.'

'Melanie, unna?'

He rolls the name around between his purple lips. When he speaks her name it is the same as his—a part of him that he can call his own.

'Well, 'ang on, Melanie, an' I'll get me radio. Wake this place up a bit, ya reckon?'

'Yes,' she smiles.

He slouches into the next room and emerges with a large, expensive, brand-new radio and a happy grin.

Turns it on so the music bounces around the room. The spiders cannot catch *this* noise, so there is joy in the icy stale house.

'Come on 'ere an' dance, Melanie,' Wolf beckons.

She comes. Rises out of the chair to become a woman. She feels the power she has as she watches the happy brown youth. She created him from a heap of broken hopes and shattered laughter and rubbish. He is all her own, shaped from her hands and peacefulness. And her friends who, even now, dance to the same old tunes of the Saturday night disco; what would they say to her now? What could they, with their empty lives, tell her now? So she dances with her creation in the small dirty room, watched only by a dubious Elvis as he counts out the money.

They fling their lithe young bodies around the wooden floor in a gentle dance. And Melanie is no longer lonely.

Elvis watches impassively as a smile rises over Perry's round face like the rosy dawn spreading over the yellow morning sky. But this time the harsh sun will not rise to turn the sky white and chase the shadows away. There is just the boy and his moon, floating above him forever.

The song on the radio finishes.

They fall onto the sofa, smiling, then stare into each other's eyes. This time the boy's elusive eyes don't look away. They gaze into her, discovering her, the only real object in the room.

Wolf reaches out an arm.

His fingers gently rub against her smooth cheek where only a while before fearful tears have fallen.

'Funny, unna? Never been with a wadgula woman before. Just to talk to, I mean. Not a real brainy one, same as you, any rate,' he says softly. 'I bet ya been all th' way through school.'

That to him is everything. A person who can read and write and add up and who knows all sorts of things. A person with a good education always gets the best things in life, he has noticed.

61 /

He left school when he was ten, but this doesn't mean he is without education. Give him a pack of cards and he can turn it from fifty-two squares of paper into a living being. Make the cards whirl in a blur between agile brown fingers. The boy's mind becomes the cards' mind. If he wants four aces in a row, he gets four aces in a row. His fingers will mysteriously find any card he wants and he can tell what a card is without turning it over.

Or... try and fight him and his enemies soon find out what he knows about brawling. And many girls have found out what he knows about love.

But ask him to read his newspaper clippings about his and Elvis's exploits, and he can only do so with difficulty. Even though he is almost eighteen years old.

'Yes, I did, Perry. I hope to go to university some day. Why don't you get a job and settle down, Perry? If you gave yourself up, then after a few years you would be set free. Surely it's better than always running and fighting,' Melanie says.

From the dusty armchair Elvis looks up. Anxious eyes always give his face a hurt expression.

He laughs now, uneasily. He hopes his laughter will pull his cousin away from the white girl who is splitting the boy's kinship apart.

'Ya got no problems there, 'oney. Us boys 'ere'll escape, quick-ways. Won't be no one 'oo can touch us then.'

'Just let 'em try, is all!' snarls Wolf, sudden rage gripping him again.

He leaps up from the sofa. Stares out of the window again, at the dark amoeba-like mass, jiggling jimble-jamble. Earth and sky, stark reality and misty fantasy jumbled together to form a storm.

He turns around with his strange smile on his wooden face. Not really a proper smile. Look at the girl and shrug.

Melanie watches him wrestle his anger under control. He wants to be so perfect for the gentle white girl.

He has never really cared much for girls. Painted faces. Shrill, nagging voices. Giggling to annoy him. Crawling all over him, trying like the police to capture him. The police take away his freedom; the girls take away his soul. But his soul is all he has, so he belts the girls and makes them cry.

But this girl is different. He watched her from the side of his eyes, in the store, in the car, in the house. He has seen a girl just becoming a woman. Lonely as he is lonely. Their loneliness joined together would form a friendship. Then perhaps love.

That is what he needs most of all—love. To be able to lie beside her and feel her warm white body pulsating, full of life and kindness. Pumping her serenity into his wild brown body. Then he will have no need for anger any more.

'Ya cold, Melanie? 'Ang on an' I'll get ya a blanket.'

Glide into the bedroom and get his own blanket.

Drape it over her.

Sit down beside the girl who has become his whole life. He only wants Melanie to admire him and not fear him ever again.

'I'm sorry I 'it ya ole dad, Melanie. I truly am.'

He has never said 'sorry' to anyone in his life. No one has said 'sorry' to him, either. The girl understands what an effort it is for him to apologise. She squeezes his shoulder affectionately.

'I understand, Wolf. I believe you.'

'Wanna read some comics, Melanie? Real beaut, some of them are.'

'All right, we'll read some comics,' Melanie smiles.

She gave up reading comics a long time ago. But they are *his* comics. It makes him happy to share the adventures in them with her.

Snuggle up close to him. A dark little shadow speaking words as soft as shadows. Yet what is a shadow when the sun goes down?

'When's Willy comin' back? It must be almost mornin' now. We gotta get away before it gets too light,' Elvis says, but he sadly knows that the girl has trapped his cousin and nothing will be the same.

'Aaah, that stupid white bugger's lost, most likely,' Wolf growls from the chair. But he is quiet and happy. He has no anger in his eyes or in his heart.

Elvis, however, is worried about his cousin. He wishes he has not taken the girl hostage now. She has been nothing but trouble. Starting the fight with Willy that could have ended in disaster, then making Perry angry all the time. And now stealing Perry away from him. Elvis wishes there was just him and Wolf—as it always has been.

Softly, disconsolately, hum a pop song. The negroes all have their spirituals and blues to keep them united. Elvis only has a white man's canned song to sing.

He finishes his slow counting.

'Jesus, Perry! 'ow much ya reckon we got?'

'Dunno,' grins the Wolf.

'Nineteen 'undred dollars. Nineteen fuckin' 'undred, eh?' Elvis breathes.

'Hooooooo—eeeeeee!!' shouts Perry.

Leaps onto his laughing cousin. They wrestle on the floor, then jump up and waltz, howling with mirth, around the dusty creaking floor. Dance for joy, while the window ledges of dead flies applaud.

The girl watches.

The boys stop in the middle of the room, gasping for breath. They cling to each other and smile into each other's faces.

'We won't *never* 'ave to steal after this, unna, Wolf? Watch all them boys lookin' up at us from now on. We bloody real crims now, eh, Perry? We the main actors, or 'oo? ""Oo's this comin' down the street? Oh, it's them two number one crims, EP and the Wolf." That's what they'll say.' Elvis laughs again.

The girl realises for the first time that Elvis has a gold earring in his ear. It is shaped like a bell, but no one can hear the music. It is as inconspicuous as its owner.

'Yeah, first thing I'm goin' to get is a telescopic rifle,' and the Wolf smiles a secret smile.

To own a gun is the last step in his initiation. *Then* he can own the world. And even when at last he dies, his name will live on like the trees and the rocks and the stars. *That* will be his soul, but it will be more famous than *any* of his ancestors.

'Siddown, an' I'll make some tea to celebrate. Wisht Willy was 'ere with our beer, so's we could 'ave one proper party,' Elvis says.

Perry sits down and stares dreamily into space.

'With a proper gun, won't be no one game enough to cheek me then.'

He turns to the girl in the torn dress, with the red ribbon drooping in her mussed-up hair.

'Never shoot you, but. Ya me friend, unna?' he says, gently.

'Yes, I'm your friend,' she returns.

Suddenly he twines his slender dark fingers between her pale ones. *His* fingers are long, his palms yellow tinged and his skin is such a deep, pure black. A rare black flower for her to nurture and grow. Her fingers warm the cold skin and feel his hot life pulsating beneath. Their life, now that she has found his soul and he has given it to her.

He pulls her to him and they kiss. Dark fingers tangle in her hair. Dark lips devour her pink tongue. To the girl, it is as though she is floating down a calm brown river. To the boy, it is like drinking sweet love milk, white and cool. To Elvis it is a moment of anguish and renewed resentment of the alien influence he feels the girl to be.

Three people in the almost dark, who cannot decide whether it wants to be Saturday night or Sunday morning.

In the middle of their kiss they hear the car.

'Willy's come at last!' cries Elvis.

'An' about bloody time, too,' sneers Wolf.

Headlights sweep over the trees and dash against the wet window. Wolf uncoils himself from the sofa.

He slouches towards the door and opens it. The cold, ragged wind sweeps in.

' 'Bout bloody time too, Willy, ya stupid great white tit,' he shouts.

Then he goes tense.

Slams the door. Spins around. Grabs his shotgun, screaming, 'The fuckin' white cunt's brought back the munadj!'

Elvis's mouth falls open and he turns a dirty grey as he sags against the wall.

'No,' he whispers, 'Not Willy. 'E's me mate.'

A megaphoned, eerie voice shouts out of the rain and swirling dawn.

'Come out of there, Dogler. Send the girl out first, then come out with your hands up. The place is surrounded.'

Wolf's face crumples into insane hate. Eyes turn yellow with rage, swimming in red. Saliva foams from his snarling mouth as he goes mad.

'I'll kill 'em,' he hisses. Then shouts, 'I'll bloody kill 'em, the white, jerk-off bastards!'

Wrench open the door.

Fire into the night.

Like an echo, three shots answer him.

He is flung back into the room, to lie, twitching and silent, as pain and death claw over him. The grinning silver skull on his shirt is shattered and red with blood. His hair, spilling over his dark tortured face, is specked with blood. From his pink open mouth dribbles a trickle of life and hope and red, red, blood; his soul pouring out onto the cold floor. His eyes that held hate and sorrow, laughter and briefly love, are dead—just as he has always been.

The girl screams. Elvis can only stare, stupefied.

Three policemen burst through the door and knock him flying. Twist his arm around his back and push him to his knees.

Big, clumsy men, dressed in navy blue, like the night. They bring the smell of mud and rain with them. They do not belong here in this house. Following the policemen comes the girl's father.

Everyone crowds into the room while love and laughter leap out of the open door and disappear forever.

The two constables gather around the still body, murmuring the last rites for the lost youth. No priest for him, just his nation's keepers.

'Jesus, he almost hit me. Not very old, is he? Shouldn't have pulled the trigger. Well, he was dangerous, anyway.'

Dismiss him. That is that. Another body for the morgue and another day's work done.

The sergeant heaves Elvis to his feet. He smiles triumphantly into the boy's wet, frightened eyes.

'Some pal you've got, Pinnell. Willy Jones got sick of your smell. So he dobbed you in for the reward. Too bad about your cousin, but he asked for it, the crazy black bastard.'

Elvis Pinnell looks so different to the stunned girl. His cocky grin has gone. He has no laughter, no money, no cousin, no chance of seeing his distant girlfriend now.

A nobody man with no place to go.

Elvis does not look at the girl, only at his dead cousin. He buries his face in Wolf's bloody shirt, so it becomes bloody too. His long body shakes with dry sobs as he hugs the lifeless piece of meat that was his cousin and friend. They lead him stumbling outside, while his tears wash his cousin's blood away.

The girl's father hugs her to him.

'Don't cry, Melanie. It's all right now. Did those ruffians hurt you?'

He will never understand that she is crying over Perry's death. At that moment she hates her father with her whole heart.

He leads her away, past the blanketed body of the boy, soon to be forgotten with all his unrealisable dreams.

The sun is just beginning to rise. Soft pinkness over the pale yellow sky. Birds sing from the exhausted trees. Golden songs to spear the morning with love.

It will be a magnificent sunrise, as all sunrises are. And, since no two mornings are the same, a unique sunrise. But she has no liking for beauty now. All her beauty lies, shattered, behind her.

Sunday morning, a time to pray. Saturday night, a time to sin. No one remembers the millions of Saturday nights and Sunday mornings. No one remembers anything at all.

The rain pierces the men, the dejected boy and the girl, with grey leaden arrows. It pierces the girl's dreams and leaves her dreadfully alone.

PENSION DAY

ALL day the old black man sits, away from everyone else. He wears the same old black coat every day. Once it had silver buttons and a silk collar and was worn in the best society—with speeches, silver and champagne.

Now it has no buttons and sits upon the hunched back of the leader of the redback people. The people who hug the dark corners and scuttle hideously from rusted hiding place to rusted hiding place. Away from the pale blue eyes that are like the sun, burning everything away so all is stark and straight and true, and there are no cool secrets left.

No one wants to know any of the secrets, anyway.

He sits in the park, the old man, like one of the war cannons that guard the perimeter and stick their long green noses out threateningly at the cars that swish by, not even knowing they are there. Today's children leap and laugh over silent steel to further demolish yesterday's pride.

There is no room for yesterday's people.

He is a Wongi from out near Laverton, and he can hardly speak English. When he first came to Perth many years ago, he huddled in the back of the police Land Rover and moaned in terror as the ground swept away before him and trees and rocks and mountains and towns and his whole universe disappeared in a blur. Had it not been for the handcuffs around his great wrists, he would have leaped out the door and ended it all then.

The white men had torn him away from his red land's breast for a crime he could not understand.

A life for a life. That was how the law had worked since before everything. The law was the law.

Yet the Land Rover lurched out to the camp and the three policemen had sprung upon him, taking him by surprise as he sat, singing softly, by his campfire.

The dogs had barked, the children screamed, his young girl-woman, already full with a child-spirit, cried, and he had fought with all his strength.

The old men had watched with silent, all-knowing eyes as he was overpowered and two policemen held him while the sergeant clipped on the handcuffs triumphantly.

He took one last look at his night-blackened land and the black shut faces in the red firelight. Rubbed red dust over his horny feet before being pushed gently into the hard, hot Land Rover. A tear slid out of his frightened, puzzled eyes before he closed his mind and hunched into himself.

He was only about eighteen then and although he wore a pair of scruffed grubby moleskins (and an army slouch hat he kept for special occasions) he had only seen white men six times in his whole life.

So that was that.

When he came out of jail seven years later, he was still strong and proud. No one had been able to touch him in there. He had worked all day and at night he had willed himself out over the walls back to his country.

Red dust and thin mulga bushes and glittering seas of broken glass from the miners' camps. Yellow-sided holes many metres deep. Black open mouths gulping in the hot air and holding white man secrets and dreams.

Just the place to hide a body snapped in two by powerful hands.

He could never go home again. He would have been killed out at the gabbling, dusty camp, if not by the relatives of his victim, certainly by the new husband to whom the elders would long ago have given his woman.

So he had no country. He had no home. He decided to learn more about the white man's ways that had so awed him.

But what could *he* do? A young man with big muscles, a quick temper, not much knowledge of English—and a black skin? After a few fights in a few country towns, he settled down, working for a produce store deep down south and doing some shearing on the side.

He loved that town. His boss was a good man who protected the angry giant from the taunts that sometimes whipped through the air. It was his boss, too, who found him a good half-caste girl from the nearby mission.

They called him 'Jackie Snow' and the name stuck: Snowy Jackson, the straight-shouldered, black colossus among his brown, sharper brethren. There was no love lost between the full-blood and the half-castes. They jeered at the way he worked so hard and refused to share his money around. But they were afraid of his physical and spiritual powers. For wasn't he one from the shimmering emptiness of the desert, a man who came with laws and secrets the brown staggering people had lost or only half-remembered?

He did not tell them that he had lost those, too.

At the produce store he was always cheerful and he kept out of trouble. His educated half-caste wife taught him a little more English, but he never learned how to read or write.

They got their citizenship rights and a little house, just off the track to the town's reserve. Every evening, especially in winter, his wife read the Bible and he stared into the searing heart of the fire with thoughtful, quiet eyes, and tried to remember before.

But this was his life now.

At shearing time they put him on the yard work. He loved to stride through the greasy, grey sea, shouting in his own language and clapping his huge hands so they sounded like the echoes from the thunder in the sky above. He would fling his head back and flare his nostrils like a wild black horse, and the sheep would pour into the darkened tin woolshed with a furious clicketty-clatter on the wooden grating floor. He felt like a king then, a leader of the people.

The other shearers respected Snowy Jackson for his size and strength. Who else could lift a bleating struggling sheep up above his head and still flash the huge white grin he wore (like his slouch hat for special occasions).

But he used to grow angry sometimes, and picking the stupid sheep up by their shaggy necks he would hurl them into the yard, sometimes killing them.

Then they put him on the shearing team alongside all the white men. He was at last one of them, and he took great pride in his new position. After he got over his first hesitation at the whining shears, he became quite skilled at peeling off the curly wool so it lay, wrinkled and ready, around his feet. Each bald, skinny, white sheep that he pushed down the chute was a new piece of juicy fruit for him to chew on, until his belly was full of white man respect.

Every night when he went home, he would try to explain his joyful day to his little wife, just as once, as a successful hunter, he had recounted his stories to his young woman way away up in the red, swirling Dreaming. But he could not tell the half-caste anything and, after a while, he would stop his broken, happy mumbling and stare into his fire. He would smile softly at things that had happened that day, while the stories came out of his eyes and nestled amongst the coals so he could see them again the next night.

Dreams, dreams.

One year, his young wife died giving birth to her fourth child.

All her relatives came down for the funeral. They sat around talking and remembering, and catching up on the news. Then they all got back in their old cars and trucks and left.

He just has the rain now, turning the sky grey and the world cold. He used to love the rain. He could stand for hours in the soft drizzle and let all the secrets from the heavy black clouds soak into his soul. But he hated the rain, that day, for it was there and his little quiet wife was dead.

He just has the rain—and his tears. All his secrets and the love the half-caste girl had taught him, dripping from his puzzled eyes.

When he was alone, he became roaring drunk and smashed up his house that he and the girl had been so proud of then went and started a brawl amongst the Nyoongah people.

He might have been getting older, but his huge angry fists put three of the men in hospital. He was put in jail.

The next morning the boss came and got him out. As he walked down the muddy street in the sultry sun, everyone stared at him, shocked or disgusted at the damage he had done. He followed his boss's footsteps like a huge dog.

So he lost even his pride and gave up.

He worked at the store for a few more years. Every time he thought of his woman he went out and got drunk. He lived in a little humpy in the bush, where no one could find him.

The Community Welfare took away his children one day whilst he was out hunting. All except the baby, whom Mrs Haynes the boss's wife was looking after.

He never saw his children again.

He did not shear any more, as he was getting too old. Beer fat lay over him, like bird dung greening a famous statue.

Just as he had been shearing beside the white men and had

gained a type of pride, now he could drink beside white men with another sort of pride. They were all brothers now—getting drunk together.

He left to wander.

He has memories of countless tin-and-asbestos towns with cold white people and whining brown people. He has memories of crowded hotels and fights, and falling asleep, drunk in the slimy gutter or under a tree. He tried his hand at boxing on a show-ground troupe. But soon he fell down, forever. His body was left to moulder where it lay, while the laughter bored into him like busy constant ants.

Boys drag lazily past, going nowhere. Cigarettes hang from their thin lips, phallus-like, to prove they are men.

The old man would like to beg for a smoke, but the wine he has drunk today thickens his tongue. All that comes out of his mouth is a thin dribble of saliva that hangs off his scraggly grey beard.

Devils dance out of the boys' black eyes. They swagger, shout and laugh loudly. The words and laughter are caught by the fingers of the Moreton Bay fig trees. Later, they will be dropped to rot away with the stinking, sticky fruit. But the boys don't know that.

Two peel away from the sly dark group and squat down beside him.

'G'day, ya silly ole black bastard. Gettin' stuck into th' gabba at this time a day? Hey, ya wanna tell us 'ow ya was the state boxer, ole man?'

'Look at the metho 'e's got 'ere, Jimmy.'

'Unna? 'E got no sense.'

'Look out, Snowman! Featherfoot comin' your way, ya ole murderer.'

'Jesus, don't 'e stink, but?'

They laugh.

He smiles, uncomprehending, and nods his head. He knows they are laughing at him. Once he would have leaped to his feet and pulverised the whole group. That was a long time ago, though. He cannot remember.

They steal $20 from him with quick black fingers. They always do, every pension day. Where they had been afraid of his powers before, now they laugh and steal from him. He has no people to look after him. Only himself.

He sits under the tree, surrounded by empty wine bottles. He staggers over to the tap and bumps into two young girls, who shriek and squeal with mirth at him.

'The Snowman's drunk!' they shriek.

Once, they would have had to respect and admire him, as he told them about the ways and laws of their tribe.

Once.

Now they have no tribe, and he has no ways.

He half-fills a bottle with water and pours the last of his methylated spirits into it. He sits and drinks, lonely.

He watches as the groups gather in circles. People wander from one group to another or stagger across to the hotel, waiting on the corner. The tribe goes walkabout. They stumble over to the brick toilets, as lonely as he is. They clutch onto the tight circles and pass the drink and words around.

Drink gets hot, words get hot in the cold wind.

The boys strip off their shirts and fight out their quarrels, while the women join them or egg them on.

The people play jackpot or two-up or poker. Some grow rich, some grow poor; almost everyone grows drunk.

Everyone goes home, to wherever home is.

He stays.

The sky gets darker and more oppressive. Then it rains.

First there are the whipcracks rattling across the sky, rolling and growling like puppies playing in the fleeciness of the clouds. The lightning leaps and bounces like children; here, there and gone. The rain starts off fat and slow but becomes faster and leaner.

He just sits there, finishing off his metho and wishing he had a smoke. He suddenly vomits up all his pension day money. All over his coat and face and trousers.

Time to sleep.

The old Aboriginal lies underneath his tree that cannot help him, for it, too, is old and sparse of gentle green leaf. The tree and the man get wet; neither cares, though.

So cold. The rain runs in streaks down his face and body. It washes the vomit off him, with soft hands. The pattering of the rain is interrupted only occasionally by short harsh coughs.

In the early hours of the morning, the cruising police van that, like the gardener, is searching for a few weeds to pull up by the roots and throw in the bin, finds him.

His rain has taken him away from his useless, used-up life. Perhaps back to the Dreamtime he understood.

No one knew the old Wongi was dead until the next pension day.

ONE HOT NIGHT

THE train smashes away the hot, still, trembling body of the night and leaves it crumpled upon the hard rocks beside the sleepers. Black and bloody and flecked with light from the dying sun and the prosperous shops or the comfortable middle-class houses or the rushing vehicles on the highway or the arrogant street lights that guard the highway. The train charges noisily onwards, high up on its embankment. It will never reach the stars, but it is too proud for the common, crowded highways. It floats on a lonely uniform course between reality and dreams.

The train rattles and rocks in rhythm to its music. Inside its throbbing belly the black boy who huddles in the very corner is rocked too.

When he got on at Guildford, the three sailors with their painted giggling girl and the old, faded, white couple in their faded best eyed him furtively and coldly.

Just a skinny, scrawny part-Aboriginal boy, with a ragged mop of tangled blue-black hair on top of his hatchet face and a black beard and moustache surrounding it and his thin lips. He holds up his head in pride. His royal black eyes flick scornfully around the carriage for a brief second before he drifts up to the other end and throws himself into the corner to stare out of the window, ignoring the world.

He had a fight with his woman and punched her to the ground. She stared up at him reproachfully with her large sad eyes. Faces going red and orange, then black again in the flickering firelight. People stood silent. Blood ran out of his woman's mouth.

'Don't go to town, Elgin. Ya know the munadj's on the lookout for ya. Specially that big Fathers. Ya wanna go back to jail or what? Ya don't even think of me, unna? I may as well be dead, as much as you care, any rate.'

'Block up, Maydene. I'll do what I wanna do, see? I'm me own boss now.'

'I was better off when you was inside!' the girl cried and he backhanded her across the face and kicked her in the stomach so she gave a queer half-cry.

He knelt down beside her in remorse, and stroked her long black hair back from her bruised face before leaving abruptly. He went away from the communal campfire that held the ever-present circle of shadowy forms close to its warmth or comfort.

People get on the train. People get off. All white. They stare at the dark, sullen youth gazing out the window.

The sailors' girl leaves. Her high-heeled shoes clicketty-clack off the platform, then she is swallowed up by the lips of the stealthy night. The Nyoongah's eyes devour her plump white body then, from the corner of his eyes, he spots the three sailors glaring at him. He smiles at them, an evil smile. Spits out the window.

The Indian ticket collector bustles along the corridor. He stares through the youth with arrogant eyes, as if no one is there. He takes the youth's money, though.

Perth station.

Full of noise and colour and dancing lights. Shouting people and shunting trains.

Early yet.

He hunches into his clothes and shuffles outside. He rolls a smoke while the cars roar and rumble around him and people pass him by. So alone in the crowded city.

Over on the other side of the river, the flats stand high and alert, like a tribe of advancing warriors. Lights flicker from balconies and rest on the serene back of the river. Soft music from record players, radios or guitars drifts around the dark shore like a lazily swooping seagull.

Tonight is a night for romance.

Little Caesar Jackell struts importantly down the cool white footpaths. He flits in and out of the shadows like a busy black hummingbird searching for honey.

He disappears.

Silent as a thought, he creeps between the trees and bushes of the garden. Only the whites of his eyes are seen in this world that he knows all too well, if only through the stories of his brothers and cousins.

No one is home.

No dogs.

Big house means big money.

He slinks around to the back and tries a window. Locked. He notices a small louvred window high up on the wall, big enough for him to crawl through.

Quickly and quietly, he drags a box over to the window. He pecks out the glass louvres one by one with agile fingers, like a black crow ripping out the eye of affluence, as it squats, powerless, in its green garden. Then he scurries through the hole he has made, to feed off the living juicy insides.

First he pulls out a packet of smokes from his coat pocket and lights one up to calm his nerves. This is only the second house he has ever broken into, and the first time he has done it alone.

Wait till his eyes become accustomed to the dark, then slip quietly through the house.

He comes to the bedroom. A photograph of an earnest young man glares out at the cheeky thief from among various bottles of perfume on the dressing table.

It can do nothing to him.

He flattens down his bushy hair with a brush and pulls faces in the mirror. Then he sets to work.

He finds a small locked metal cashbox with a lucky-sounding jangle inside it, various rings and necklaces in another box and a watch that takes his fancy. In the kitchen, he takes two bottles of beer and a flagon of riesling from the fridge. In another room, he finds more cigarettes, three cigars, and a $10 note. He shoves the biggest cigar into his mouth and grins into another mirror.

On top of a cupboard, his searching fingers feel a hard, cold object.

It is a rifle. A telescopic .303. He searches the drawers of the cupboard until he finds four packets of bullets. This truly is a prize.

He shoves all his loot into a bag he finds, and lowers it out the window. Then the .303, then himself.

Same stars, same people, same lights.

He goes.

Lack of pronouns

Keeps to the back ways as much as he can. No one sees him—or would care if they did.

He reaches the riverside and lights up another cigar. He decides to dump the bag and .303 and come back for them later.

'Takes me, unna?' he brags to the waves that gently slap-lap-lap against the shore. 'Pooooh! Ya one solid man, Caesar Jackell.'

Takes one of the bottles of beer from the bag and wrenches off the top with his white teeth. He pours his cold, golden triumph down his throat. Starlight and city light glint off the bottle. No one is at his celebration party. Only the waves, and the floating rubbish and a few drifting ghostly gulls.

Across the water, the city beckons with crooked fingers and winks from tempting eyes. The buildings dance the dance of the night people, the street people, the nobody people.

His people.

Caesar finishes off the bottle and tries to open the cashbox.

He curses and swears and rips his knuckle open before he smashes the lock with a rock.

Open it eagerly.

Shells.

'Shit!'

Hurl the useless box away, spewing beautifully patterned shells into the air.

He still has the $10.

Drinks the other bottle of beer. Slowly. He relishes the bitterness, and remembers he has robbed a whole house—a big, rich house—all on his own. Last time he was scared as he squatted under a tree chain-smoking, with his eyes darting about nervously, keeping watch for the others. Now he has proven he is as good as they. No, better, because he has a .303 and bullets.

He is drunk now.

Pats the barrel then aims it at the curious gulls.

'Bang, bang,' he mutters softly and smiles.

He hides the gun and bag, then stumbles away.

He staggers across the bridge and along the freeway, a small insignificant, drunken moth going to boast and be a big spender for at least one night in his miserable life.

The people pour onto the footpath in a noisy flow. They whirl and eddy, and cling to the sides of cars or heroes in bobbing groups. Inside is a comforting blast of music and synthetic gunfire as the youths become pretend cowboys or soldiers or gangsters or racing-car drivers; all fantasies that are so real for them. Then they squeeze out the door, to become black boys gazed upon in contempt or fear or black girls sitting on the seats, giggling and shouting, eyed over by the white man.

Big Murry James leans into the darkest doorway across the street from Crystal Palace, watching all the Kings and Queens and Princes and Princesses amble in and out.

He is the Court Jester.

He was fostered by a white family and lived with them for fourteen years. Last month, the murmurings of his people stirred in his heart and he wandered home again to Lockridge camp.

Very black, with large round eyes—and a deep voice. A small squashed nose and a low forehead. He hardly ever talks, for it takes a long time for him to work things out. He leaves the thinking to his cleverer cousins and friends while he just gets on with living.

Despite his huge size, he is gentle and kind.

Puff on a cigarette, and dream about the girl he would like to take to bed. The other boys shout and yell their love across the rooftops and drag names from dirty lip to dirty lip, sweetened by knowledgeable laughter. Then they will swoop in and rip a girl off the footpath like an owl pouncing on a squeaking, cowering mouse.

Not Murry. His woman is like a drink kept secure in a bottle so no one but he can partake of her. Her name slides down his throat and warms him whenever he thinks of her.

He sees her now, lost in a crowd of grinning girls gathered around two blonde-haired brothers who came out of Riverbank last week.

Saunter across.

'G'day, Lynette.'

'Look 'oo's 'ere! What ya doin'?' she shrieks.

Small and young with a beautiful body, a permanent grin and sparkling dark eyes that have not yet been dulled by brutal sex. She is only fourteen and still a virgin. He is sixteen and shy and not yet used to this dark world that laps around the marble pedestal he has stood upon for so long.

'Nuthin'. Wanna Coke?'

'Get away!' she cries, grinning at him. Then her grin fades to a half-smile, as she looks deeper into him.

'Orright then, if ya like,' she replies.

She understands. She always did from the first, when she caught him staring at her silently across the campfire the first week he drifted in.

He is tall and strong and handsome—in an ugly sort of way. He is quiet and gentle and kind. When he does make love to her, he will not be cruel.

They walk down the street to a coffee lounge.

'Lets go to Beaufort Park, Murry.'

'No. Ole Billy 'Owes died other day. The place is packed with 'Oweses now.'

'Elgin Broppo oughta look out, then. 'Im an' Mantan 'Owes 'ad one big fight, unna?'

'Yeah.'

'Ya got any boya, Murry?'

'Yeah.'

He is proud of the job he has at the panel beater's. He grins down at Lynette then away again at the staring, glaring lights all around him. They rip into his love like fruit fly boring into a delicate, delicious fruit. Get away from the harsh forest of lights. Go to the sea of darkness and shadows and softness and bushes down at Supreme Court Gardens.

'Stick around me, Lynette, an' we'll 'ave a good time.'

'Orright.'

They grin in unison and she moves a little closer to him.

Elgin Broppo slinks into a darkened, rutted lane way near the Beaufort Hotel and peers around the corner at the crowded park. Obscure figures flutter from one circle to another. Furtive mumblings and occasional yells of recognition. The Howeses drink to the death of old Billy.

An ebony trio is squeezed from the park and ambles across the street towards Elgin. He tenses, ready to run, then notices his cousin Jimmy Olsen.

Grins and soft punches as the cousins meet.

'Hey, Elgin, brother. Doan' 'ang round 'ere, budda. Manny 'Owes is drunk as all buggeries.'

'Shootin' off 'ow ya fought 'im dirty, like.'

'Go an' get 'im, Elgin.'

'Doan' talk silly, Larry. Mantan 'ud kill 'im with 'is own mob,' Jimmy growls.

Elgin's sombre eyes gaze thoughtfully over the park. He lifts his lips a little in a suggestion of a smile.

'Another night, yeah.'

'Let's buy a drink, you fellahs.'

'Oo's got the boya?'

'Jimmy busted into a shop, unna? Ya still got monies?'

They troop over to the bottle shop leering out at the dark parked cars.

The proprietor eyes them in an unfriendly way because last night there had been a big brawl in the front bar where the Aborigines drank. But money's money, so he sells them a flagon of Brandevino and half a carton of cans.

Fade away behind the toilets, in the grubby, scuffed sea of dirt. Broken bottles blink their last as they drown in the sea.

The youths drown, too.

Caesar Jackell stumbles into the light-blasted circle outside Crystal Palace. His stage light. His big performance.

'Hey, Donny, I got a gun, ya know.'

'Yeah, an' I got a million dollars.'

'No. True'sGod. I got a real gun. Bushted thish 'ouse. Easy as pissin', it wash.'

'Look 'ere! Caesar drunk, or what?' a girl shouts happily.

'Yeah, 'e's drunk. Finished.'

'Caesar drunk!'

They gather around him, gabbling and grinning. All blurs and noise. Caesar clutches hold of Donny's sleeve.

'I got a fuckin' gun—and bullets.'

'I'll give ya gun right up ya bony 'ole d'rectly, if ya don't bugger off.'

'I got ten dollars, too, if ya wanna know. I'm fuckin' rich, me.'

They gather closer. Caesar smiles around the group, then swaggers into the poolroom. He nearly trips over his feet and is saved from the disgrace of falling on his face by two girls grabbing him. Everyone howls louder than ever at the joke.

Caesar dances over to the counter. Everyone of importance gathers around, and he is a hero to the drifting night people.

Slaps the $10 note on the counter.

'Fill 'er up, buddy,' he grins.

'Gimme a lend of a dollar, Caesar.'

'Caesar, give me a few bob, please. Go on Caesar, baby.'

'I'm ya people, Caesar.'

Five dollars go.

'I'm keepin' the rest,' he says.

Staggers over to a pinball machine, which blinks at him with
the knowledge of an old friend. The people disperse and only two
bony, scraggly-haired girls hang around him in the hope of more
handouts. He becomes lost in the world of bright lights and bouncing balls and flashing numbers. The only world he wants to know.

Murry and Lynette huddle on the corner with all the white people.
They sip their Coke silently.

'Let's go down to Supreme Court Gardens, Lynette.'

She is thoughtful for a moment. Looks up at simple Murry's
kind face.

'Yeah, orright.'

They cross over, rubbing against each other in the crowd.

Up the street, with busy people and screeching buses and windows full of white man things.

The gates: and beyond the gates is sweet obscurity that swal-
lows them up.

The Gardens are quiet and cool. The young couple go down past
the Court House and through the trees onto the lawn.

No one is there.

They lie under a spreading tree and let the silence and peace
blanket them. They finish off their Coke, talking in whispers.

Murry forms the words in his mind and repeats them over and
over before rising up above her. She stares up and the whites of
her eyes glint in the city light.

'Lynette ... Lynette, ya wanna be my woman?'

'Get away, ya silly bugger.'

'No. Ya know I'm mardong for ya, unna? I just gotta tell ya,
that's all.'

She grins uneasily, yet knows that she *does* love him.

Soon, one day, a boy will grab her and suck what he wants from
her, then toss her away. She would rather it was this boy than any
other.

Murry's large clumsy hands encircle her and she gives an in-
voluntary yelp before his face buries into her own and his lips
devour her untainted ones. She struggles for a moment before
relaxing. She is fearful of the unknown, yet happy in the comfort
that will be her new life.

He peels her jeans down while his heavy fingers fumble around her body. Warm brown skin touches warm brown skin, and a unison of young, gentle, love is born.

The buildings, like stern priests, gaze down. The moon runs in naked freedom across her field, while the stars, clustered like daisies, wait to be put in a chain around her head.

personification of Night

The night—the hot, dusty night—presses down upon the city. Its misshapen head peers over the mountains of tall buildings while its grotesque fingers feel along the streets.

People go home.

Aboriginal children linger in large pulsating groups, sucking as much fun from the night as they can.

Elgin wanders up from Beaufort Park with his cousin Jimmy Olsen. Both are half-drunk and happy.

Caesar Jackell slumps in a dingy doorway, feeling sick. Drags listlessly on a cigarette.

Money all gone. Friends all gone. He is just like everyone else now. Waiting for the police to come and send him on his way.

'Give us a cigarette,' Elgin mutters and sits beside his little cousin. He grins up at slim, watchful Jimmy.

'What ya reckon, J.O.? Our main man is pissed as a parrot, yeah.'

Ruffles the boy's wiry hair. Caesar turns bleary, dull eyes on Elgin, his hero.

He remembers, and clutches at the straw that is going to save him from drowning.

'I got a gun, Elgin,' he mumbles as he extracts the crumpled cigarettes.

Elgin and Jimmy grin as each takes a cigarette.

'Yeah, I got a gun too. Right 'ere, unna. Big shotgun.' Elgin grins and jabs a finger at his groin.

The older boys laugh.

Caesar sits dazed.

'No, I *'ave* got a gun, ya know. An' jewels, I even got a watch.'

No one listens to him. Jimmy Olsen squints down the street.

''Ere come them 'Owes, budda. Time we was movin'.'

Half-drunk Elgin stares away, with his quiet eyes in some far-off thought of his own.

'You c'n go, Jimmy. I'll wait 'ere. Go later, yeah.'

'Doan' you get in no fight, Elgin, that's all I ask, or else ya

'istory. None of our people around tonight, ya know, 'cept Murry—
an' 'e's gone somewhere—an' this silly little prick.'
  'Yeah. Well, see ya, J.O. See ya t'morrow, then.'
  'Yeah.'
  Jimmy disappears.
  Just Caesar and Elgin and the city left.
  'Ya gunna fight Mantan again, Elgin?'
  'Naw. Fightin's stupid. Where's fightin' get ya? In jail, that's
where, brother.'
  'If ya get me gun, ya can shoot bloody ole Mantan full of 'oles.'
  'So ya truly 'ave got a gun.'
  'Course. An' jewels an' a necklace an' everything.'
  They puff away on another cigarette.
  Some Howeses wander by and look the two over with hard
Oriental eyes.
  'Goin' to be a smash, directly, Caesar. Let's get goin' and find
Murry.'
  Elgin, the boss, climbs off the seat. Everything is going hazy,
but he still walks with a sort of pride. His grubby little page boy
swaggers behind him.
  Big cousin Elgin who held up a bank and has stolen a dozen cars
and beat up two munadj. Big Caesar who broke into a house.
  Black boys who idle along. Shy of the bright white lights that
expose them for what they really are.
  They go up Murray Street.
  Past the fire station where the firemen whistle and shout and
jeer.
  They sit down on the low wall outside the nurses' quarters
where girls in short, tight uniforms glide between the iron gates,
comfortable in the knowledge of their whiteness and virginity.
  No one notices the two Nyoongahs in the shadows under the
huge Moreton Bay fig tree that erupts from the footpath in a green
volcano, It leads a doomed life, one day to be chopped down by the
hands that nurtured it. Just like the people it shelters now.
  'Hey boy, 'ow'd you like *er*?' Caesar grins and spits as a pretty,
buxom, young nurse walks past.
  'Roasted, with two eggs,' Elgin grins.
  Eyes follow her as they would a dream.
  'Yeah, just like I was thinkin'.'
  Elgin glances at his little cousin and bursts into laughter.
  'Listen to 'im talk. Ya couldn't 'ave a moony to save yaself. Don't
try foolin' me. I'm almost ya brother, yeah.'

'I done all right with Jenny Doolan.'

'Garn. Y'never touched 'er, even. I was there.'

'Any rate' Caesar sulks, 'I thought we was lookin' for Murry. What we doin' up 'ere?'

'Walkin',' Elgin grunts.

Staggers to his feet. 'Let's get goin'.'

'What we goin' up 'ere for? I wanna get me gun before some jerk finds it, ya know.'

'I'm goin' to say a prayer to turn me white.' Elgin smiles, and his eyes take in the cathedral that looms down upon them, its spire silhouetted against the sky. The Virgin Mary looks out over the city that surrounds it like broken eggshells.

'What ya reckon we steal the cashbox, Elgin?'

'Don't talk silly. 'Ow'd ya know God won't blast ya to bits, eh?'

Caesar laughs loud and young, while Elgin gives a mocking smile.

They leave the cathedral with its awesome shadows and tranquillity up on the hill.

Past the now-silent school. In the daytime (with all its blue heat and flies and dust) green-clad schoolgirls shout in play and hide their self-conscious womanhood behind starched uniforms.

Past the mint, looking like a caged animal behind the iron bars and twisted barbed netting. A snarling white man's animal.

The two descendants of the kings of the old civilisation glance from hooded eyes as a police car swishes past.

Elgin digs his hands deeper in his pockets, and his sharp eyes flick over to the taxi parked beside a block of flats that rear up into the sky. It taunts him with its sleek whiteness. The sleek white owner is upstairs in the flats, fondling his white girlfriend between white sheets.

'Ya can't even pinch a car, Elgin,' Caesar sneers, still sullen from Elgin's gibes about his sexual prowess.

Elgin's eyes flash.

'Couldn't I, ya little jerk? Just you keep watch, budda, an' I'll show ya 'ow one Nyoongah can steal a car.'

The wiry youth crouches beside the taxi and his teeth pull back in a grin. His thin fingers find a crack where the window is wound down and he heaves with all his might. Puts in his hand and unlocks the door.

Caesar stands, tense and afraid, under a tree.

A utility glides past.

Elgin leaps onto the other side of the taxi, while Caesar melts into the tree.

Door open. Silver paper on the fuses.

Two shadows pushing a taxi down the hill. The gentle crunch of tyres on cement. A sudden kick, and the engine bursts into life. Doors slam and Elgin lets out a howl of laughter as he screeches around the corner.

Caesar clutches the door in fright.

Elgin Mortimer Broppo lets all his drunken frustration bubble out in one long whoop of joy.

'*Now* we'll get ya bloody gun an' shoot bloody ole Mantan so full of 'oles 'e'll look like a piece of lace, yeah,' Elgin cries.

Caesar lights a nervous cigarette.

'Not so fast, couz. I wanna live, ya know.'

A faint, persistent thought hammers at Elgin's mind.

Back to jail; back to jail
E.M. Broppo back to jail

The wheel between his thin agile hands whisks the thought away. It bobs with the coloured lights here, then is gone.

Down in the cool peace of the gardens, Murry lies beside Lynette. She smiles serenely at him and he rubs a calloused hand through her hair.

She has become a woman tonight. In the way she dreamed about, down at the dusty camp, when she was small, and read, over and over again, the tattered book on 'Sleeping Beauty'.

Caressed and kissed and loved on this hot night. And her man is still here beside her, tracing patterns in her hair.

'We'd better go soon, Murry. The 'Owes'll be everywhere.'

'They won't bother us,' the giant rumbles.

The girl realises he is still white, in many ways as well as in his manner of making love. She sits up and takes out cigarettes for them both.

'They will if they know ya one of Elgin's people.'

They finish their cigarettes. The incense-like blue smoke drifts around them and the tree squats above them like a buddha. They kiss again, never wanting to leave.

But there are Lynette's father and three brothers to think about—and her uncles and cousins. Just as everything is going well, Murry doesn't want to start a feud of his own.

'Better go.'

They amble up into the lighted city that is becoming dark and empty now.

The buses are all gone.

The Howeses are all there. Too many glowering, hunched Howeses stalking the streets for gentle Murry and feminine Lynette to fight.

They slink back the way they came and down towards the river.

'We'll get a taxi, if there's any goin'. I got the money,' Murry murmurs.

Elgin and Caesar, on their way to get the .303, find them.

The squeal of brakes rips out the guts of the night. The taxi reverses back to gaping Murry and surprised Lynette.

'Shut ya mouth an' open the door, Murry,' rasps little Caesar, eyeing Lynette. He feels more sure of himself now, and happy that—at last—he is going to get his rifle.

Elgin cocks his head over his slight shoulders. Bright eyes twinkle at Murry.

'Where ya been, Murry?'

'Where ya think, Elgin? Down Supreme Court Gardens, unna, Murry?' Caesar says before Murry can answer.

'Ya *wanna* punch in the 'ead, Caesar Jackell, ya big prick?' Lynette snarls.

'Da's true,' returns Caesar, and nudges Elgin. Their teeth gleam as they shudder in silent laughter.

Lynette glowers.

'Ya steal this taxi, Elgin?' Murry mutters as he slides in.

'Nah! 'E bought it, unna?' Caesar cackles.

Elgin smiles a superior smile.

They drive over the bridge. Elgin idles along the riverside slowly.

'Where ya goin', Elgin?' Lynette asks from the back. She is the only girl there. She has heard about these sort of rides before. After all, the two in the front *are* Murry's cousins. Share and share alike is their code.

'Just gettin' some of Caesar's stuff.'

''Ere. Turn off,' Caesar orders. He is the boss again, just as he was up in front of Crystal's.

The taxi rocks and bumps down the gravel track until it reaches the water's edge.

Caesar leaps out and searches in the long grass until he finds the .303 and the bag. He holds them up and shouts a challenge to the soaring flats and the dancing moon and the cold, white, impassive stars.

The cab screeches back onto the main road, spitting dust and gravel in defiance.

Caesar produces the flagon of riesling. Drunk and happy again, he hands out pieces of jewellery to everyone. He keeps the .303 on his knee and the watch and two earrings in his pocket. He takes a long swig of the flagon, then hands it to Elgin.

'Ya smart little bugger. 'Oo'd of believed it, eh?' Elgin gives Caesar a proper grin. A man-to-man grin for the new hero of the clan.

Caesar aims his rifle at buildings and boats and the occasional bird, Murry and Lynette snuggle up close to one another and take the odd sip of wine from the offered flagon.

Elgin drives, drowning in bitter riesling and his own thoughts.

They will be looking for the cab by now. When they catch him, they will make sure he goes to jail for a long time, if Big Pig Fathers has anything to do with it.

He thinks about his woman, lying alone in their tent out at the camp. Her round, bright eyes and quiet voice, and the gentle smile that can calm his wildness.

A still part of town.

A tired sign above a building, flashes blue and red: LAWSON HOT L.

He swings the taxi into the gloom of the parking area.

Two o'clock in the morning. No one around.

The others stare at him in curiosity as he grins around the dark cab.

'We just goin' to break into 'ere an' get some beer. 'Ave one big party, when we get back to camp.'

'Yeah?' Murry, uneasily.

'Nothin' to it, Murry. Wait 'ere a bit, you mob. Be back d'rectly.'

Elgin slips out and scuttles over to the wall. A sharp crack as the window breaks. Protesting squeaks as it jerks open.

A low whistle.

Murry clambers out noisily, not used to this sort of thing. Caesar floats beside him, holding his .303. Lynette huddles in the cab, with just a cigarette and the riesling to keep her company, feeling terribly alone, without big Murry beside her.

Elgin's head peers out of the window like a fox glancing out of his lair. A sly, thin, black fox, about to grab the fluttering white chickens and make them squawk.

'Come 'ere, Murry. Caesar, keep watch.'

The two coloured boys stand inside the murky lounge, while their eyes become used to the gloom. Elgin leads the way as they sneak into the storeroom.

'We right now, baby,' Elgin whispers. 'Fuckin' Christmas, unna, out at camp, when we deliver this little lot.'

Murry is afraid. It is strange that he is here, in someone else's place, taking all this beer. The pictures on the wall scowl down at him. He passes out the carton to drunk Caesar, who staggers over to the cab.

Carton after carton of bottles and stubbies and cans.

Murry is a criminal now. If he gets caught, it's an end to all his dreams. And all he wanted to do was go home.

'Grab some gnummerai, Murry. Geeze, do ya 'ave to be told everything?' Elgin hisses as he dashes past with an armload of spirit bottles. Murry gets a small cardboard box and quickly fills it up with cigars and packets of cigarettes. His strong hands wrench open the till and he stuffs about $200 in notes into his pockets.

'Come on, Murry, ya ole woman!'

He rushes over to the window and leaps out.

They roll start the taxi. Head for home. Home amongst the gaunt trees, beside the wide river flat.

They weave through the streets, keeping clear of police vehicles and taxis. Out on Guildford Road, Elgin pushes his foot down hard and lets the power and freedom of his body and mind echo in the taxi engine.

Reedy voices crackle feebly over the two-way in a vain search for the cab. Black Elgin is supreme once more. For the second time in his life he has the radios of Perth spread like a spider's web to catch him as he buzzes along.

'What ya reckon they'll say out at camp when we roll up?' he grins.

''Appy birthday,' Caesar laughs.

A train roars past and Elgin tries to beat it.

The only car on the whole lonely road.

Caesar pretends to shoot the people in the train.

Lynette sniggers, 'Look 'ere at Clint Eastwood!'

Caesar turns and laughs with her. All he can do now is laugh. If he stops laughing, he will spew up. He sways and rolls and clutch-es his .303 even tighter. His smile is a fixed one.

Lynette is only happy-drunk. She leans against broad Murry and his big hand covers her child's breast. He broods about the crime he has committed, then thinks about the money that will buy his woman a lot of joy.

Elgin is remote from the others. Just him and his car and the road.

They are almost at Guildford when they zoom past a speed trap.

Caesar hears the eerie wailing and jerks around.

'Hey couz, bloody munadj 'ave got us!'

Fear settles like a mist over the remnants of the tribe.

"Old tight. When I tell ya to run, ya bloody run—understand?' Elgin says, through clenched teeth.

More cars join in the chase: two blue vans and a CIB car. They bay and howl like hounds after the fox.

'I'll stop 'em!' screams Caesar, and loads the magazine of his .303.

Six bullets.

He leans out the window of the swaying cab so the wind whips his hair back and shrieks through the curls.

He fires the rifle and the bullet whines away. Fires again and again.

On his last shot, the bullet smashes through the windscreen of the foremost van so it slews to an abrupt halt. The RTA car also stops, but the others come relentlessly onwards.

The CIB car comes up alongside them. They think they are Starsky and Hutch, in their olive-green Kingswood. Elgin sees the fat, pale face of Detective-Sergeant Fathers peering in at them.

Slides over to the other side of the road in an attempt to block off the CIB car.

It only comes up on the other side of the road, so Elgin rams the taxi into it.

Twice he smashes the taxi against the car, desperately trying to escape. He has visions of smirking Fathers and his mates, like white toadstools growing on Elgin's black rotting body, down in the forest of Central police station.

The second time he rams the CIB car, Caesar Jackell's arm breaks with a snap like the click of his stolen rifle bolt.

He gives a cry of pain.

Just over the Swan River bridge, Elgin slams on the brakes. The taxi careers up onto the footpath.

'Run! Run!' he yells, and is out sprinting even before the car has stopped. Down over the bank and towards the river.

Caesar stumbles across the road, in the headlights of the pursuing CIB car. He scrabbles painfully down the opposite bank from Elgin, and staggers across the paddock, trailing his .303.

Dull Murry is stunned for three vital seconds and Lynette clings fearfully to him. When he explodes from the taxi, the area is surrounded by police.

He has more to lose than the other two boys. He has his pride at never having committed a crime and his good job and his girl whom he *does* love. He pushes Lynette down the bank after Elgin. Turns to face the approaching horde with the anger of a cornered wildcat.

He lifts one policeman off his feet with a powerhouse right and smashes huge Fathers in the mouth, rocking him.

Six police pounce on the giant Aboriginal and grapple him to his knees with punches and kicks. Hurl him into the van where he crouches in the corner with dead eyes.

'Who's your mates? Who was drivin'? What was the girl's name? How old was she, sonny? Do you know what carnal knowledge is all about? What's your name, arsehole? You 'ad the gun, eh, Jesse James? Well, who did, then? Where did you get all this beer and grog, matey? By Christ, you're in the shit now. Tell us who the others were, or we put everything on you. Hey, sarge, one went down along the river. Where'd that bloody girl go? I wouldn't mind arresting her, eh, Billy? ... Hey, sarge, Central want you on the radio: Get every man you can down here, a mob of Abos have split everywhere ... one of them is fucking dangerous ... got a gun ... took a shot at one of our cars ... No, no one is hurt, only shaken ... Listen, Jacky, yer better start talkin' soon, before I belt yer bloody ears off ...How's Mal? Pretty crook, that boong's got a hard punch. Yaaah! They all think they're Baby Cassius.'

Words, words. Going round and round inside Murry's battered head. He drops his eyes and chews on his bottom lip while white faces gaze in at him as though he were a monkey in the zoo, not a human at all. Hard eyes, contemptuous eyes, wondering eyes: slit mouths and Hitler moustaches.

White faces, blue uniforms.

Being the only one caught is such a bitter feeling. The loneliness is more acute. He remembers Caesar joking and Elgin grinning, and Lynette smiling and pressing against him—so close—in a world so far away.

They take him to Midland lockup.

Caesar huddles, moaning, down beside the river. He stares at the blank brown water. His arm hurts now and tears run down his face. He sniffs noisily and wonders if he has killed anyone. The excitement of the chase wears off and he feels sicker then he has ever been. Leans over and vomits all over the ground. Fades among the trees as he hears the droning of a car bouncing over the paddock. Two yellow eyes stare out of the darkness and pick him up, cringing against the tree.

Car stops. Doors open. Feet crunch on the dead grass.

'Look out! He's the crazy bastard with the gun!'

'G'day, Caesar.'

Fathers and company.

'I never meant to kill no one.'

'No one's dead, Caesar. Now, suppose you give me that gun.'

'I busted me arm, ya know.'

The men close in around him.

'Well, we'd better get it looked at, then, hadn't we?'

He is escorted to the car.

The stars watch from above. His people.

They can't help him now.

No one can.

Inside the CIB car, on his way to Midland regional hospital, with the stale fingers of the evening's enjoyment ripping at his small body, he babbles out the truth of everything.

Just as the sun is crawling over the hills to begin a new day, Elgin creeps into the camp. He has run and slipped and swum his way along the river, then over the paddocks.

Safe back at home, in his tent.

His young woman stares at his silhouette in the tent opening with chiding eyes. He is angry, yet ashamed, of her disapprobation.

'Where ya bin, Elgin?' she whispers, tired of asking the same question. Tired of trying to settle her thin husband's turbulent soul.

'Nowhere.'

He throws himself down on the blanket and lights up a cigarette. He cannot meet her dark, all-knowing eyes.

Blood from a rip in his arm where he got caught on a barbed wire fence, trickles down the brown skin like a teardrop.

'Ya badly 'urt, 'oney?' she murmurs.

'No. Go back to sleep, Maydene.'

'It's almost mornin', an' ya been stealin' again, Elgin! 'Ow *can* I go to sleep, with yaself moonin' all over the countryside?' she cries. 'Ya only come out of jail last month, too. Ya *want* ole Fathers to flog ya again, or what?'

And Elgin was going to ride into camp on his white horse and unload all the beer. Everyone was going to gather around, and there would have been jokes and laughter and fun. His woman would have smiled at him and hugged him, and forgiven him—because he had brought some light into the dusty reserve.

He digs his hand into a pocket and pulls out one of Caesar's necklaces. His feral eyes meet her bruised ones.

'I got ya this, Maydene,' he mutters.

'Ooohh, Elgin! What ya tryin' to do to me, boy?' she weeps.

Elgin gets up abruptly, and moves outside. Muffled sobs pierce him like the first shafts of the orange-red sunlight from the new day.

HERBIE

THERE weren't many Abos in our town; only the Corrigans and Herbie's lot and, as the Corrigans and Herbie's cousins were all grown up, Herbie was the only boong to go to our school. Perhaps this is why we all taunted and teased him, because he was different and us kids don't like anything different.

Since this is all about Herbie, I reckon I'd better have a go at describing him. But this is real hard, because he was all thought: I mean, like, he'd look at you with those big, brown scowling eyes and he'd look right into you, so anything you knew, he'd know. Those eyes seemed to take up almost all of his face, then the nose, flat as a board and all nostrils, took up the rest. You never noticed his mouth, because he rarely spoke and never smiled. He'd flit around the shadows like a crow—he was black as one, too. His legs were long and thin like a crane's and his arms were long and skinny. His hands were abnormally big and his fingers long, so he was clumsy. He wasn't big and he wasn't strong, Herbie, and they reckoned that was because he never got enough to eat. But he was an Abo, and they never do.

Whenever he came to school, he'd only sleep, so it weren't really much good him coming. And us blokes used to smash him up, every break. Once the three Morgan boys locked him in the boys' dunny and left him there all day. The next day he was caned for six for wagging school, but he never told. That was the good thing about Herbie: no matter what happened to him, he never told—not even on me, and I was one of the worst.

Herbie was a bad scholar, but there were many other things he could do well. No one but Herbie knew where all the wild bees hid their sweet, rich, brown honey. No-one but Herbie knew where to get the baby rabbits in spring, or where the foxes hid in holes in the Dongeran hills. Only Herbie knew where the ducks laid their eggs or where the kangaroos grazed. Only the thin, silent outcast could climb to the top of the highest trees and get the young birds or eggs out of the nests. And he knew where the few emus we still had in the district hid among the pink salmon gums. But most of all only Herbie, out of all of us blokes who had lived in the bush all our lives, really understood the hidden feelings of our land—or his, really, I suppose. I mean, like, he'd spend hours staring at a plant or pretty flower; he could lie still, hidden in the tall yellow grass, watching wild animals all day, and they wouldn't know. Or, if they did, they never ran away. They were his mates and they, too, seemed to shrink away from us white fellahs: shy, silent and wild.

Yeah, we used to give that kid hell. Just some of the things we used to do was bury him in the sand by the footy goals or tie him up to the old bent redgum, by the hut in the middle of the playground where we'd have our tucker. Once me and Joey Gruger the German kid stuck him in a petrol drum and rolled him down Mile Hill. He went full belt into a black stump at the bottom, which must have nearly killed him. Then we all got around him while he sat on his knees and chucked up all over the ground. We laughed and Ally Moore rubbed Herbie's face in the chunder and we laughed even louder. I reckon we all feel bad about that now.

We used to chase him around the footy oval, but usually we gave up before he did, because he was a good runner. Only Herbie could run ten miles non-stop—well, he had to, didn't he, to get away from us blokes. But once we got him stumped when Kelly Ryan bought his Dad's best stockwhip to school, and we all ran behind him, lashing him, just like mad old Jay Hiskee did to his horses in the team he still used.

Once we went too far, when Alfie Morgan painted 'boong' all over Herbie's books: then his two brothers painted 'boong' all over Herbie, stripping the frightened boy naked 'like a proper nigger ought to be' as Jimmy, the wit of the Morgans, said. That night Dad brought a rumour home with him from the pub, that the Warandas (that's Herbie's family) had had a fight with the four Morgans—old Evan and his three boys, and had won, too, but since Dad was drunk as he could be, I hadn't believed him. But the next morning, when I saw Alf's face and the way Jimmy limped and the fact that Mick, who always came to school if only to annoy Herbie, was absent, I knew the old man was right. None of us asked the Morgans, of course, but the word went around the school.

I reckon we was scared a bit after that, but summer come on and Willy Harris nearly drowned Herbie in the waterhole and nothing happened to the Harrises. Of course nothing would, if the Warandas had any brains. There were only four Warandas now, since Dallas was in Freo, and ten Harrises. Still, being scared never really stopped us from bullying the thin, silent Herbie but the Morgans let up a bit.

The Morgans lived on the other side of the railway from the Warandas. Old Evan owned a couple of sheep and a cow, and a vicious Alsatian-Labrador. The dog was a real racist because he hated the Warandas. One day, Herbie was daydreaming along the street when the dog rose from the shade of the Co-op wall and charged him. Herbie got a bad bite on the leg, which left a white semi-circular scar. The dog chased the boy up a gum tree and kept him there for an hour before going away. The next morning the dog was found stiff as a drunk man, with a dirty big stake sticking in him. No one really knew who done it of course, 'cept old Morgan reckoned he knew. So that's why the Morgans and Warandas was at war.

Like I said before, Herbie wasn't liked by us bigger blokes, but not all the school was against this lonely outcast. The little kids liked him, and he loved little kids. He would show them baby rabbits and foxes and birds, he would carve them toys out of wood—and he was a good carver, too. He made my brother a real beaut dingo standing on a rock and I reckon all his skill must have gone into making *that* little figure. But that's because he really adored my little brother. Yeah, Herbie loved the young 'uns of our town.

Then come the day I aren't never going to forget. It was hotter then hell, and everything sort of wilted in the hot, white glare of the sun. It was after school, and us kids was all out around Herbie; pushing him around until he got so dizzy he fell on the ground. All us boys were showing off to the girls, who shrieked their applause like a mob of cockatoos. Suddenly big, shaggy Kevin Andrews, who had brains the size of a sheep turd and a face like a cowpat, yanked the scared kid to his feet and boomed out, 'Yer gunna climb Big Smokey, boong, or I'll piss all over yah an' smack yah flaming face in. Orright, yah black c—t?'

Of course, the big nit had done both these things before, but this new torture sounded good fun so, with Andrews dragging the sorry, skinny figure, we all set off for Big Smokey.

I suppose I ought to tell you what Big Smokey is or else you won't see the whole point of this new ordeal we was about to put the kid through. See, there's this big old pine tree, dead as Banjo Patterson, right outside of town, a mile off. No one knows how it got there, but it must be a hundred years old, and it's a good hundred feet high. Once when it was still alive, a fire come through and burned it. They reckon it smoked for three months and whether this is dinkum or not, us kids give it the name of Big Smokey. But, you see, no one was allowed to climb it on account of it being rotten.

Well, we got there and the jagged framework of Big Smokey towered away up into the sky. The tallest building in town was the pub, which was thirty feet, and only Ally Moore, who reckoned he was tough, had ever climbed onto the roof. We was all quiet while we waited for Kevin to do something. I reckon the dopey bugger was feeling bad at sending the kid up the tree, but to stop now would mean being beaten by a blackfellow, so he grunted, 'Get up that tree an' climb to the top, yah black bastard. If yah don't, me an' the others will be waiting 'ere for yah, see? An' this time, we'll give yah one proper workin' over.'

Herbie was packing them, but he scurried up the tree. When he got out of our reach, he turned and scowled and called us names, so we got him with boondis and honky nuts. Mick Morgan hit Herbie fair on the bonce, so he climbed higher.

He kept right on climbing till he was well over halfway, until he was just a thin black speck on the greater, thicker, black trunk of the tree. All us kids was silent as a graveyard because we was sort of awed by the way he had beaten all us white blokes the way he had climbed so high.

Then, of course, it happened. None of us saw him grab the rotten branch, because the dying sun was in our eyes, but we seen him fall one hundred feet. He come down, breaking the smaller branches and bouncing off the bigger ones, then he hit the ground— splat! His yell sort of stopped halfway down, and then there was only silence except for a few girls screaming, us blokes with indrawn breaths, and Kevin Andrews chucking up.

Course, we'd nearly all seen an animal die, and the Harris's and Ashtons had seen humans die—the Harrises Mum, who took a month to die of cancer; and Johnny Ashton's brother, who fell among the plough. We was all old enough to know what death meant. But Herbie was different, because we all knew he should never have climbed the tree and we all knew we'd killed him.

I don't know if you can picture our return to town. At first we were too scared to touch the still, crumpled black body, then Joey Gruger took off his grey greatcoat, which his dad had had in the German army, and placed it over Herbie's body. After that, Skinner Flynn, whose Dad was a roo shooter, and Mick Morgan got their sheath knives out and we made a sort of stretcher. We put him on it, then we sort of went home.

It's funny, but the only thing I thought of as we went home was that day, maybe two years back, when I had mucked up the kid's new shirt. You see, old man Waranda was on the dole and he never got much money; all he did get went on beer or V.O. port. All Herbie wore, summer or winter, were a pair of dirty blue levis and an old T-shirt. Then one day he come to school in a new red-and-white check shirt. He was real proud of that shirt: we could see by the way he kept touching it with his hands, like it was a young rabbit, or fox, or bird, or something. Well, at break, us kids surrounded him and belted him up a bit, then I yanked him up off his feet and I said something like, 'This shirt's too good for a dirty black boong like you, so I reckon I'll have it.' Then I tore it off him and messed it up, then ripped it up and laughed into his face. He cried a bit, but he was an Abo so didn't cry for long—he only hated me. I see now that it must have been the only absolutely new thing his family or anyone had ever given him.

The kids from town decided to go down to Waranda's house on Saturday. They didn't know what it was: curiosity, a chance to say 'sorry' or perhaps just something to do. The drooping gum trees along the dusty main street threw haphazard shadows onto the brown grass patches or white hot pavements. Down in the pink dam by the railway crossing, the water was still and flat, unbroken by the usual crowd of happy young children fishing or swimming. Today all the kids were at Waranda's house, down opposite the line.

They had been there before, to the drab, faded weatherboard house. Then they had gone laughing, with pockets full of boondis to hurl at the large, lumbering Mrs Waranda, in the red-spotted dress she always wore. But today there were no cries of, 'Boong-man, boong-man; the Warandas are all boongs,' or, 'Tommy

Waranda is a drunk old boong bugger,' or, 'Come out an' fight, yah stroppy black bastards.'

Today the children were stealthy, guilty and silent, because Herbie was dead and they had killed him.

The house stood on bare, grey sand. Over by the wood heap, a chainsaw stood alone, unattended. The peppermint tree by the verandah drooped in the midday sun that shone viciously from a cruel blue sky. The battered old ute of many colours, the Warandas' transport, stood underneath the crooked twisted tree. Once, there had been a chook yard under the trees too, but the chooks had all died or been eaten; now remained only a broken, rusted wire fence, a lopsided tin shed, where snakes and spiders lived, and a big, white heap of manure.

All so quiet in the middle of the day.

The children stood around, staring. In there: in that dark, dirty house lay Herbie. It was hard to realise that the boy who had been so well and truly alive only yesterday afternoon, was dead.

Suddenly, old Mrs Waranda was framed in the rotten, grey doorway. The children scattered like chaff in the wind and only the yellow dust from their feet remained. The dust and the boy.

He was big and strong and brown, the boy, but he looked small in the emptiness now all his friends had gone. He was almost six feet tall, with curly hair and hazel eyes, one of which was pulled down in a squint.

For a long moment, he and Mrs Waranda stared at each other, the boy with a shifty, guilty, perhaps embarrassed look; she with a sour, sad, beaten look. Suddenly the boy looked up and moved to the dogleg fence. It seemed the Aboriginal woman retreated a little into the house. The boy cried, 'Hey, Missus Waranda, I got somphin' for Herbie. For his grave, like, from us fellahs up home.'

For a bit Mrs Waranda hesitated, then the fat old woman moved down the wooden steps and waddled across the brown dust patch. She reached the boy and looked up at him with fear in her eyes— and with just the faintest trace of hate. Mrs Waranda had never hated anyone, really. She was too humble and afraid to hate the white kids who teased her, and the white men, who had put her oldest boy in jail on a false charge, and the white women who stared at her as though she was the filth of the nation. But I knew she hated the white kids who had killed her youngest son.

The boy reached into his bike basket and pulled out a bunch of wild flowers, wilting now from the sun, and pushed them into the scarred black hands. The boy mumbled, embarrassed now. 'From me an' Malcolm, Missus Waranda.'

The faintest trace of a smile flitted across the woman's thick, purple lips and she said, softness and tears in her big, brown eyes, 'You a good boy, Davey Morne, you and ya little brother, Malcolm.'

And how I wish she could have been speaking the truth about me.

Violet Crumble

THE lines of cars crawl along the ocean road. On one side glittering blue water leaps up in reflected-white peaks to catch the impassive blue sky: on the other, red and white brick-and-tile waves crash against the grey lost road that does not know where it is going, and does not care. On one side a vast living emptiness; on the other a vast crowded stagnant pool, swirling in the backwaters, with oil tanks and wheat silos, and railway lines standing out of the cesspool in dirty splendour, like rank ugly weeds.

One of the cars staggers out of the holy procession to the God that civilisation worships. It burps to a sleazy stop in front of the drab girl hitch-hiker crumpled like the thrown-away paper from a chocolate bar beside the road.

Where you going?

Oh—nowhere.

Well, hop in. It's bloody cold tonight.

She is thin. Thin blonde hair, bleached white by the sun, thin red lips, thin fragile fingers, fiddling with her gaily coloured beach bag.

Thanks for the ride.

No worries. Watch out for my dog.

The boy is as young as the car is old. Apart from that, they are the same. Derelicts wandering nowhere, anywhere, any time. The dog is a mongrel pup, mostly collie—no special colour.

Eyes that don't care any more glance over at the girl's silhouette.

You have to be careful out here at night. Plenty of places for guys to drag you off into the bushes.

That's funny.

Funny?

She does not look at him, only out the window. Occasionally street lights peer in at the two dropouts, lighting up the twilight world the pair have buried themselves in.

Have you got a cigarette, mate?

Sure, and the name's Ron.

Mine's Linda.

Well, where are you going, Linda?

Don't know.

She lights her cigarette and draws in deeply. She still stares out the window at all the dancing, mocking lights.

Wow. Well, I'm going to find a hamburger joint. I'm hungry— how about you?

You *must* be rich! You picked me up a few minutes ago—and now you offer me a meal.

She takes another furtive puff of her cigarette and hugs the smoke inside her. Then she looks over at him with her washed-out blue eyes. He smiles shyly.

I can only offer you a hamburger. I was hassling crayfish up north, on a cray boat. Good money. Kalbarri. Ever been there?

No. I've lived all my life on a farm. Well, you know, the occasional trip to Perth. For the Royal Show and that sort of thing. Twenty-two years that bored me to death.

Said bitterly. Memories of flat-footed farmers' boys and clumsy attempts at love in a prickly hayshed, or among greasy wool, or in the warm sensuality of a virgin green paddock in spring. Dances in the town hall—same old faces, same old jokes.

The waves at Kalbarri are out of this world, like—they're something else. Tubes? Wow, you haven't surfed until you've been to Kalbarri.

Ron is happy and brown, with red-brown flowing hair and green eyes that can read an ocean, if nothing else.

One day I'm going to be a famous surfer. Then I'm going to move over to Hawaii. They say that some waves there are over eighty feet high. And there's a place in Indonesia where you can get a ride for a mile. A mile-long wave. What a magic wave that would be!

His eyes sparkle with joy and the girl smiles.

They pull into a dreary kiosk. All around on the dark dirt lie broken bottles, cans and discarded ice-cream papers. A few surfers stand in a grinning group, eating greasy hamburgers.

The boy gets out of the womb of the car, a new child born into the universe. Stars litter the black sky above while rubbish lies upon the ground around his bare feet.

Two hamburgers please, and a big bottle of Coke.

The kiosk cannot decide whether it should leap over the crumbling edge of the cliff onto the slimy reef below and end it all, or whether to stay there, selling greasy second-rate food to the used-up dreamers.

The surfers see the surfboard on Ron's roof rack. They see he is one of the brotherhood of the wandering lost.

Hey, man, where you been at? Haven't seen you before.

Kalbarri.

Yeah? What's it like up there?

Kalbarri's a mean piece of water isn't it, man?

Ask Colin about that.

Colin: a skinny blue-eyed boy, with a rhythmic swing to his loose body and big feet that could stay glued on any board on any wave. A real surfer.

Man, he came out of that foam crying like a baby.

Well, Jesus, Joe. My board was snapped in half. A two-day-old board.

A gangling youth, with an incessant grin, says to Ron,

What sort of board you got, man?

Swallowtail.

Swallowtail? Christ, man, they're murder.

Give us a look at it.

OK.

They drift over to the car, staring in at the washed-out girl. But they are more interested in the surfboard reclining on the roof rack. The boy called Colin runs his hand over the smooth green body.

Good board. I bet you get good vibes out of this one.

Well, it sort of grows on you, you know?

Right.

Hey, man, what's your name, anyway?

Ron. Ron Doorie.

Well, I'm Clancy. That's Colin and the mountain behind is Joe.

Joe is small and dark with short curly hair, an Italian. The other two are thin and brown with long blonde hair and squinting eyes, from looking at too many sunstruck waves, and coloured shirts with board shorts or jeans torn off at the knees. Feet swathed in thongs or Indian sandals.

They shake hands. A cigarette or a handshake, and you have an instant friend. That's how frail friendship is for them; all they really care about are the thundering, gliding waves.

Hey, Ron, where you going to now?

Ooh, just wander, Joe. Cruise down south, maybe. I might go to Margaret River.

That place is bad news. The way those waves come into the riverhead, you know. Well, remember Bobby Campbell? He's dead, man!

No shit?

Ron breathes sharply at this momentous piece of news, awe-struck for a second by the ocean's ever-present violence. You can forget about it and it sneaks up on you like a wave licking the beach.

Yeah, man, about a month back. Wasn't it, Clancy?

That's right. It was a hairy wave, anyway, from what I heard and he wiped out, man. You just can't afford to do that at Margaret River.

He must have been sucked under a rock or been taken out to sea. They never found him again.

There is a silence as the youths remember their comrade, flicked like a speck of dirt from the turquoise suit of the ocean with an arrogant white-nailed finger, then crushed like an offensive bug.

Ron thinks he can remember Bobby Campbell. A tall loose-jointed youth with crooked front teeth and wiry ginger hair that no amount of water could uncurl. His favourite drink had been rum, which he could drink by the bottleful with no ill effects. He had been a good impersonator of Billy McMahon, ears and all. But the great green God—or demon—they all loved had embraced this human in its liquid arms and coral encrusted lips had kissed the pale white face of the youth as he gurgled his last breath.

It happens, man.

Ron murmured gently and forgets about Bobby Campbell quick-ly. Forever. That is how it has to be.

You watch out for those pigs, man. Bastards'll bust you, sure as eggs. You got long hair, you got dope.

Yeah, that's how they think, man.

Over in Queensland it's worse. If you've got a surfboard on your car you get hassled more than if you've got a gun.

Colin is speaking again. The surfer, the traveller, the knower of all things wise. Clancy shrugs and grins.

Yeah, man. But you know Queensland.—Give me the west any time,—or Indonesia.

It is time for Ron to go.

Well guys, it was great meeting you. See you around, maybe.

Yeah, cheers, Ron. Hang loose, OK?

Remember about the pigs.

Good surfing, man. They say there's bulk waves down at Yallingup.

Yeah. Right.

The old station wagon lurches off, while dusty hands reach up to grab it back. They reluctantly slide off the mauled car's body.

They leave the kiosk and all he has are two hamburgers, a bottle of Coke, going hot, and hot words going cold.

Wow, Linda. *Those* guys have been over to Queensland—even Indonesia. That's what I call living.

The girl smiles at him. He seems younger than she. He smiles back at her and hands her a hamburger.

You're so kind, Ron. Thank you.

Well, when you've got money there's nothing much to do with it except spend it. Right?

They laugh softly. She puts an arm around his shoulders and reaches her thin face up to his brown cheek, kissing him. He wraps a gangling arm around her waist, touching the soft womanness of her breasts. He hugs her to his side and she rests her head in the nape of his neck. Her fingers pull through his long red hair, claiming him as a mermaid from the sea will claim a lovesick sailor.

Can I stay with you, Ron?

Stay with me? I don't do much though, Linda. Surf here, work there—you know. Mostly I just bum around.

I don't care. I feel at peace here with you.

Right. Peace is what makes the world go around.

They smile once more into each other's eyes. Throw out the half-eaten hamburgers to be devoured by the wind.

He pulls up, a little way off the highway in a hidden cove near the mumbling ocean. Just the boy and the girl and the blackness, all vagrants, all ready to slink off when truth and reality burst radiantly over the horizon.

His arms encircle her waist. She is no longer thin and ugly but beautiful to the boy who has searched for beauty all his life and

104 /

never quite caught it between his eager fingers. The girl tries to bite his full sweet lips with her small white teeth. His tongue flickers in and out of her mouth, which tastes of honeycomb, old lipstick and hamburger. Her fingers scratch down his hard hairless body in ecstasy. They lie down on the faded front seat and tear off their scanty clothes.

There are no words, just laboured breathing and cramped movement. Animal noises. There is something graceful yet ugly about making love. Especially love in a 1963 model Holden.

The girl lets her pale body relax, cool and clinical. The magic has gone out of lovemaking for her. Ever since she was fifteen and tried it out behind the girls' toilet at school, all interest in it has left her and it has become a mechanical process.

The boy is clumsy, like all the others were, and shy, like some of the others were. He is gentle and kind, like none of the others were. He brushes a big hand over her forehead, whispering, Don't be afraid. I won't hurt you. I never hurt anyone.

They share the experience together, rising and rising with their united passions. She arches her back and moans, while her fingers claw all over him. She bites his neck and runs her tongue over his hot, sweating body.

Afterwards, silence. They sleep, tangled nakedly together for warmth.

In the morning, there is a clear blue sky and a hot sun. Birds flutter through the leaves and wake the young couple. Ron wraps a holey brown blanket around himself and steps tentatively out onto the grey sand. He stands and stares with sleep-dulled eyes, uncomprehending, at the morning glory.

Isn't it a nice day?

He turns around to the naked girl sitting in the lotus position on the car seat.

He grunts, sleepily.

She grins and slides sensually (she thinks) out of the car.

What's for breakfast, Ron?

She is even skinnier with no clothes on. Her ribcage moves in and out as she breathes and her hipbones stick out. But he likes her, perhaps even loves her.

For you, an entrée of fresh boiled octopus. The main course was going to be chicken a 'la supreme—except I might mistake you for the chicken.

They laugh and embrace while the blanket slithers to his feet. It lies crumpled on the dirty ground, like a brown snake waiting to strike or the wrinkled skin of his former empty self.

Ron, I dare you to drive into the next town, like that—with no clothes on.

That would be an easy way for me to go to jail. Then you could pick up your next boyfriend.

He smiles, but she turns away from him swiftly and coldly.

If that's how you think of me, I'll go away now.

No! No, Linda, I was only joking. Please, honey.

His hands cover her bony, shivering shoulders and he swings her around. She is crying, so he pulls her to him.

Come on, honey. Hey, don't cry. I've never made anyone cry— please don't let you be the first. Come on, I was just joking.

He kisses her on the forehead then kisses her tears away. She looks up with wet, hurt eyes and gives a pale smile.

It's silly to cry on a lovely day like this, but I really have a feeling for you, Ron.

And I for you, Linda.

No, listen. I mean, last night you made me feel like—like—like something else.

They both laugh at her usage of his expression. But she loves and needs him, just as much as he needs the Kalbarri waves.

Come on, honey, let's go and see what's what at the beach.

He hugs her briefly and they smile again. The dog romps stupidly after an escaping magpie.

The sea is an indigo blue, throwing arms wide open to welcome its children, and roaring with happiness because it is almost summer and the surf's up. Laughing because for once it can offer joy instead of cold, mysterious danger.

The part of the beach to which the boy drives is miles from anywhere and almost deserted. A white Kombi van and a battered old yellow panel van, with flowers painted all over it, stand on the cliff edge, sniffing at the salty sea breeze with rusty dented radiator noses.

Ron gets out and waits for the girl. He clasps her to him and they idle over to the panel van. Two youths hulk in the front seat, staring fanatically into the humped back of the blue animal they worship. They hardly glance at Ron and his girl.

Hey, man, how's the surf?

The closer, younger youth has tried to grow a beard that hangs sparse and brown from his smooth cheeks, but he still looks young and useless. He intones, like a prayer,

Good swell. Left-hand breaks are cool. Bit freaky out there, though. Bit heavy, man.

Right. I'll still give it a try. You guys know a Sammy Saydlaw? An Abo kid?

The other boy turns to look at Ron and the girl, interest in his coal-black eyes.

Sambo? You wouldn't think he'd miss a top day like this, do you? He came with Keeley and Charlie Yo-Yo.

Still got his same old board?

Yeah, still as fluky as ever.

The old-young boy grins. He holds up a plastic bag full of green leaf, saying, If you're going out, man, tell him to come and have his joint before me and Billy smoke it all. You and her can have some too.

He nods at the girl, who is slightly shocked at the casual display of illegal wares, and looks at her with a knowledge that is older than his age.

I'll hang loose today, man.

Ron lifts his fingers in lazy farewell. The boys have already forgotten about them; they are in a trance again, hypnotised by the rolling ocean. Ron and Linda go back to the car. She squats in the car's shadow and puffs slowly on a cigarette; watching him wax his board with loving care, then wriggle into a wetsuit. He touches her gently.

You'll be all right? I won't stay out for long.

I'm OK. I'll go for a walk along the beach.

She pauses and stares into his dreamy green eyes and the green board he hugs as closely as he hugged her. Behind him the green-blue ocean crooned a love song to tear him away from her. She feels jealous. Last night had been intended only as a one-night stand, like all the others were. But she likes this warm brown boy with the sea-green eyes.

Do you smoke that stuff?

What? Gunja? It's good for you, baby. Makes you non-violent and gives you good dreams. You'll have to try some soon. Not today, but. Another day, another way.

He smiles again and touches her sunny shoulder with a bony lemon-yellow finger.

OK. See you, sweetheart.

He kisses her pale freckled cheek. Then he sets off down the slope with his easy, loping gait: the black knight going out into the towering blue forests with his faithful steed—to win a white-crested castle, all by himself.

For a while she watches him, mesmerised by his graceful movements as he soars through the water. She smokes another cigarette and shades her eyes against the glaring, hurtful sun on the water. This is the true God, pounding the waves into formation with its white heavy fist, turning the half-dozen or so surfers into black shapeless dots on the dancing water. A pack of wolves waiting, and once every while chasing a white or blue or green wave ceaselessly towards the beach, where it crashes in death.

She goes for a walk along the shore. She comes to a lumpy green reef with sand-swirling hollows carved out of it by a bent, scaly, old green-haired man, who only came out at night and wove spells with the stars and created the reef for her to find—only her. It seems to rise and fall above the rushing white foam: overbearing, mysterious, full of magic things for her.

It stretches green fingers out into the blue sea. At high tide, white waves roll over it scornfully, but at low tide the reef emerges like a huge crocodile—or a mouldy rotting log, green and grey and undestructible.

She loves the reef, wedged between the fine white sand and the pure blue sea; lonely as she is lonely, and wanting a friend. But only as a friend—not as a conqueror. Several pieces of chewed-up surfboards are scattered on the wet rocky shoreline, to show everyone that no one will tame its waves.

And she *is* a friend. She stares out over the sun-blotched water that makes her squint her eyes like Ron. She listens to the stories that the waves sliding languidly up the beach tell her. Stories of sunken ships, and huge silent fish and exquisitely coloured shells at the bottom of the sea. Sitting in the warm sun, she can see the black depths where no man had ever been before and thus she is knowledgeable—more so than Ron or anyone else who only skimmed airily across the surface.

The reef lets her slide her body into the swirling blue water of contentment.

Gentle strands of seaweed touch her face, like the boy's fingers last night. In one deep hole she finds a glorious, orange-green, curly shell like a trumpet. She would like to blow out a sea song so it would explode all over the silent white cliff and shatter into fragments onto the wild, white beach torn into sandstorms by the grey wind's wily hands, and let everyone know how happy she is.

Before she leaves the reef she wraps a strand of seaweed around her head and interlaces it with yellow and pink beach flowers. The queen of the ocean is going to meet her lover.

The sun reaches down hot lips, kisses the water from her body and reddens her pale skin. Whom to love? The rider of the sky or the rider of the water?

When she arrives he is emerging from the water with another youth.

He smiles over at her, admiring her flowery crown.

You look beautiful, Linda.

I found a fascinating reef about half a mile away. There are so many things to find there.

Ron's companion speaks, in soft lilting tones.

You look out for those reefs. Plenty of sharks around there. A person could disappear in a wave forever.

He is tall, with huge muscles and a sleek chocolate skin. Orange board shorts cling wetly and lovingly to his broad legs and slim waist.

This is Sammy, Linda. He was the top surfer in the state for junior, and soon he'll be top surfer in Australia. Maybe even the world!

Sammy looks away shyly and, embarrassed, wriggles his long black toes in the dry white sand. Then he glances at the white girl. His eyes, too, are strange, a brilliant green—white man's eyes in his dark face. Like Ron, he can read the ocean. Better than Ron, because he grew up practically in it. Now he has achieved what he wants—to be the top Western Australian junior surfer and one day soon he will be the best Australian surfer.

His eyes look at the girl and there are no dreams in them, for his Dreaming is over. Only pain and liquid shyness. He has many friends now, because Sammy Saydlaw is the tops and they are all at the bottom. That is why he continually has to improve his technique. His friends only surf on waves; he surfs on monstrous, billowing life, right on the crest where he can wipe out or cruise in to victory among the white man's cheers.

Yet he is different from the other surfers, not just in his quietness and skin colour. He thinks differently from them about the ocean that was his ancestors' feeding ground for centuries. He can tell you where hidden middens lie, holding the skeletons of shellfish and stories going right back to when man's footprints first touched a truly virginal land. He can tell you where fish and crayfish reside in the nooks and crannies of a thousand jagged reefs. Unlike the white surfers, whose language is often inarticulate and sparse at the best of times (unless they are stoned when they have the chance for eloquent, drugged words, or unless, like Colin, they have been world wanderers with stories to tell) Sammy speaks of his ocean with a knowledge and love that no one, not even Ron, could hope to understand. This is why he speaks differently sometimes. Like his skin, this can set him apart from the rest of the youths, as well, of course, as the slight nasal twang that betrays his Aboriginality.

He shrugs his powerful shoulders and smiles softly at Ron.

Pretty soon now you'll be taking over, Ron. You had some good rides today.

Oh, it was OK.

Sammy punches Ron softly on his chest.

See you round, Ron. Nice meeting you, Linda.

He wheels around and glides up the eroding cliff towards the panel van like a shadow.

Good bloke, Sammy. One of the best.

All the boongs on the farm were either drunk or in jail, and they were *all* no-hopers.

Well—yeah. Not all, though, baby. Sammy's a good bloke.

You're a better one.

They hug each other's wet bodies and he tastes the salt on her face.

You be careful on that reef, Linda. Sammy's right. He knows every inch of this coastline.

Ooooh, pooh! What sort of shark's going to eat a skinny little chicken like me?

They laugh and drift up towards the car. Ron has his board in one arm and his girl on another: he is content.

For the rest of that week, Ron and Linda take life as it comes. It stretches over the horizon in a warm lazy yawn and sinks to rest in the sun-red sea at night. The boy surfs and talks to his people, and sleeps in the sun. The girl goes for peaceful walks with the boy's mongrel: through the stunted slinking growth creeping up onto the sand dunes (but never quite getting the courage up to rush in and attack the ocean), along the innocent beach, the dog chasing birds that he never caught (and knew he couldn't) or digging holes when he knew there was nothing to find. The girl would laugh and stroke his matted fur. She loves the dog as she loves the boy—both are the same.

She loves the reef, too, though after Sammy's soft warning she doesn't venture out too far. Once, in a patch of clear water, she

110 /

fancied she saw a shadowy grey shape that glided as quietly as the Aboriginal boy in from the deep. She swam frantically to the shore, fear freezing her. Afterwards on the safe beach, she laughs at herself for running from shadows. She curses Sammy for turning her Eden into a hell with his words of knowledge.

It is lazy weather for the lazy people who are just lying around. Once Ron and Linda drive to the angry square town, with its littered streets and horrible constricting houses and the inevitable policeman. They wander together, oblivious of the grey wrinkled people on the grey wrinkled seats. They come to a delicatessen and brush away the fly-wire door. Ron grins.

Sweets for the sweet?

Oh yes, Ron. I'd really love a Violet Crumble—I'm crazy about Violet Crumbles, I could eat them forever.

If you don't look out, you'll turn into one.

Perhaps I have already.

Then you're all the better to eat, dear Gretel, and I am about to build you a house of Violet Crumbles.

What about the witch?

Witches are out of date, babe. Who needs a witch, anyway?

They laugh together over their secret, standing barefoot on the dusty floor, with all the people mumbling around them, about them. But they don't care. They have each other and all the secrets of the sea.

So that's how the days go. Every night she makes love to Ron rolled up on the sand, in blankets, beside the flickering fire and every day she makes love to the sun. She becomes brown and glorious and happy.

One day, while she is sleeping in the sun by her reef, a wavering shadow covers her. She looks up with a smile on her lips for Ron. She sees silent, soft Sammy, who squats down beside her.

Oh, hello.

She turns her back on the hunched powerful, dark form.

Hello, Linda. Sorry I woke you. I see you still come to the reef.

Yes. I like it.

He stares out at the turmoil with gentle eyes.

Can I offer you a cigarette?

No, thanks.

You don't like boongs, do you?

The quiet question spears her. She wriggles on the ground, like a captured bardee grub; fat and juicy and ready to be eaten, soul and body, by this boy with the awful silence. The calm green eyes pierce her now, reading her disgust.

No.

Neither do I much.

She stares at him to see if he is lying. But there is a faint cynical smile on his lips and pain in his eyes.

My mob used to hang around me like flies. Every prize I'd win, the whole tribe would be in for their share. There'd be none left for me. One day I had a big brawl and told them all to clear off. I shifted over east for a few years and haven't looked back since.

But there are always the jagged rocks waiting for him below the surface, below the wave he rides so well. So he can smash into them and they will tear his beautiful black body apart.

Ron's my best friend. I hope I will be your best friend, too.

He glances up over her head.

Here comes Ron now. We're going fishing.

He raises a hand in welcome, pink-nailed, a little yellow on the criss-crossed palm. Ron leaps down the side of the sand dune. Linda smiles at him as he slithers beside her and solemn Sammy.

Sammy found you, then?

Sammy gives a mocking smile.

Set an Abo to track anything down, he'll find it.

Got a cigarette, Ron baby?

Sammy's got the fags today.

A dark hand holds up a white packet of cigarettes. She takes one tentatively. Dark fingers strike a match and cup it from the wind.

Thank you.

It's all right.

Well, come on, people, let's go hassle these fish. Sammy and Keeley are coming over to tea tonight, honey.

Then we'd better catch plenty of fish.

They set off down the beach, Ron with Linda, Sammy with the rollicking mongrel.

That night, Sammy and Keeley and some others looking for a free feed come over to Ron's camp for tea.

Ron and Sammy have caught many fish that day. Sammy has caught a rare wobbegong as well. Keeley has brought some steaks. Gren Woolley has brought some marijuana.

They sit around the fire that flickers across their faces and draws out their souls to dance with the pungent wood smoke and frying fish smells evaporating into the night sky.

Hey Ron. Still got that old plank you call a board, I see.

Don't knock it, Keeley. A guy gets to love a board and it's his whole life, know what I mean?

Wally, the wise old-young youth with the sparse beard, is speaking. His mate, Billy the kid, grins.

Yeah, man. Doesn't matter what sort of board it is, as long as you can ride it. It's just the same as a woman, really.

Sammy smiles over at brooding Linda.

Let's not talk about boards tonight. Linda must be bored.

Bored with boards, eh, Sammy?

Ron laughs happily and hugs Linda close to him. She smiles up, full of love.

Gren's slow voice creeps over the fire. Heavy-lidded brown eyes gaze at Ron dopily.

Hey, Ron, Piglet's coming down soon, man. He heard you were hanging out here.

Piglet?

Now that's one guy I can't handle.

Who can, Billy? He's a spoilt little brat.

Not so much of the little, man.

Yeah, how can a guy that size handle a board?

What's it matter to him, Charlie? If he breaks a board his old man will buy him a dozen more. He only owns half of Australia, after all.

Yeah, I remember once when he got a little dent in his board and he went right out and bought a new one. A hundred dollars, man.

That's nothing, Billy. What about when he didn't like the colour of his board? I mean, there was nothing wrong with it. Just that Ian Cairns had a cream board or something. So Piglet bought a cream board.

I mean, he can't even surf, man.

Laughter mingles with the smoke and disappears. Ron has sat silent throughout the conversation, with Linda staring up at him, trying to read his mind.

Oooh, cool it, you guys. Piglet's OK.

Well anyway, I was only telling you.

Billy, eager to get some free enjoyment out of life, nudges loose, sleepy Gren.

Well *I'm* telling you, Gren, you freaked-out drug dealer, let's have these reefers you promised us.

Gren's fingers roll the joint expertly. It is the only thing he can do half right. He can't even surf properly. He is only there because he knows where he can buy cannabis and hashish or even heroin or cocaine. One day he will get caught, like his cousin, and maybe sent to jail.

Ladies first, man. Never let it be said that Grenwall Woolley is not a gentleman.

Oooh, wow—three cheers for our man, Gren.

You're just a big poofter, Gren!

Amid the muted laughter, Ron hands the girl the joint.

Look at that lovely creation. You can count on Gren to roll a first-class joint.

No thanks, Ron.

Go on. You can't be a proper surfer's chick if you don't have a puff of grass once in a while.

Ron hugs her reassuringly, so she is tempted. Across the fire Wally winks at her with his wise eyes.

Go on, Ron's girl, where's your form?

And amid the laughter of her people, she takes her first puff, at the beginning of the trip into Ron's world.

So they sit around the formless fire that is their God when the sun goes down (for everyone needs an idea to huddle up to when everything else is dead) puffing sedately at the joint and handing it around, like a tribe of wandering unwanted Indians smoking their peace pipe. When the first joint is finished, Gren rolls another and yet another—until it is all gone and he can sink back into oblivion for a while.

Words and laughter tangle together like lovers. They drift outwards in the air and cover the fire, the boys, the girl and the sleeping dog so they are all in one world of their own making.

Linda huddles against Ron and listens to him telling the others about his job on the crayboat. His drugged eyes sparkle as he tells of the one big thing that has happened to him in his tattered life. She glances over at Sammy and sees he is watching her, hidden in the shadows that the flames throw away. She is embarrassed and pulls the blanket around herself.

At last the youths straggle away to wherever they camp. The boy and girl make love on the midnight sands beside the dying coals and sleeping dog. They create love all that night and sleep in for half the next blue day.

Piglet comes in the afternoon. He hurls down the track in a brand new Rover with two new surfboards gleaming on the rack. He pulls up with a flourish between Ron's old station wagon and Billy's flowered panel van.

He is huge and white like an exposed, wind swept sand dune, with medium length sandy hair and round blue eyes in a fleshy pink face.

He peers suspiciously in, at dreaming untidy Billy and Wally, then strides down to the beach. Clean well-cut trousers adorn his long legs and a gaily coloured Hawaiian shirt flaps around his heavy body. He raises a meaty hand and roars, like the ocean.

Hello, men. What's the surf like?

None of the surfers answers him. Tiny Charlie, the wedge-faced Chinese boy, mutters, Oh, I think you could handle it, man, with a little help from your old man—God.

Piglet tries again.

Scarbs is flat.

Yeah, it would be, Big Boy. Coming out today?

Sammy is speaking. Piglet is one of the rocks that Sammy must ultimately dodge or smash into. Piglet hardly glances at him as he speaks to Keeley.

Yeah, I might go out for a ride. Is Ron Doorie around? I saw his car.

He's not surfing today, Big Boy. He's off in the scrub, making it with his chick.

His chick? This I *have* to see. I'll wait around.

He pulls out a packet of cigarettes.

Any of you guys want a smoke?

No one appears to hear him. At last Gren speaks.

No, man, I'm going out in a minute.

I'll have one, Big Boy.

Sammy's green eyes stare into Piglet's pink face, amused at his discomfort at having to give the Aboriginal boy a smoke.

Here.

Thanks, Big Boy. Got a match?

No answer as Piglet sticks a cigarette disconsolately between his big rubbery lips, and lights up, then blows out the match.

Sorry. Windy day, you know? Wind blew it out.

Yeah. Tell us about your new board, Big Boy. You don't mind if I sit with you, unna, koordah?

Sammy adds the last two words sarcastically and contemptuously, for he lives in a white world now and his people are in the past—except to someone like Piglet.

I'm going for a walk. Get some fresh air.

The mountain rises and lumbers off back to his new car.

The bastard grows a foot every time you see him.

Pity his brain doesn't grow.

See his face when he had to give Sam a fag?

Yeah, you showed him, Sammy.

I wish I didn't have to show anybody anything!

Sammy gets up quickly and wanders off, just as he has always done since he was a child, when he was being moved and pushed around with his family. Always being blamed for the stolen sheep or car, seeing his uncle taken away, accused of being drunk, seeing his older brother punched up behind the police station in one small town, just another cheeky boong who got what he deserved—or a bit of fun for the bored white men, hearing about his aunt who was raped by two of the local cockies' sons. No justice there, and he cried into his mother's faded, crumpled lap, the only comfort he knew in those young years. His father was always drunk because he had given up. His cousins and brothers were always stealing, getting as much fun as they could out of their second-rate lives. His sisters were always pregnant and whining. So Sammy's music was the crying and the whining and the swearing and the fighting and the complaining, and when it all got too much for him he would wander away, disappearing for days into the bush and letting the harsh peace rub into his tormented soul. He promised himself he would be better than his family and *his* music was the rolling, curving, crashing tune of the sea. And he knew that one day he *would* be famous and everything would be better than the life he was forced to live. Now he is almost famous—but everything is the same. So he wanders as of old, brushing angrily past Wally, who has finally made an appearance.

What's hassling Sambo?

Nothing, Wally. He's just an unpredictable boong. Doesn't matter how famous a guy gets, he'll still go walkabout like any other nigger.

Cool it, Yo-Yo. Does Sam ever call you a Chink? Uh? Or a yellow gook, like Big Boy would? And did, too, man—remember?

AH, Jesus, Keeley, I can see right through you, man. If Sambo was a shit surfer, you wouldn't be giving him a ride in your wheels now, would you? I'm honest, like my Jewish mama, God rest her soul.

Little bandy-legged Yo-Yo picks up his board and goes down to the water. Then he is shooting swiftly out towards the breaks. The others stand around on the hot sand that is bubbling and heaving in the wind like a volcano, ready to erupt into more violence on this sweltering, sultry day.

116 /

Linda and Ron have gone down to Linda's reef. The jagged green teeth grin evilly from the water and swirling white saliva drools through them in mad joy.

They run into the flickering surf and dance with it. She screams happily as the water rushes over her, claiming her. They are clutched lovingly to the cold salty breast and sucked out into the deep by the next wave. They roll and tumble in the surf, laughing with love—for themselves, the sea, the sun and life. The waves lick over them as an animal licks its babies, so that the babies stay clean and warm and alive.

Out of the shining water they burst, and up onto the soft dry sand that clings around their wet bodies warmly. They sit cross-legged like two Buddhists praying for salvation, crying out upon the lonely beach and watching the falling sun. Ron stares moodily up at the sun.

Clouds coming up, sweetheart. Tomorrow might be a bad day.

For surfing, maybe. Not for other things.

He smiles slowly down at her and runs his fingers through her lank yellow hair and across her thin, peeling face.

He leaves to do some surfing while she explores the rock pools she knows like her own mind now. Small striped fish swim around in frantic circles: round and round, all day, until the tide comes in. Crabs scuttle busily over the rocks. She wades out until the ocean whips around her tiny waist. The wind whips her hair around and covers her with its salty breath. She is so far out and so alone in the sea, with the whole ocean salaaming at her feet, that she truly feels like a goddess of the ocean.

She sees a rare porpoise drifting out of sight into the green water at the end of the reef, like a thought too gentle for the cold dark world it is entering. She sees several huge, grey, slow fish. Then the deep frightens her, as though she is standing on the edge of two worlds. One little step and she will hurtle down, out of the sunlight forever.

She goes back to the shore.

She lies on the sand and undoes her bikini top. The gentle hands of her new friend, and Ron's old friend, the sun massage her forlorn freckled back, and send her into a contented sleep.

She feels someone watching her and opens one eye warily. A huge pink youth is staring at her frankly, with round blue eyes. She sits up, embarrassed, doing up her bikini. She snaps, to cover her embarrassment.

Who are you?

I'm Big Boy. Ron Doorie's mate. You know Ron, of course?

Yes, of course.

Good bloke, Ron. Got a few stupid ideas, though.

His eyes rove over her in the way his father surveys his vast tracts of land. She hugs her arms around her and snaps again.

Well?

Well—cigarette?

Arrogantly spoke, as though he is sure of himself.

She accepts a cigarette and he smiles his infuriating, triumphant smile.

So you're Ron's chick?

Perhaps.

Not bad-looking. Ron picked a winner for once.

Look, what is this? The local horse show?

Just having a friendly chat, that's all.

She knows she ought to get up and leave. But this presumptuous giant's power holds her back. She stares silently out over her reef, sensing the blue eyes feeling her, making love to her. The reef is of no use to her, so she turns back to the giant, awed by his size. He has taken off his bright flowery shirt and the muscles beneath his fat skin roll like heavy swell in an oily sea.

Why don't you piss off, Big Boy?

Because you don't want me to.

Want a bet?

Before the girl can do anything, Piglet's meaty hand squeezes her breast. The other arm curves around her waist as he pulls her to him. Big lips smother her cries and his body rolls on top of her as his hands crawl over her thin body like crabs.

Up on the cliff, under a scraggly tree that rears in distorted silhouette against the sky, an invisible black form watches Piglet and the girl impassively. Sammy has been watching the girl all afternoon, where he has sat hidden from mankind. He loves her languid movements and the way she seems to melt into the water, and become part of the ocean he loves and needs.

He thinks he should go down and stop Piglet from fouling his dream. But neither of the two likes him; it would be a waste of time. Piglet would only beat him senseless, then go back to raping the girl.

If it is rape.

He sways to his feet, like a snake emerging from the snake-charmers basket, lured and lulled by the music of the sea. He tears away from his shadows under his tree, and walks away.

Down on the shore, Piglet has peeled off Linda's bikini top. She bites his hand and rolls away as he rears in hurt surprise. She sprints for the curling ocean and dives into its protectiveness.

On the shore, just out of reach of the waves, Piglet bellows, You can't fool me, you little slut! You were just begging for it, *I* could tell.

He dangles the white bikini top in his massive fist and laughs cruelly.

White for the virgin, I *don't* think! See you soon, sweetheart.

He drops the bikini scornfully on the ruffled white sand. He gives a defeated laugh, picks up his shirt and walks off without once looking back at her.

She stays in the cold water that tosses her to and fro without any fun until she is sure Piglet has gone. Then she crawls out of the slithering waves and cries on the friendless beach.

For Piglet knows what she has been trying to hide from everyone else, especially simple, happy, clumsy Ron: especially herself. She is just a drab butterfly flitting from one drooping flower to the next, getting a little enjoyment before she flutters away. She thought she has found her happiness in Ron Doorie, but she knows now she will leave him, one day—for another flower. Ebony Sammy, the black tulip, perhaps, or red Big Boy, the pink pig face.

She moves down the beach after the giant.

Out on the green sea, the land looks far away and unreal amongst all the wavering fantasy. Suspended between the rolling water and the windswept sky, it doesn't seem to exist for the windwashed, sun-scrubbed pack of black-clad boys on their boards.

There is a strange, unspoken hierarchy out on the water; almost a type of pecking order, really, that doesn't exist on the land. Probably because a surfer can float all day on the idly moving back of the water and perhaps get only five or six good rides, so it is a hierarchy based on good manners and skill of performance. That is why the surfers are glad Big Boy doesn't come out, because he has yet to learn this highly complex code. If a person waits on the outside break all day for a ride then, just as he gets it, someone slides in on the inside, causing him to pull out or wipe out, it can cause bad situations and is even dangerous in white water near reefs in high waves. So courtesy is extended to everyone; if one surfer sees another in the prime position for the wave, he pulls out and lets him go. There'll be another wave soon—waves are as countless as the stars in the universe. Of course, the more experienced surfers are usually those who get the best places, but in keeping with good manners no top surfer ever hogs all the waves; sometimes he will pull out of a good one to let a less experienced rider have his chance. Of course there are times when a surfer feels he is as good as the surfer in the prime position and *will* drop in. Then things can get a little tense and nasty. But in all the seven years Ron has been surfing he has not seen one occasion turn into fisticuffs; mostly, after a few sharp words, the two antagonists drift further apart. Back on the shore, the quarrel is almost always forgotten. Anger, for them, is as loose as the sliding clouds changing and moving all the time, just as they did before man was even thought of. It is a time for idle talk out here as well, a time to get to know your companions even better as you squat or kneel, sit or lie on your gently rocking boards and survey the blue horizon for the wave of the day.

Ron hugs his slender, polished, green board between his wiry legs and his green eyes hypnotise the huge green wave bearing down on him. All green—all supreme and harmonious.

He catches the great green wave and flies through the rushing water, suspended between the watery foam-flecked pit below the wave and the blank blue sky above: right on the crest of his wave. He is really moving now. Several others compete with him, then two catapult off and there is only one—Sammy Saydlaw. They cut spinning patterns into the gleaming green side of the wave, with their boards performing perfect movements. Then the crest seems to bow before its god and the wave forms a tube. Ron shoots into the tunnel with Sammy tailing him. Glorious blue greenness with its own special muted light and roaring all around, as though he is in the very belly of the wave; water all around him and everything moving fast, without his knowing where they are all going. He crouches on his bucketing board and skims out of the tunnel, up over the curving back of the wave and down into the valley. He subsides back onto his board and watches the wave crash onto the rocky shore.

So huge, so magnificent, created and moulded by the cunning, clever hands of the sea; an idea from the sea—and he has mastered it, controlled it and made it die. The biggest and best wave of the day and only he has ridden it all the way to victory: no, only he and Sammy.

Ron turns and grins at silent Sammy, coming up behind him. He shouts in ecstasy.

120 /

Man! Man, did you see that tube? Wow, what a spacy wave, and I took it all the way. And did you *see* that tube? That blissed me out, man.

Yeah, I saw it. It was good.

Sammy smiles faintly and his green eyes flicker away over the shimmering water. He can read and understand waves, but girls and love he can't. In that way he is very much like Ron, his best and only friend. He has to tell Ron what he saw, although it will hurt them both. He has too often smashed on unkind rocks to know otherwise.

Ron pushes his russet hair from his green, shining eyes and off his brown, radiant face. He glances out to the horizon in search of another wave. But there are none worth capturing after the demise of the one he just rode.

He turns to Sammy, who has drifted up beside him, and smiles into the dark, worried face.

Hey Sam, you going to that show tomorrow night?

Beverley's?

Yeah. Jesus, man, every time I go there, there's a fight or rape or attempted suicide—and always pigs busting us. Man, something *always* happens at Beverley's.

Sounds like fun. I might come.

It wouldn't be the same without you, man. Everyone'll be there. All the guys, chicks. Even Piglet, I suppose.

Piglet? I got something to tell you about Piglet, Ron.

And he tells him. Out there on the empty sea, with their disjointed reflections squirming beside them, captured by the sun and water, with the blue sky above that reflects all that the youths want to see and be, and the thin ragged strip of land in the middle beckoning like a crooked dry finger. Asking Ron to come off his rolling green dream: asking Sam to come back and be a black man, as he should be. Beckoning and sighing for the sheep to come home.

That night, around the cold trembling fire, Ron stares sadly into Linda's masked face. He plays with two burning twigs, then glances shyly at the skinny girl on the other side of the fire.

Piglet was here today.

Was he?

Yeah. I saw his car on the top of the hill, when I was surfing. You couldn't miss it with all the boards on it. More boards than a chicken's got feathers.

A weak laugh that is lost in the smoke. No joy in it at all.

121 /

Did you see him today, after I left you on the reef?

No.

Oh, I thought you might have. He must have gone down that way because he wasn't on the beach or in the water.

No. There was no one there.

Right.

He stares at her alabaster face shielded by the flames and knows now that Sammy was right; she will spread her legs for any animal, and when she gets sick of him, she will leave.

Linda pretends to eat her food and wonders why she does not tell him what really happened.

So they both sit there on the freezing white sand with the jagged fire between them, separating them.

Oh, yeah, that's right. Beverley's holding a party tomorrow night. Have a change of scenery, eh?

OK, Ron, a party sounds like a good time.

Ron grins suddenly; determined to hold on to his girl.

Yeah. A good time will be had by all.

They arrive at the house at about eight o'clock. There is a buzz of mosquitoes from the verandah and a noise from a stereo and people down the hall. All around outside, cars huddle into the shadows of the trees and the night, as though ashamed of their shabbiness. Only Big Boy's new Rover stands brazenly under the one humble light in the street.

Beverley lives on the outskirts of a small coastal town, hidden away in her own Garden of Eden. Everyone knows about Beverley. At the moment, she is growing a crop of marijuana, a couple of kilometres away, in the bush. Next time she may be selling heroin or her own body—it's all the same to her. Either way the police always catch her. She is that kind of girl with that kind of luck.

Ron and Linda and silent Sam stand by the fly wire door until Beverley comes to greet them. She is short and sloppy, with waist-length red hair and huge, placid brown eyes like a cow's. In her small hand she holds a joint which she hands to Sam while she squeals and hugs Ron.

Ron, baby, where've you been? Sambo, too. Wow, what a buzz! Hey, come on in, anyway. Keep that joint, Sam sweetheart— there's plenty more. Hi, you must be Ron's chick, huh? All the guys are sold on you, I can tell you.

Down the skinny dirty passage, past a couple making drugged love on the floor. Into a maelstrom of music and voices from the two dozen or so youths sprawled around on the stained carpet.

Christ, is that Doorie? I thought he was in jail.

Got a lovely sheila there, mate.

G'day, Sammy, sweetheart. Come and sit here with me.

Give us a try on that joint, man.

Hey, Ron, how's the surf down south, babe?

What was the cray boat like, man?

Fuck, man, I haven't seen you in yonks.

Ron falls down on an empty beanbag and drags Linda after him. He holds her close to him protectively and smiles around the room. Sure enough, there is huge Piglet, holding up a wall and swilling beer from a bottle almost lost in his massive fist. He eyes Linda over with his small round eyes and grins confidently. Ron scowls and glances at Linda, but she is listening to Gren tell one of his stoned jokes. He forgets about Piglet and settles down to have a good time, drinking and joking and smoking Gren's joints and keeping a gentle hand on his woman's thigh, to remind himself, that he still has her.

About two o'clock in the morning, when everyone is stoned or strange and several people have staggered out to be sick in the tangled weeds and perhaps go to sleep there; when couples are naked and rolling on the dusty splintered floor, getting what love they can before the sun rises and it's tomorrow again, it is then that drunk Piglet staggers over to sleepy Ron. In the corner Sammy stiffens beside his murmuring girl for the night, alert and ready, as he has been since the party began.

G'day Ron, my old mate, and how's things with you?

Good.

That's marvellous, boy. Marvellous. And I hear you were actually working?

On a cray boat. You ought to try it some time, Big Boy.

On a cray boat? Do you call that working, Ron? Come on, you didn't do any work.

I did.

Ron sits up warily, coming out of his marijuana dreams. He has been proud of the work he did on the cray boat. Now, flushed and drunk, Piglet is tearing his pride apart with brutal words.

Why, Ron. I think you were back in jail again. Isn't that the truth?

Oh, shut up, Big Boy.

Piglet leans close and breathes stale beer all over thin Ron. He leers.

Shut up? Oh, I understand. You don't want certain quarters to know of your previous sinister dealings. Well, sssshhhh, Big Boy.

Piglet chuckles deeply and stares at Linda with wicked red-veined blue eyes, while he places a huge finger over blubbery lips.

And how are you today, sweetness?

That's Linda.

I know that's Linda. That was her name yesterday, wasn't it sweetheart?

Piglet bares his teeth at Ron.

How's your pal Sambo going?

Good.

Piglet turns to the quiet Linda, who tries to disappear into the beanbag.

You know what, Linda, I forgot to tell you one thing yesterday. On the beach, remember? Sammy and Ronnie baby here are very close. *Very* close, isn't it, Ron? They share everything—*everything*.

He stares at Linda with innocent yet cold eyes, a shark circling around his prey in a dark sea. Then he turns back to bristling Ron.

Isn't that right, Ron?

Go away, Big Boy, and play with your bottle.

Play with my bottle, uh? What do *you* play with?

Ah, piss off.

Tell me one thing, Ron. Has Sam had your baby yet?

Ron's eyes go cold and flash over to Linda who sits, astounded, beside him.

That's not funny. That's dirty.

Come on, Ron. With all the screws you two have, I felt sure that you'd be a proud father by now. Or am I wrong? Is Sambo the lucky father?

Fuck off—*Piglet*.

What?

You're a real Piglet, man.

The name's Big Boy.

The name's *Piglet*. You big, slobbering, pink Piglet!

Ron shouts now and someone giggles. Piglet has got what he wants at last, a chance to fight lucky Ron who has a pretty girl. The giant grabs Ron by his shirt and drags him to his feet. There are screams and shouts as people scatter. Joey, the Italian, cries, Look out, Ron, he's drunk as a brewery horse. He'll murder you!

Then a heavy fist smashes open Ron's eye and he gags. He tries to get out of the grip but he is no match for the giant. He is punched in the stomach then thrown across the room and kicked in the head, so he is knocked out.

In the corner, Sammy slides away outside and waits under the shadows of a jacaranda tree. His business is not for the drugged eyes of the idle clan inside, but for the trees and the moon and the yellow rainstorm clouds and all the ghosts of his people.

When Piglet swaggers out of the door, Sammy falls in beside him.

G'day, Big Boy.

What do *you* want?

Why don't you leave Ron and Linda alone?

The giant stops and sneers down at the Aboriginal.

You can't have it both ways, Sambo honey. Which one shall I leave you ? Would you know what to do with a piece of crumpet?

Big Boy, you are about as dirty as white can get.

Piglet brushes Sammy aside contemptuously.

Bugger off, you useless black poofter. I've got better things to do tonight than talk to a smelly nigger who shoves it up white assholes.

Sammy's eyes turn an evil bright green. In one movement he scoops up a piece of wood and slams it down on Piglet's turned back.

Then they are fighting beside Piglet's car. Only the impassive trees see the violence spilling bloodily on the ground, with grunts and harsh gasps puncturing the serene night.

Just down the road, the police car starts up slowly.

I knew there'd be trouble, sooner or later, tonight.

There always is when Beverley holds an orgy, sarge.

Jeeze, look at that boong go, will you?

They pull up and saunter out, powerful; two blue shadows crawling from their hole, then crawling back again to whatever they came from.

Rightio, you two, break it up. The fun's over.

The old sergeant turns to a sullen Sammy and stares at him with bleak grey eyes.

What did you attack this bloke for? Don't think you can lie, because we saw it all from just down the road. You come out of the trees and whacked him over the bonce with a nulla-nulla. Eh?

Sammy says nothing.

Right, sport, if that's the way you want it. Get in the car.

Sammy stares, cold yet defeated, at Piglet.

Go on. You going to be trouble, are you? Eagerly said by the thin young constable with the agate eyes and pale lips pulled back in a slitty grin.

Sammy gets into the back of the car.

Piglet stands, bloody yet victorious, while the police sergeant admonishes him then sends him home to bed: and maybe that is because of his size, or his colour, or the fact that his father seemed to own half the state and is well known in high circles. Whatever, the policemen sends him home. Tonight is Piglet's big night.

In the car, the sergeant glares at Sammy beside him.

The driver sneers; Look at him, sarge. The crazy boong.

They all think they're David Sands or Hector Thompson.

But they're just baboons, eh, sarge? Every one of 'em. Their mums are baboons, anyway.

Yeah, too right. Are you a baboon, dickhead? Perhaps he'd like a couple of rounds with me, or you, Donald. Would you like that, matey?

Perhaps he doesn't understand English, sarge. Say it again in nigger talk.

The sergeant pokes Sam in the stomach while they laugh. Their laughter mingles with the roar of the waves on the shore. Both are so real in Sammy Saydlaw's life; only he has tried to forget the laughter that ties him down in chains so he can never really rise but will sink beneath the waves forever.

Ron wakes up late the next day, feeling sick. His eye is swollen purple and yellow, while his stomach and head hurt. Nearly everyone has gone and the old house smells weary, used up and hopeless. He staggers out onto the oily back porch into the warm sun where cicadas are singing a hymn (or perhaps it is just a dirty song).

Jesus! Oh, Jesus Christ!

Ron sits down groggily, and holds his head in his hands.

He won't help you, man. What you want is a cigarette.

Ron looks over into the weeds and sees Colin the oracle, Colin the great surfer, Colin the drunk, sprawled among the dandelioned rubbish. Colin groans to his feet and lets his thin body zigzag dizzily up to the steps. He offers a half-empty flagon of hot red wine to Ron, who shakes his head. They roll shaky cigarettes.

Some night, eh, man? I mean, Piglet really got heavy on you, didn't he?

Where's Linda?

126 /

Linda? Oh, your girl! Yeah man, she went to the beach for a swim, I think.

Where's everyone else, then? What about Bev and Sammy—and Piglet?

Wow, man, where've you been? Sam got picked up by the pigs last night. Bev's trying to bail him out today. Nothing new around here.

I'm going into town for a walk.

Right. See you when I see you if I see you, Ron, man.

Yeah.

The road is hot and dusty and it is a long way into town, it seems. Still stoned from last night, Ron idly picks some dandelions and makes a chain to put around his neck. He puts a yellow dandelion behind his mongrel's ear, but the dog promptly sits down and scratches it out, so it lies forgotten on the hot grey road.

In town he remembers the last time he and Linda came, and decides to buy her a Violet Crumble bar. He stands alone in the cold shop, with his drooping dying necklace around his skinny neck, with his ugly black eye and smashed lip. All the people's suspicious stares crush him into the dry boards. He buys her one, bright beauty caught in his weblike fingers.

Ron goes reluctantly to the stern, red-faced, brick police station. The sly constable stares scornfully at him.

Saydlaw's gone, chum. This dopey sheila bailed him out. Course, Beverley Owens would screw *anyone*.

Back he goes to the sagging house in the untidy bush.

Linda is sitting in the shade of the jacaranda tree, floating on a sea of soft, dead, purple flowers. She does not look at Ron when he squats beside her.

Hi sweetheart, what's the beach like?

Where've you been?

Her face is thin again, with hard eyes. All that morning she has lain on the beach, thinking. She has decided it is time to go. She will go up to the house and break it off. She is good at doing that.

The tentative smile that has begun to form on Ron's battered lips disappears. He looks down at the shadows grovelling on the rocky ground at his feet.

I went to see Sammy. He was in—

Sammy! Sammy! All the bloody time it's Sammy. Well, do you know where you and Sammy can go?

Linda.

Softly spoken, shy of her rage. He notices her flowered beach bag lying tiredly beside her.

Hey, sweetheart, where are you going?

Then he remembers the present he bought her and drags it out, sticky in its bright purple wrapper.

Look, I bought you a Violet Crumble.

Stick it up your bum! I'm sure anything'll fit up there now!

She shouts, knocking the chocolate from the boy's placating hand. It spins gaily through the air and falls in the dust, where, after a cautious wait, the mongrel sniffs it, then eats it, warily, watching for a kick.

Listen, you hopeless bastard, Big Boy came around today and I'm leaving you just as soon as he comes back to get me. So you and little black Sambo can be very happy together.

Linda, did you believe that crap Piglet said?

You *were* in jail. Everyone says so, not just Big Boy.

Ron draws circles in the sand with a crooked brown finger, then rubs them out again. He doesn't look at Linda.

Yeah, I was in jail for burglary. I broke into a supermarket and got a load of food. But that's all past now.

The time in jail when he was eighteen was a time he could not forget. He had been as lonely as a seagull circling high in an empty sky. They had sliced off all his hair and torn off his beach-comber clothes and ripped off his necklace with the gleaming white dugong tooth hanging from it.

He would sit in the corner of the exercise yard and his yearning eyes would gaze at the cruel blue sky where the clouds floated so free above him, fat and sleek like basking seals. His nostrils would twitch at the smell of salt that the Fremantle Doctor brought on its windy breath each afternoon. The smell of the sea he loved and needed, as a heroin addict needs the fine white powder.

It was because of this need that he made friends with Sammy, whose calm green eyes and gentle smile accompanied his deep lilting voice, as he told tales of surfing feats and huge curling waves and lovely white beaches that Ron Doorie in all his wander-ings, could only dream of. They had welded themselves a special friendship; the thin brown white and the tall, quiet black boy. When Ron's cellmate left, they arranged to have Sammy trans-ferred to his cell. The talks of wild coasts and images of leaping waves and bucking surfers helped feather the blows that each harsh new day brought when the walls, grim and hard, threw back the waves that crashed in their dreams. The touches and caresses the two traded were part of killing loneliness and a way to feed the hunger of their souls aching for sunny, water-drenched freedom again.

And that's where you learned to love your fellow-man. And I mean love, baby.

Ron glanced at Linda with subdued eyes.

Piglet's bad vibes, honey. Don't hang around him any more.

Don't tell me what to do, Doorie, you fucking nigger-lover!

She slaps him three times across his shocked face just as Piglet's Rover squeals to a confident stop.

Coming, Linda, gorgeous? We have to hurry if we want to make it to that hotel tonight.

He grins coldly at Ron, who watches the girl get into the car.

Then they are gone.

Ron leaves without saying goodbye to anyone. He and his dog drive down to the waiting beach.

No one is there.

Only Sammy Saydlaw, staring out at the meandering grey merpeople.

Ron unhooks his board and idly begins to wax it, with a sterile imitation of the love he once had for the board that has been more than a board; an escape from his troubles, he had thought.

Sammy wanders over to him, but before he can say anything, Ron spears him with angry words.

Just where the fuck were you last night when I needed you?

Sammy replies softly, a shattered black silhouette against the glassy ocean. I was in jail, Ron.

I know that! If you had come at Piglet when he was fighting me, we might have got somewhere. Now Linda's left me, and where were you?. In bloody jail. Christ!

Hey, Ron, take it easy.

He sits down and puts a gentle arm around Ron's slumped shoulders.

Come on, Ron. We've both had hassles just lately.

Ron's brown skin cringes from the arm as though it is a snake to be feared and not a comforting crutch to lean upon, as it has been in days gone by.

He shrugs the chocolate-coloured arm off abruptly and leaps to his feet. He snarls down at the shocked Aboriginal.

Don't touch me, you black nigger bastard ... It's all your fault Linda left me. Just go away from me—I don't want to know you, see? No one wants to know you, you boong poofter. You're out of class, man, understand? You think anyone cares you're top surfer? You're fucking black jail meat, baby.

He grabs his surfboard and stamps down the falling-away cliff. Behind him, stunned Sammy lets a tear slide down his dark cheek. Then more tears come and obscure the magnificent view of his ocean. He sits there alone before dragging his dreamless body to thumb a lift from the snaking highway, back to his people—who are waiting.

Ron walks a long way until he comes by chance to Linda's reef, where they had such good times. Now everything is as empty as the phlegmatic blue sky, while anger and bewilderment throb dully in his vacant mind like the thudding of far-distant surf.

He sits his dejected body on a scabrous rock that sticks into him derisively. His miserable eyes gaze out over the sea that is as grey as a dead man's dreams. Nothing seems real any more.

It is high tide and the sea roars like a dragon. The dragon dances while the shells sigh and the birds cry. The dragon howls for blood and spits out spray. Love can die, friendship can die, even dreams die—but the blue-purple-green dragon will always be there, dancing on everyone's grave, alive as the sun.

Suddenly he grabs the calm green board that has taken him to truth and fantasy and made him someone important so many times. He smashes it against the monster heads of the rocks. Once, twice, thrice, then it snaps into ragged halves—useless. The boy gulps in salty air, and pants hopelessly, while the mongrel puppy leaps around him, uncomprehending and the sun looks down imperiously from the blue sky.

FISH AND CHIPS

SOMETIMES I can close my eyes and pretend I'm right away, all alone in the heaving clouds, up in the air, where there is peace and quiet and the warm sun lying beside me like my girlfriend, kissing me before it goes to bed. Everything will be soft and red-yellow-purple, like everything good spilling across the sky. I will be right in the middle of it, playing with the wind and telling all my secrets (that I couldn't tell anyone, not even Mum) to the moon and stars.

Then Auntie Nira starts fighting with Mum or Uncle William, and I'm back home again.

Mostly, there are sixteen of us living at home. We're all Whittys together: there is no hope for us if we don't stick together. Mum was an Erwell, but she is one of our people now.

Gwendoline came home after running away and Dad gave her a proper hiding. Her legs were black and blue and all swelled up. She was crying too much for me. I went to watch TV until it was my turn to get belted.

Darryl and Louis have just come in, really pleased with themselves because they broke into a house and found $500. Tomorrow we'll have a wicked feed-up, and for that I'm glad, because I haven't eaten properly for a good three weeks. They found out Dad had come back to Mum, so they took away her Social Service monies, and we've been doing a real starve 'cos Dad don't spend his dole cheque on anyone except himself.

Darryl tells how a big dog made Louis shout when it come for him. Darryl reckons Louis was swinging in that tree like a little monkey. Uncle William busts himself laughing at that. Louis is Uncle William's kid. He is only about nine, but he smokes like a chimney and when he is drunk he wants to fight everyone, even Dad or Clancy, who are both over six foot. I tell you, that little Louis can make you laugh. Now Darryl's learning him how to break into shops and steal cars. He's pretty good, too, because he is so small and black that no one sees him.

All Uncle William does is laugh all day. Even when Auntie Nira broke a bottle over his head last night, he just laughed. He's mad, I reckon. I would have made Auntie Nira jump. She bosses us kids around and cheeks Mum, when Dad's not here. Jimmy said he'd take a machete to her one of these days, but I don't think he ever would. He just likes to hear himself talk. He's in Fremantle now, and I really miss him. He might not have been able to fight, but he was a solid dancer: his legs were rubber and his body was elastic, so Mum said. You should hear his impersonations of Elvis Presley and Humphrey Bogart.

But he assaulted a policeman who took him up into a back alley to belt him around.

Peter and Coran are huddled over by the window. They aren't talking or laughing, or nothing. They're on the run from work release. There is always a Whitty on the run; it's how life goes. Coran's going to dye his hair black so he'll have a better chance of escape. His hair's all pure blonde and long and beautiful, like a moonbeam or the sunlight creeping through the trees. He was so proud of his blonde hair that is like a crown, really, I suppose, because we're black all over. Now he has to give his crown away, since there aren't too many blonde Nyoongahs running around and he's too easy to spot. Those coppers are going to make Corry piss blood, they told me and Darryl.

Peter's just skinny and dirty and scared. Peter is Uncle William's other kid, my older cousin. He's the same age as Jimmy and they're good mates. When Jimmy was taken away, Peter went all to pieces. He thought he'd be the big man and help Coran steal a car. They were rolling it down the hill when Coran saw the munadj coming up the other way. So he jumped out and left Peter holding onto the passenger door. What the police van saw was a driverless car shoot past with a skinny bag of bones fluttering in the breeze like a flag at half-mast. Funny? We laughed for weeks, about that. Even now, if someone asks how Peter's stolen cars are, everyone busts a gut laughing.

But they still got caught.

They're out now, for a while, though. Coran stares at his feet and broods, while Peter doesn't even play cards; that's how scared *he* is. He mightn't read too good—none of us can, except the older ones—but he can do anything with a pack of cards. He's the best card cheat I know, except for Clancy. Clancy learned in jail when he had nothing better to do, then he came out and taught Peter, who never had anything to do. Coran and Peter only had another month to go, but they got itchy feet. Now they sit by the window all day, waiting for the police to come.

Dad's a Thursday Islander, a big bloke and a boxer once. He can still fight, but only when he gets wild. Then everyone had better look out. Uncle Joey was a good fighter too, until he got killed by a featherfoot. Last night those girls played a spirit game and brought him back. I was thinking of ghosts all night and when a sheet flapped out on the line, I nearly turned white for good. After that, I got into bed with Clancy.

Sally thinks she's really important because she has been all the way through school and has a job typing. But she won't give us any money; she doesn't want to own us now. She lives in a flat by herself, and is having a baby by a white bloke. Do you think he cares? He's gone away up north and he won't be back, either. Sally will be back, though. She can't stay away from home forever. No one can.

Gloria's got two babies, and she's only seventeen.

She's Uncle William's only daughter (at least, until he and Auntie Nira get together and stop fighting). Her man is in Fremantle, right now, for stealing cars. He's good to Glory and hardly ever beats her around. When he gets out he's going to get a job as a mechanic and settle down in a house; just the two of them, and the babies. That's *his* dream.

Those little babies are fun and we all love them, especially Clancy. He can hold one in each hand, right up in the air, so they look like little brown bees buzzing around a black flower. Clancy makes them laugh every time and when they do, a slow smile will drift over his own quiet face.

He was put on parole six months ago, after doing time for killing one of those Moores. The Moores are enemies of ours from some fight long ago. Anyway, it was the Moores who killed Uncle Joey and burned out Cousin Paulie's stomach so he died, too. One night, in town, the Moore boys came picking Clancy and Coran and some other cousins of ours. Pooooohh, boy! Clancy went wild and started throwing pool balls and smashing into those Moores with pool cues. I was only ten, so Clancy shoved me under a pool table. But I saw *that* fight.

Coran belted into two blokes and laid them both out. One of my cousins got a busted head from a pool cue. Then Clancy grabbed hold of big Gary Moore and threw him halfway across the room. He kicked him again and again until blood spurted out of that boy's mouth. Then Clancy grabbed a bottle and smashed it over Gary Moore's head and jabbed it in his stomach. Blood was running out of Gary Moore's head like a river, and I saw my first dead man. You, see, Paulie had been Clancy's best cousin and he was upset when Paulie was killed. Gary Moore was one of those blokes who shoved newspaper in Paulie's open stomach, then poured kero in him and burned him up.

Clancy was in jail for five years. Now he's grown up, with short hair and long sideburns. He told me, when he came out, 'Artie, don't you ever go to jail, boy. Let them white blokes rub you in the dirt, spit on you, shit on you even. But you keep right out of jail. It's a bad place in there, brother.'

Clancy's big like Dad, and doesn't talk much. No one knows what he's thinking or what he's going to do, so he's the most dangerous of us Whittys. On his face you can't see whether he is smiling or frowning, or what.

Our neighbours don't want to know us, really. Mum tries to keep the house clean, and us too. We have a bath every night but, as Darryl jokes, we never get any whiter. But it's not really a joke. No matter what we do to become like white, we're still black, and that's what it's all about. We can't even have a fight or have our relations around without all our neighbours minding our business.

They tell us to get a job.

Dad did work on the railways until he got a bad chest from the colds we're always getting. Darryl was working in a meat store just down from our place, but he almost cut his fingers off with one of those big knives they use, so he gave *that* job away. It was the first time Darryl had ever worked, heaving those big frozen kangaroos around. I went to take Darryl his lunch, so I know all about it. There were bulllets through the head, the stomach, all over— but the head, mostly. And all those dead eyes watching you, following you all around the room. I wouldn't work in a meat store.

When Darryl left, he went back the same day and stole the cashbox. He'd seen it standing on a shelf. Those white blokes never learn. But the police came straight to our place and caught him. They always come to Nyoongah houses first. Darryl went to Riverbank that time, but as soon as he got out, he and Louis went breaking into houses. Darryl's got a joke for everything; he doesn't care at all.

Our house is like our world. Sometimes it's dirty and sometimes it's clean. None of us have our own bed. We share everything when we got it. Out the back Mum's got a bit of a lawn growing, and she waters it every day. There are always bottles and flagons by the bin because Auntie Nira drinks like a horse. So does Dad and Uncle William too, a bit. Down by what was the back fence, there are two car bodies. Darryl has smashed all the windows now, just for something to do. They look a bit like what we're all going to be, I reckon. Perhaps that's why we surround ourselves with old rubbish. We are all going to be old rubbish when we die, or before.

In the house everything's broken or dirty, no matter how hard Mum tries to keep things clean. I feel sorry for her because I know how she feels. But you can't keep a house clean with sixteen or more people living in it and only Mum doing all the work.

So at our house we sit around: playing cards or drinking or fighting or laughing. Sometimes a couple of us go and visit our cousins. We've got cousins everywhere; we'd be no one without cousins. Always there are some of us in jail, or Riverbank or Bandyup—or some place. The Whittys get around all right, yet we never really get anywhere: we never move. There'll always be a Whitty family like us.

The one sound I hate most of all is the knock on the front door when the police come. I grew up with that sound. The police are always coming to question or arrest someone. When they came for Jimmy there were five, all with guns. Sweat was running off Jimmy and he was crying for Dad. He was shaking like he was a hundred and ten, instead of only just eighteen. We all laugh about that now: the night the munadj took Jimmy away; because, really, laugh is all we *can* do about it.

Well, now we've got some money and there's a programme about Charlie Pride on the radio. Everyone is happy and there's a good movie on TV.

Tomorrow there'll be fish and chips for tea.

That'll do me.

COOLEY

I

He shuffled down the narrow, meandering track still dotted with puddles from the morning rain. Overhead raced the heavy grey-black clouds and the wind that tore into the leaves of the trees bit through the frayed old coat of the boy and into his skin.

No one liked him much, this boy: the white children because he was a half-caste, the Aborigines because his parents were both white and he came from a different area, up north. He had only his brother Ben to take his part. Now Ben was up in Perth, playing football for the state, too busy to worry about his brother who was shuffling home from school.

He kicked a stone with his old dusty boot and watched it sail up into the air and land with a splash. That was Ben. Rise up to fame and then come home again. Back to shrieking kids and a grumpy dad and useless whining mum. Cooley spat. Not his mum—she was dead and the boy greatly wished she was still alive. It had been fun on that station, although Cooley couldn't remember much of it. Only his grandad, old Bandogera, who could tell great yarns and knew how to make a boy laugh. He had been only five when his mum died, and Ben had been eight.

The men had come in at sundown, when the sun had turned earth and sky the same deep red. The last of the sun's rays jumped off the tin roofs of the humpies, flashing in the coming darkness like drops of water. The last of the sun's fire joined the newly awakening flames of the campfires. Now the stories of the day could join the stories from the night and keep everyone warm with their words.

But not this story.

Even before the men reached the area where the tribe lived, they knew. Old men looked out from the shadows of their eyes. Young girls stood as still as stones. Old granny hugged the two boys to her dried-out dugs and softly moaned.

Her three brothers and behind—alone—her husband.

She had been riding flank when the herd spooked and wheeled towards her. Oh, how she had laughed! With her white teeth flashing in her dusky face like the sunlight's rays catching the windows of the station house on top of the hill. Oh, how she could ride on her huge black horse! She had been a part of the night herself, her stockwhip cracking like lightning over the herd's back.

But her horse had stumbled and she had fallen. The maddened herd had charged over her like the incoming tide of the irreversible ocean. All that was left was a confused riderless black horse in the midst of bucking red backs.

So Jurparri, known among the white people as Lucy Fluter, died. She was only twenty-five.

The station owner heard the keening of her people and his wife heard the story from the kitchen staff, so they went down the hill. They found her husband standing alone beside the eternally chuckling creek which cared not what happened in the frail world of humans, night or day, life or death.

'Come on along now, Nat. This is native business.'

'Couldn't even find all her body,' he cried in disbelief.

'Come up to the house. Have a drink,' the station owner murmured, and gently led the stricken man away.

He never went back to the camp again. He hardly talked to his two light-haired sons who played with their full-blood cousins and friends at the waterhole or out in the dusty plain.

A year later Nat Cooley married again. This time he married a white woman who came up as cook in the station kitchen. Then they moved down from the north into this little town that hugged the banks of the wide, slow river. It only survived because it was a milk depot on the road to Bunbury. It had a state school where the district children went, supposedly hungry for education, at least until third year, when, if they were good enough, they could go to the high school in Maidstone. There was a petrol station where thirsty cars went and where men could often pick up a juicy morsel of gossip in the dusty sun or drizzling rain, as well as a hall where dances, pictures, elections, meetings and church services were held and a hotel, a general store, and a few houses for the families who worked in the depot. That was Herron River settlement.

Cooley's dad lived on Packer's Road in the bush, about two kilometres from town. Every day Cooley, Sam, Linda and Rebecca would walk to the school and back again. Usually, big Cooley had to look after the screeching infants, even though Sam thought he was old enough to look after himself. But tonight he had let them find their own way home, and he savoured the peaceful quiet, broken only by the warbling of an occasional magpie. He reached home when it was dusk. His father was waiting for him.

'Where have you been, you lazy bugger? Down at the camp with them boong Quinns or Garpeys, I suppose. I ought to beat some sense into you. Leaving the kids to walk home alone, and you coming back late. Now you get and do those chores, else Mr Packer'll skin you!'

Cooley moved off the verandah and into the dark again. That was his life—work all day at school and work for Packer when he got home. Dad might kiss the ground the bastard walks on and lick his boots, but I couldn't give a stuff for Packer and his farm, Cooley thought. Geeze! What's his two sons for, anyway? Cooley spat. But it had been his dad's idea to give him chores to do. They kept him out of trouble, having to come home after school.

Cooley reached the feed shed and, stooping, picked up a pile of boondies. In the small, dark room there were always rats and mice and sometimes, as a bonus, one of the wild cats that lived under the sheds. Cooley sneaked up and suddenly switched the light on. Fast as a spear he hurled his three boondies, killing three rats. Then he booted another one up into the air as it tried to run past him. He laughed at the evening's entertainment and some of his anger left him. Then he began hauling out bags of oats and bran and bales of hay for Packer's pigs, cows, and horses. Some day I'll be a farmer too, thought Cooley.

After he had fed up the stock, he wound his way over to the shearers' quarters, where he had his shower. Packer lived in the big house a few kilometres further down, in the cleared green valley. His workman lived in the crowded asbestos house in the bush, right near the cattle yards. During the branding season, they were kept awake by the lowing of unhappy voices calling for their freedom and by the tramping of countless captive feet. In the daylight dust settled on everything: Mrs Cooley's clean washing, her cooking and her house.

If the children wanted to go for a swim they had to walk five kilometres to the pink clay dam, if it was full. The Packer children had only to walk three hundred metres and they were at the waterhole for which the farm was named: 'Yolganup'. It was cool, with fresh yellow-brown water and there were reeds all along the bank where wild ducks, swans and long-necked grey cranes made their nests. The banks were of sticky, warm, black mud that made good mud bombs, or, plastered over white bodies, prevented sunburn. The banks were riddled with gilgie holes and the trails of big tasty marrons or turtles.

But the workmen or their families were not welcome there, though occasionally the Packers condescended to let them come. That was no fun, though, because it was the Packers' waterhole and everyone had to do what the Packers said. Often as not, a fight would break out between angry Cooley or his independently minded brother Ben and the sneering Packers until at last the Cooleys were banned and the Packers' white mates churned the water to mud and scared away all the nesting birds from the old waterhole whose name they couldn't even pronounce and wouldn't know what it meant anyway.

Cooley returned too late for supper with his family, so he ate his cold. While the others watched television he had to do homework.

The next morning they set off for school again, with the three white children messing around; Sammy throwing stones at puddles and trees and the two girls crying out, 'What's this, Reg?', 'Carry my case, Reg', 'Give me a piggy-back, Reg', and scaring off the magpies.

As they reached the school-ground, Morry Quinn and Shaughn Garpey, the two Nyoongahs, yelled, 'Here comes ole Mum Cooley,' and 'Look 'ere, the walkin' talkin' skeleton comin'', while they laughed and lounged with their younger brothers and sisters under the shade of a depleted, wounded old peppermint tree that had survived the ravages of children for some forty years. Even now, young Leo Garpey scratched his new love's name into the flesh of the trunk, finding a space among the names left by previous generations of inspired carvers.

Cooley moved over to the group and spat on the ground.

'What about a weed, bud?'

'Yeah, Mum,' said the short, stocky Morry Quinn, and his face lit up in laughter again. A faint smile played around Cooley's mouth. Always laughing, Morry was, until he got angry. Then the person who had caused his anger was in trouble—like that third year boy last year whom he had picked up and thrown out of the door then off the verandah, because he annoyed him too much, or like that Rocky Gully cricket player who had his jaw almost broken this summer. Morry was boss here.

'Molly Clare give a bit to me last night. I made 'er squeal,' said Shaughn, in his solemn tones. He was big and sleepy and peaceful.

Morry turned laughter-filled eyes on his mate.

'You and Molly's suited. She's a slut and you're a garbo. Garbo Garpey, what ya reckon?' he said, and this time Cooley laughed, as everyone eventually did when around Morry.

They made their way across the pot-holed playground towards the far boundary of the bush. They crawled through a tunnel in the honeysuckle creeper that covered the wall of the toilets there, and, reaching out long tendrils, had enveloped and transformed two old bushes. Morry leant against the sunny brick wall, the king's seat, while the other two sprawled in the dirt. This was the Aborigines' spot and had been since time forgotten. The white boys took themselves down to the pipes if they wanted a drink or a smoke or a game of cards before school.

'Gnummerai, Koordah' the king ordered, and a crumpled packet of cigarettes appeared in Shaughn's yellow palm. The two south-west boys lit up while Cooley rolled a smoke.

There was always that difference—in small things—that kept him apart from these dark southern children. Morry and Shaughn were cousins, with people all over the state. From as far north as Geraldton to as far east as Menzies and Norseman there were brothers and sisters, uncles and aunts. They had their own stories and legends and fears.

The stories that old Bandogera had told him had no place here, even if he could remember them. The songs that his mother sang to him, these boys, almost as dark as she, would not understand, nor the dances his Uncles Banjo, Yarraman and Cockle had danced around the fire as they told the day's stories at night, their mouths open in shouts of laughter and their brown eyes melting in tears of joy down their faces as they chased an elusive goanna or got out of the way of a charging bull or were bucked off a horse—or all three in turn. Or at other times, when the big corroboree was on, when men spent hours painting and preening and everyone waited with great expectations for the dance to begin—with all the tribesmen there, their horny feet pounding on the red dirt, the red dust rising up to their bodies, scarred in manhood.

Oh, he could remember that! In his mother's thin arms, as black as snakes. He could remember that love. One day I'll dance as well, for my mother and sisters and a wife as black as you, Mummy. One day I'll have the sign of manhood ripped into my chest by a piece of sharp rock or broken glass. I shall cry tears of blood and learn the ways of my mother's tribe. Old Bandogera will initiate me into the ways of my country and I shall dance in the red dust made by my uncle's feet.

Cooley sat in the brown dirt and smoked his lumpy cigarette and listened to strange birds in this green bushy land. That was all past now.

'Done ya 'omework, Reg?' said the king.

'Aw, yeah. Bit.'

'Hey, Reg, I seen Ben got two goals in the footy game yesterday.'

'Yeah, we'll kill them crow-eaters. I seen Jimmy Quinn's photo in the paper, Morry,' said Cooley.

'Yeah. Us blokes are fuckin' muritch' said Morry lazily, then put his ear against the wall. 'Shh, youse mob. Coupla yorgas comin' in.'

They fell silent and moved slowly up to the wall. Carefully they pulled out a loose half brick and all looked in. Molly Clare and Diana Grey were there, giggling at girls' secrets, not even guessing at the black eyes watching them. Diana was changing into her sports clothes and admiring her blossoming body. As she bent to pull up her shorts Morry shot her with his shanghai and Shaughn let out a piercing wolf-whistle. Cooley only stared until he was dragged away by Morry's dark hand after it quickly slammed the brick back into place.

They scuttled out through the bushes to roll in abject merriment on the ground.

'Oh, shit! You see 'er jump?' Cooley said, and set off laughing again.

'Like a rabbit, unna?' gasped Shaughn.

'That was somphin' not to miss. Diana Grey's big pink kwon,' whooped Morry, the happiest of all.

They all tried not to laugh as the two girls stalked out and stared suspiciously at them. Then the bell went. The dusty children lined up on the hard cement playing area and glanced anxiously at the grey sky. They were a tatty lot, the Herron River state schoolchildren. All carried bags as grey as the sky above.

They were about as happy as the sky looked, too. Only one or two had the complete uniform, though most wore some part of it. Morry Quinn wore his elder brother's hand-me-downs. At the end of this year his clothes would go to Jonny, then to young Ricky.

The principal glared down at the upturned faces. The dark faces of the Quinns and Garpeys (Morry grinning up at the teachers with his hands in his pockets and his little compact body in a slouch), and the sharp brown face of the half-caste Cooley, with his hook nose and sly, slanted, sneering eyes, contrasted with the blotchy white faces of the farmers' sons and depot workers' children—as did the olive face of the storekeeper's daughter, Annetta Milano.

The principal said prayers and they raised the flag to the tune of 'Advance Australia Fair', just as they had done countless times, so the ceremony had no meaning any more. The children mumbled away and passed sly notes. Staccato coughs sounded from all areas of the assembly.

Then the kids trooped inside the dusty classrooms with creaking floors. Ned Grey scowled at Cooley.

'See you after, you filthy black prick,' he said, and Cooley was scared. Diana must have told on them.

The three Aborigines sat up the back. Shaughn decided to have a sleep. Cooley began catching up on the adventures of *Vampirella* and Morry copied out Cooley's homework. It was only English now but maths straight afterwards, and even Morry was a bit in awe of Big Merv McKenzie, who had a black belt in judo and taught maths.

It began raining and Kathy Sumpter lit the old black heater. She brushed herself against Gary Degill and wriggled her pretty hips so the boy went red. Poor Gary, so shy, so studious. The only third year student who looked like passing the exams.

There were those who said that Kathy Sumpter lived for just one thing, ably told in one of the Herron River change room songs:

I up and pumped 'er
That Kathy Sumpter.
Just bumped and bumped 'er.

They said that she and her sisters were as bad as their mother and that each of them had a different father. The Sumpter girls just couldn't help exuding sexiness, with their swaying hips and huge, long-lashed blue or deep green eyes that could turn a man's thoughts to sin if he merely looked at them with their milk-white breasts oozing from tight dresses and their shapely bodies turning a man into a confused jelly.

The plainer women nurtured all the unpleasant rumours about the small family that lived on the outskirts of town near the reserve. They would huddle in the tiny store of Giuseppe Milano and tell how one girl showered with the bathroom window open so the locals going home could get a good glimpse of her; it would be surprising if one of them didn't rape her one night—if someone hadn't already done so. And this girl had been seen in a highly revealing position in Lenny Jackson's panel van at the Katanning drive-in, with a crowd of boys outside waiting their turn. Oh, yes, that was disgusting, and the noise! No one could watch the film! The Sumpter girls were just a menace and the quicker they got married, the better. 'They say the older one is pregnant. Well, I can only say that finding a needle in a haystack would be easier than finding out who its father is.'

But the boys in Cooley's class grinned and muttered sly remarks about Kathy Sumpter, saying that after school, if you had $5, you could go and visit her in the culvert pipes, abandoned behind the football oval.

Cooley thought, 'I'd lay her any day,' and spent the rest of the class dreaming about himself and Kathy Sumpter.

In maths, Shaughn Garpey was sent to the office to be caned for sleeping and Morry laughed so much he was sent up, too. Then homework was collected and Marcia Quinn and Paul McCauley were caned for not doing it. The previous night, they had been doing far better things than maths. Cooley was glad he'd done his homework because the week before he had been caned by Black Mac for smoking, and it still hurt.

At break the kids had to sit on the verandah, as it was still raining. Cooley, Morry and Shaughn were in a corner, laughing at some joke, when Cooley noticed a big crowd of white boys coming towards them led by Ned Grey and Wally King, who was over six feet tall but didn't have any brains.

Ned yelled, 'Come here, Cooley! What's all this about you firin' a shanghai at Di?'

Cooley replied sullenly, 'I never fired a bloody shanghai. I ain't got one, 'ave I?'

Rick Mizen growled, 'None of your cheek, Cooley. You come here or we'll come there, you black bastard!'

Cooley slouched out alone, but he sensed the two Nyoongahs

cold and alert, behind him, leaning against the weatherboard wall.

Wally King, Rick Mizen, Ned Grey and the Packer brothers, Lou and Ken, stepped forward.

'You think you're the boss just because your brother sucked his way into the state footy team. Ben Cooley a footy player? Shit, my old Mum can play better than that useless boong. Why, he's just a big black poofter, and not worth a monkey's shit anyway,' sneered Lou, who was thick everywhere, and fat, who had failed third year and was repeating, so was a year older than most of the class.

Cooley stiffened as the gibe went home, but he was scared. He didn't know whether the two Nyoongahs would join forces with him, and, even if they did, the odds would still be three against five. He didn't know what to say, so he said, shuffling his feet, 'Wasn't me fired the shanghai. Why don't you ask these blokes?'

Out of the corner of his eye, he saw Morry step forward with a reluctant Shaughn behind him.

'Yeah, youse fellahs, why'nt youse ast me, bud?' said Morry, scratching his jaw.

'All right, then,' grunted big Wally, who was the only one not afraid of the small dark youth. 'Was it you?'

'Yeah, bud,' murmured Morry, then sprang forward as fast and furious as a wildcat. He punched Ken Packer off the verandah and into an orange puddle, then ducked Wally's powerful right and hit the giant in the stomach, but went crashing back into the wall when he in turn was punched in the stomach. He tried to rise but Wally hit him in the same place again and the boss was winded.

Meanwhile, Shaughn Garpey backed into the corner, then lashed out and knocked Rick Mizen flying. He gave Lou Packer a bloody nose, then was tripped and Lou began wrestling him.

Cooley shaped up to Ned Grey and tried to remember what Ben had taught him about boxing.

'Keep ya guard up, baby brother. Look a man in the eyes now. Shuffle them feet around, eh?' Ben had laughed at Cooley's flailing fists and thin arms going like a windmill. 'What's this 'ere, brother-boy? Two butterflies?.' Past Cooley's flapping hands had come two lean brown hands to pat him gently on the cheek. 'You as useful as tits on a bull, budda,' big Ben had grinned.

Never mind Ben now. This is serious. Come on, Cooley—can you hear the crowd roar for you? Come on, Dave Sands Cooley, we'll show this white bloke a thing or two.

But Ned Grey was the under-seventeen boxing champion and he

pushed Cooley all over the place. No one cheered for him. The Quinn girls and Jenny Garpey cried out for their stricken champion brother and gasped for their brave cousin, who was now swamped in a white maelstrom of angry bodies. There was no one to cry or cheer for Cooley, who was beaten to his knees and given a black eye. Poor Cooley.

The principal broke through the yelling crowd and there was silence.

Ned Grey said, 'These blokes insulted my sister, sir, so we got 'em.' He didn't worry about the insults they had poured on Cooley.

Cooley, Quinn and Garpey were caned for 'disturbing the orderliness of the school'.

Afterwards the three argued among themselves about why they had been silly enough to fight. As usual, Morry put the blame on Cooley.

'I dunno whaffor you go actin' big. Ya shoulda tried to run off, then I wouldn't 'ave this fuckin' guts-ache.'

'Run off! I don't run from no one!' Cooley scowled.

'Aaaahh, you winyarn, bud. Ya couldn't fight if ya'ad eight fists, same like a spider, any rate.'

'Aw, shut up, you. Wha' for you go jumpin' in on Packer and King? We mighta bulled our way out of it but for you,' sulked Cooley. 'I thought youse was me mates.'

Mates, Cooley? But you have no mates, boy. Or didn't you see that? Did you think you were the main actor, or what? There you go, dreaming again.

'What for I go jumpin' in? What, ya want me to see ya smashed to pulp? We the same colour, bud. But I tell ya straight, ya got no sense. If ya hadda shut up I wouldn't be feelin' crook.'

'Yeah, Reg,' grinned Shaughn, who hadn't really been hurt and had punched Ricky Mizen a beauty. 'You get beaten up properly, you don't come to school, Morry—he don't get no free gnummerai, see?'

And Morry, who couldn't stay angry for long, smiled.

'Tha's true, cousin. Let's 'ave a smoke now and settle me stomick down.'

But Cooley went home in a bad mood and pushed Sammy over into a puddle when the boy annoyed him. Sammy told his mum, who told Cooley's dad, who belted him.

'Some time I'm goin' to beat that bastard up real good,' Cooley thought as he tossed the bags of feed around, practising judo holds.

145 /

He imagined himself beating up his father and forgot to feed the pigs. So the next afternoon Mr Packer yelled at him, then his dad yelled at him. Bad luck, Cooley.

II

The cold, grey days dragged along like a snake in winter. They were boring days of work in the dreary classroom, with the yellow peeling ceiling and paint-flaked, dirty white walls. The heavy jarrah desks and the hard chairs screeched when you moved them. Moon-faced, fat Miss Dayne, the history teacher, was fifty if she was a day, even though she smelt of sweet, cheap perfume that made a man sick, painted her face and chased all the single men (and maybe some married men if the incessant rumours were to be believed). Black Mac Merv McKenzie's huge bulk loomed, with hard opal-blue eyes and black hairs all over his body. Some said, he could sniff out a cigarette from twenty paces and many who had been caught believed that. Thin, stammering Mr Kennedy taught English and there was also the straight, brown, hawk-eyed, hook-nosed principal, Mr Davis.

One day, as the three Aborigines sat in their honeysuckle hide-out, Morry said carelessly, 'Come down to the railway bridge tonight, koordah, because we 'avin' one party ya never goin' to forget.'

'Yeah, Cools,' said Shaughn, catching small Morry's dark eyes. 'Big mob of yorgas goin' to be there, unna, cous? Plenty of drink and all.'

Cooley was pleased because this was the first time he had been invited to one of these parties. He often heard the next day of the fun the two cousins had with the rest of their people. But he shook his head.

'Ah, no. You fellahs know I gotta feed up Packer's stock,' Cooley murmured. 'Dad'll get worried if I don't go home.'

'Get away! Friday night t'night, look. No school t'morrer. No footy practice. You come to this party,' Shaughn urged.

'Someone wanta see ya, Cools,' Morry grinned.

''Oo?'

'Never you mind. You come and find out.' Morry smiled.

'Tell ya what, koordah, us mob'll give you an 'and to feed ole Packer's animals,' Shaughn suggested, and Morry reluctantly agreed.

146 /

That afternoon the two Nyoongahs joined the Cooleys on the walk home along Packer's Road. Sammy and Linda and Rebecca were silent and kept throwing glances at the two strangers whom they usually saw only on the other end of the playground or heard about in whispered stories on the side of the playground reserved for the junior classes. Morry and Shaughn joked among themselves and thought it so funny when Cooley adamantly refused a cigarette that Morry nearly split his sides laughing.

'Hey, boy, this ain't a stick of dynamite, ya know,' Morry spluttered through his tears of laughter.

'All right! Dy-na-mite!' said Shaughn, in a good imitation of an American black.

But Cooley was aware of Sammy scowling at him and in his imagination could hear him later: 'Hey, Mum, Hey, Dad. Reg was smoking. I seen him, eh, Rebecca?'

'Yeah, Dad. He was with that Morry Quinn from the reserve. Him and Shaughn Garpey.'

'And you know, Dad, those boongs come right up to the farm.'

More trouble for Cooley.

At the scattered selection of farm buildings the three younger white children left and headed up the hill for home. Far out in the river paddock Cooley's sharp eyes could see a man on a tractor at work ploughing, and he hoped it was his father, who therefore would not hear the news and come and spoil things for him.

The three youths set to work, or, rather, Morry supervised from his throne of soft bran-filled bags while the other two sweated in the small stuffy shed. In no time at all the stock were fed and they were headed back towards town and the Aboriginal reserve beyond it. They had finished so quickly there was still a grey light in the sky.

They reached the corner road, where the old hall stood; the two cousins in front, arms around each other, and Cooley behind, trying to roll a cigarette.

A battered old red ute spewed up gravel and yellow sand all over them as it slewed to a stop beside Morry and Shaughn. Cries came from the crowd of Nyoongahs in the back.

''Op in, you fellahs. We cuttin' off into Maidstone to pick up some yorgas,' Lindsay Pepper grinned from the window. Beside him the two Peters brothers laughed as they thought of the fun they would have, and passed a bottle of wine to Morry.

'What's Cools doin' 'ere, cous? Daddy let 'im come out, did 'e?' Johnny Peters chuckled. ''E's 'ad 'is monthlies, 'as 'e?' Lindsay laughed.

Last year sly Lindsay and big Johnny had been expelled for annoying the teachers and scaring Miss Dayne. They had had a fight with Black Mac and been thrown all over the room. The next day they had been told to leave, and they now spent their time thinking up new devilment against the townsfolk. Only last week, with an air rifle, they had shot out every light on the town's one street. They were out on bail now, waiting to appear in court for that spree.

Cooley wondered if he was wise in going along with this mob.

Look out, Cooley. These boys may be going to break into the co-op, or the baker's, or anywhere. You know that even Morry goes stealing at times. You'll go to jail, Cooley. You might as well be dead, then, boy, 'cos your dad'll kill you anyway.

'Come on, Cools. What, ya frightened of a ute? 'E won't bite ya. Norris got it trained,' Morry laughed.

'Come on. We gotta get goin'. Pick up some beer too, eh, what ya reckon?' smiled Norris Peters.

At nineteen, he was the oldest of the Herron River mob. He owned the ute and was the only one able to get beer. He was Ben's mate, so that decided it for Cooley.

The three clambered up into the back amongst the crowd of younger Quinns, Garpeys, Peppers and Peters. Even little Joey Bunyol was there. He wrapped an arm around Cooley's hunched shoulders, leaned his curly head close to his ear and shouted above the wind.

"Ave a charge, koordah. We bin drinkin' all day, us mob 'ere. Too, too drunk, *I* am!' he cackled, and Cooley took a swig of the warm beer, then passed it on to Morry, whose eyes were alight with laughter at Joey Bunyol.

'Tchoo, little man Joey. You properly charged up, eh?' he chuckled.

After a moment's thought Joey's bleary eyes gazed at his older friend and he murmured solemnly, 'Da's true. Trues' fuckin' t'ing you ever did say, budda,' which only brought more guffaws from the happy clan. A faint smile even appeared briefly on Cooley's thin face.

The township of Maidstone was nestled into the craggy breasts of the mountains (they were really hills, but people called them mountains because that sounded grander). The highway towards Albany, or Perth, depending on which way you were going, passed about sixteen kilometres from the town. It had many shops and two hotels and, possibly not unconnected with the latter, a white brick courthouse; at the back of the little police station was a single lock-up cell. Here the locals sentenced for minor offences spent their two or three nights and the daytime part of their sentence tending the policeman's garden. Occasionally someone receiving a longer sentence filled in his first night here while awaiting transport to the far less friendly confinement of Fremantle jail. It had a silo for storing grain. It had a level, well grassed football oval where players had no fear of dodging bushes or falling on rocks and where, indeed, all the district matches were held. It had a big high school to which students from the smaller schools in the district were brought daily by a network of buses. Soon, some said, a hostel would be built, and older students would go to Maidstone to finish their education, rather than to Albany or Katanning as at present. It had a huge co-operative store and a main street that at night was alive with lighted shops and window shoppers. It had an elegant hospital, sleeping amid peaceful gardens. Outside the town there were bowling clubs, a rifle range and a go-kart track that could accommodate motor bikes as well. Last, but not least in the eyes of the children, a contractor was even now building a drive-in cinema. They would no longer have to drive half the night to the one in Katanning. No more sitting on hard seats in the hall in the dripping wet winter or sweltering summer. As a local comedian said, 'The Herron River hall is the only one in the sou'west that keeps out the cool in summer and lets the rain in in winter.' It was right there, scrawled on the men's toilet wall, along with other memorable information about who loved whom, what old Clare could do with his prize ram and where old Degill could stick his interfering nose. It also mentioned who was the best root in town and why—but this was a strongly arguable point.

Best of all, there would be no more shouting, stamping of feet or attempts at cuddling while the projectionist (old, old Mrs McCauley, president of the Herron River CWA) tried to untangle yet another broken reel.

Civilisation had come to the district at last, along with a Space City full of electronic games and a disco.

Mindful of the police station, the central feature of the town to them, the Herron River boys stopped in a clump of she-oaks just before the township and finished off the last two bottles. They left all the youngsters there to avoid possible trouble from the police, then the ute, with the six older boys, clattered and backfired off towards the sleepy town, followed by such warnings as, 'Hey, you buggers, don't leave us 'ere, either, Norris.' 'You don't go sniffin' around them girls too long. I know youse mob, too good.' 'You leave us 'ere and I'm tellin' Dad, Uncle Charlie too, what you fellahs doin'.' The two cousins in the back responded to such remarks with finger gestures, and Cooley, who was beginning to feel the effects of hot beer, gave a silly grin.

The old red ute let out a defiant blare on its horn as they departed. Lindsay let out a wild howl and hurled an empty wine bottle out the window to sail off into the bush. All along the sandy track a grinning Norris fishtailed the ute and did snakies on the corners, while the boys shouted in joy.

Friday night. The night of fun, where there were no worries or problems. Friday night, the end of the week. The night of dances and parties. Sometimes, if there was a band or a pool or darts competition, the pubs would stay open until eleven or twelve o'clock.

It was dusk when the boys reached town and pulled up outside the hotel that served Aborigines. Norris did a whip around to get some money for beer. Most of the boys had a few crumpled notes in their pockets. Lindsay, who had had a good run on the cards that day, produced a $10 note. Not much money altogether, though.

Five dark faces turned to Cooley, dreaming in the back.

'What about you, Cools?'

'I got a bit,' he returned warily.

'All them rabbit skins ya sold to ole Kelly, unna? Bring in some boya, I reckon,' came sly Lindsay's soft murmur.

Then Cooley knew why he had been invited to this party. Norris worked on the Kellys' farm and Maude Pepper worked in the kitchen. One of the big things in Cooley's life were those rabbit skins. He had trapped sixty rabbits in three months. He had cured the skins then stitched them together at night when everyone thought he was asleep. There had been grey skins and black and many shades of brown, even a rare white one. He had sold them as a bed cover to Mr Kelly for $150 only the Tuesday before. It was the greatest sum of money he had held in his hand in his entire life. How he had dreamed. He would buy a car, he would buy a new coat. He could do anything. The money was kept in various places among thin Cooleys' clothes, so no one at home could find and steal it. He could imagine his father believing he had earned so much cash! He would certainly say it was stolen money. Even if he believed his son, he would take it away from him on some pretext.

Now, like a pack of pariah dogs, these slinking youths wanted a part of his juicy sweet dream. Better give them some, Cooley; they'll only roll you, anyway, and take the lot! Cooley thought he couldn't fight even one of the Peters', let alone both, and their cousin Lindsay would come in on the side, ready to king hit a bloke. But he felt vaguely bitter about the business.

'I'll give ya some for two cartons only.' he said.

'Hey, that's too loverly, Cools! We 'avin' Christmas 'ere,' Big Johnny Peters grinned.

'Git some gnummerai, koordah,' called Morry to a departing Norris, then turned to a sullen Cooley.

'Someone want to see ya, Cool Cat. Hey, you must be a solid man, or what?' he said, to cheer him up.

A glint of life came into Cooley's slitted yellow eyes. "Oo wants to see me?'

'As long as it ain't the munadj,' Shaughn grinned, while Johnny and Lindsay's eyes shared the secret with the other two.

Cooley felt uneasy. He had never become really drunk before and he had a feeling he would that night. In fact, he had very rarely drunk beer: only once, just before Ben had gone away to Perth, had the two brothers bought half a carton from the Herron River Commercial Hotel and taken off down to the dam at night. That had been good, listening to the frogs and the night birds and the distant thump of a kangaroo across the yellow-stubbled paddock. The two brothers had spoken of brotherly things and recalled almost-forgotten stories from their own mob far away in a red-burnt land of pale green pools and purple mountains.

But this! All these dusky boys had been joined together by blood ties that had united them for thousands of years. He sometimes felt as alienated as the whitest man. So he felt uneasy, despite Morry's wicked grin and Shaughn's wild cackle. He didn't like jumping into places where he couldn't see what might happen. That was like charging on a horse into the blackest part of the bush on a cloudy moonless night, he thought.

Johnny's shrill whistle broke through his thoughts and he glanced up to see four Maidstone girls drifting over the railway line from the reserve.

He didn't know any of the Maidstone people because he spent most of his time in the bush, alone or working on Packer's farm. He stared at them with suddenly shy eyes as they wandered into the pool of yellow light that bathed the ute.

'Well, look 'ere. That rough mob from ... wassa name of that place? London?' one girl demanded.

'What you doin' 'ere, anyways?' another asked.

'Lookin' for yoks,' Lindsay cackled from the semi-darkness that he liked best.

'Keep lookin' then, Lindsay Pepper, 'cos *I* wouldn't go with you if ya shit was silver,' cried one girl, who remembered Lindsay and his ways. She was the oldest and biggest of the girls, so Lindsay faded back into the darkness while the two cousins on the back muttered, 'Tchoo, shame, girl,' and, 'Where Norris? 'E most probably 'avin' a drink 'imself.' Big Johnny hugged himself in silent laughter on the other side of the ute.

Cooley stared at the girl. He realised she was staring back at him and ducked his head. 'Yeah, 'oo you starin' at, bud? Want me to turn into a vampire for ya, do ya, mate?' She demanded.

There might have been further trouble had not grinning Norris burst from the pub laden with cartons of stubbies and cans.

Norris was the local hero. Like all the Peters, he was tall, and he was strong and fit because he didn't smoke and he drank very little. He was an amateur boxing champion and a good football player. He was Ben Cooley's best mate and it was only bad luck that he had not been chosen to play for a city team as well; a broken finger had put him out of most of last season's games, when Ben was picked.

He gave his easy smile. It was always easy because no one ever fought him. Even if they did, they couldn't touch him.

'Narali Jensen, what you splittin' ya big 'ole for?' he asked.

'Ya want me to shout? I'll shout,' the girl cried. 'Awooooo!' Then she gave a cheerful cackle.

'Look at these Herron boys, eh? They shit when ole Narali come along.' But she was happy now that Norris was there.

'Old is right. She got two kids already,' muttered Morry, but his dark eyes shone at the girl's humour.

'Where are you goin' with all that beer?' one of the other girls asked.

'Us boys 'avin' a party. You comin'?' said Shaughn, feeling it was now safe to talk without fear of getting bawled out by heavy Narali.

'Yeah, why should we go with you, ya fuzzy-haired monkey?' someone cried, starting an outburst of giggles.

'Suit yaself. We only ask once, unna, Morry? Ya missin' out on one good time, but.'

'Yaaah! We'll go pick up some of those pretty things cruisin' round Collie,' said Johnny, and he opened the door, while Norris dropped all but one carton in the back and jumped in the driver's side, grinning over his shoulder.

'Ya comin' or stayin', or what?' asked Lindsay as he also jumped in the front.

Of course they came, giggling and whispering as they clambered into the back. The boys had known all along they would. It was a game they played among themselves, a type of courtship.

As they set off into the gloom, one girl with blonde streaky hair was rubbed against Cooley. She murmured, as shy as he was, "Oo are you, budda? You from Perth?'

'No, I'm from 'ere. 'Erron River.'

'I never seen ya before.'

'Naw. I keep to meself, see.'

From the other side of the rocking ute Morry called out as he ripped the top off a stubby, 'Hey, Janine! 'E's a wongi, Cools is. 'Is mob come from wa-ay up north, unna, Cools?'

'That's old Cool Cat Cooley 'ere, youse girls,' said Shaughn, drinking. 'This is Janine and Narali and their cousins Suzy Blackstone and Moira Bunyol.'

The girl next to Cooley seemed to move away slightly while she stared at the youth's dark shape.

'Truly,' she breathed, 'A wongi? I'd never of believed it.'

'Dad's white,' he said, sensing he had lost her, even before he had begun to find her.

'Still and all.'

"Ave a charge, Cool Cat,' grinned Shaughn, who was on the way to getting drunk.

Cooley caught the thrown stubby expertly, as he would a football. He realised yet again he could never really be a part of these people. He was still a wongi even after eleven years in this bushy green-brown country that sometimes he could love like his own mother and in which at other times he could feel so alone—as though he were the last of his tribe.

'Moira, ya little nephew is blue drunk, waitin' out 'ere.'

'What, Joey, ya mean? You boys want to 'ave more sense gettin' 'im drunk at 'is age.'

'It was 'is idea, any rate.'

'Brother Clem'll bloody kill youse when 'e finds out.'

"E don't even drink any more. 'E'll make you jump, anyways, Morry Quinn,' Narali said.

'Aaahh, no 'e won't,' Morry murmured. 'Be 'is brother-in-law directly, look,' and he wrapped an arm around plump Moira.

They arrived at the she-oaks where the four younger boys waited, nervous now. The darkness and all the spirits darkness holds had scared most of the drink out of them and they climbed aboard the ute gratefully. It hadn't helped that Ricky Quinn had been telling ghost stories meant to scare the younger ones but in the event scaring them all.

'What about one of you girls 'oppin' in the front 'ere?'

'Piss off, Johnny Peters,' called Narali.

'We wouldn't want *you* in 'ere, anyway, that's for sure. Put us off our drink, you would,' whispered Lindsay.

'What about puttin' Norris off 'is drivin'?' said Johnny and there was a muted burst of lecherous laughter from the front.

'It's gettin' too cramped up 'ere. I'll get in the front,' sighed Janine.

Then, everyone being organised, they set off.

Cooley drank and stared at the bush rushing past him and listened to words rushing past him, whipped away by the wind.

There were two places where the Herron River Nyoongahs drank. One place was the sand quarry, but they didn't go there much now because, about five years before, Joey's older and only brother Percy had suffocated in a sand cave-in when he had been drunk on sweet sherry. The other place was the old railway bridge, about three kilometres from town.

To get there, the car had to be hidden in the bush then they had to walk about five hundred metres through prickle bushes and stunted banksia and a few big red gums. There was a small, quiet creek running between two almost sheer, low cliffs covered in suckers and jumbled grey rocks. A railway bridge and a tunnel in a hill further along had been built, but the railway line never came through here because the planned sawmill never eventuated. Instead, the trains ran through Maidstone so only these two lonely reminders were left, as well as a few rusty rails along the grassy embankment between them.

By the bridge was a sandy bank that lay, virginal white, upon the brown earth. Reeds grew thickly on the other side and sang a soft song of the creek as the wind moved among them. Bush and all the things of the bush towered around them. It was a place for quiet talks and jokes and good times. The Herron River mob never fought among themselves and rarely became involved in the family feuds that existed throughout the South-west. They were too far away and too peaceful to be worried about feuds. The police had not yet found this place and wouldn't have cared if they had, since there was very little trouble at the camp.

It was a beautiful bridge, made of the big red-orange rocks from the area, with thick jarrah woodwork and two huge karri logs, brought up from Pemberton to support the trains that never came. No one saw it, though. Hardly anyone remembered it was there.

Cooley slipped and slithered upon the grassy bank and found a shadowy spot beneath the bridge. He began to roll a cigarette and wondered why he had ever come on this party. He had lost $30 to these boys' greedy hands; most of them he hardly knew. He knew only Morry and Shaughn and, if he faced the truth, he didn't really even know them. After school was over each day, all the Aborigines went off down the road and down the track into the bush, a dark, skylarking crowd, kept safe from the whites' scorn by numbers and kinship. After school was when Cooley felt loneliness— walking home with his pale, screaming white brother and sisters.

He certainly didn't know any of these girls, for he had hardly ever been into Maidstone and his father discouraged him from meeting any Aborigines and making friends with them. Once, when they first arrived, the Cooleys had gone to a football match in the town. Nat had gone straight to the bar to make a few mates there and Mrs Cooley showed admiring women her new little Sam. Ben disappeared somewhere and Cooley wandered over to watch the game and to play with some stones that his dreaming mind turned into soldiers. He had an old football that Ben had found on the dump and patched and pumped up. So at half-time some of the dark-skinned children who had been watching him with possum-shy eyes sidled up to him, while the oldest boy scratched a leg with a long toe and asked if he'd like a kick. He had been enjoying himself, showing even at that young age the skills he would keep when he was older. His thin face was split into a grin and his light yellow-brown eyes sparkled with joy. He learned the names of some of the others and made many friends. It was like being back home again; suddenly the world was not the cold unfriendly place it had become for him, so recently departed from the people he had understood and loved.

Then his father came from the bar, grabbed him by a scrawny shoulder and spun him around, saying angry words.

'Keep away from this bloody mob, do you hear? They're nothin' but a mob of thievin' mongrels; a load of bludgers these bastards are, and you're keepin' right away from them. If I catch you hangin' around them again I'll belt the bloody daylights out of you, all right?'

One bare foot had kicked the ball towards Cooley and in a forlorn dive, it had landed in his arms.

'See ya, mate,' came a soft musical voice.

But he never had seen them again, except from a distance. He watched them grow up and get girl or boyfriends and sometimes disappear up to Perth or down to Albany. But only from a distance. There is beauty in a distant mountain, dancing in the heat haze on the edge of a plain, mauve and blue and pink. Dry desert mirages look like Paradise from a distance, but there is no such thing as distant friendship.

Someone turned on the wireless, and Kid Creole and his Mob of Coconuts brought sophistication even to those wilds. The Peters brothers searched for firewood so they could have a fire to keep warm and (who knew?) maybe roast a stolen and killed sheep later on for a feed.

'Look at ole rubber-man Joey go, eh? Can 'e dance or can 'e dance, or what?' one of the girls called out.

'I'll show ya 'ow us Garpeys dance,' grinned Shaughn and he was on his feet swaying all over the ground.

Cooley felt someone slide down beside him and turned to see Morry's dark shape, with the starlight glinting out of his dark eyes.

'Be glad when Big Boy and Norris get this fire goin',' Morry murmured. 'They say there's an old woman down along this creek, ya know. If you 'ear someone call out to ya and ya turn around, well, then might be that ya die.'

'Yeah?' Cooley breathed.

'Fuckin' oath. Danny Jensen one time before turn around when that ole lady call 'im, and ya know? 'E could never talk again.'

''Ave a drink, Morry. Don' scare me with these yarns.'

'Just tellin' ya,' Morry said, then grinned and leaned close to the thin, dark face of the half-caste. 'Now, you don't get drunk too much, 'cos I got a yorga lined up for ya, see.'

Cooley stiffened and turned to see if Morry was joking. He scratched his stomach nervously.

'Aaah, get away, Morry. These womans is scared because of Mum bein' from up north. I don't know any wongi ways, ya know. I left there when I was five.'

'Nah, you don't worry about these black things 'ere, buddah. I got you a wadgula woman. She'll be 'ere d'rectly.'

Cooley was apprehensive. There was no way he would tell Morry that he had never been with a girl before. He hadn't even kissed one, so he was suddenly very nervous. He was reading a book in which the hero was in the darkened streets of Chinatown, being followed by three Chinese whom he suspected intended to kill him. At that moment, he felt just as the hero did; as though a pile of rocks was rolling around in his stomach.

"Oo you talkin' about, Morry? Those white fellahs are my enemy. What if this girl is the sister to—oooh, shit, Morry, it better not be Carol King!'

Morry's bubbling laugh echoed from under the bridge and the light from the newly awakened fire caught his pink tongue and snow-white teeth.

'Cooley become a coldie, or what? You scared, Mr Cool Cat, unna? Don't you worry, mate. This yorga I'm talkin' about got no brothers, only sisters. You wait 'ere till I whistle. Don't want them other boys to spoil ya own fun, unna?'

Then he was gone and Cooley sat there and drank two more stubbies to nerve himself for the coming adventure, then another two, until he felt drunk and relaxed. A lazy smile spread over his sharp face and his eyes half-closed. He joined in the talk around the campfire from his shadowed seat: jokes and ghost stories and camp stories. Stories about the old people.

The moon came up in the turbulent sky, round and full; full of a certain kind of beauty, like a pregnant woman. The shadows deepened. Cooley, staring into the wavering face of the fire, re-called other fires in other lands and softly began to sing a half-remembered children's song that his mother often chanted.

'Hey, listen to old Cools go! Is 'e Elvis Presley?'

'Come on, Cools, give us a tune.'

The boys began a dance that they made up, stumbling on the sandy uneven ground of the beach by the creek, giggling and waving stubbie bottles in the air so the brown glass winked as red as rabbit eyes in the light of the fire. A sad yet beautiful corro-boree from the new tribe the white men had made. But the girls were frightened that Cooley might be 'singing' them and, anyway, he forgot the rest of the words, so the song lapsed into silence. Then Johnny turned up the wireless and the white man's words embedded themselves in the group like arrows of madness, and they danced more and more frantically.

More stories, more drink. Little Joey Bunyol crept off into the bushes to be sick and go to sleep. The other boys got down to the serious business of conning up individual girls.

Then Morry's whistle penetrated Cooley's fuzzy brain and the youth zigzagged over to the bridge.

'Now, big Cools. She waitin' up on the bridge there for your big 'ot thing,' drunken Morry grinned lecherously. 'Go to the other side so them boys don't see ya. Specially that Lindsay, 'cos 'e got just 'is friend Mrs Palmer ...'

'... And 'er five daughters,' Cooley broke in, chuckling, so Morry stared at him and grinned even wider. 'You right, Cool Cat. You charged up now. Man can do anything when 'e's charged up. Now, take these stubbies so's ya can 'ave a good party. Give 'er one for me, all right.' A heavy hand pounded Cooley's thin arm and, cackling, the youth went away, to disappear into Moira Bunyol's black arms.

Cooley slowly straightened up and bumped his head on the jarrah top. Thinking this funny, he giggled to himself, then made his way through the bush, dropping a stubby now and then and having great difficulty in finding it each time. He climbed up onto the railway line where the ironstone and the few remaining rails caught pieces of the moon.

Here we go, Cool Cat. Into that dirty dangerous Chinatown, full of Chinamen with knives and opium dens and pretty ladies peeping from windows. Full of all the sins in the world. Lose your life or lose your virginity. Look out, Cooley!

The moonlight caught the girl and bathed her in its pale light so she seemed a part of the moon itself, a moon lady. Skin and dress so white, like the moon's rays. Hair as flaxen as the moon itself.

Kathy Sumpter.

'Hullo, Reggie.'

Cooley's mouth fell open but no words came out. Only the other day, he had been dreaming of her—the prettiest girl in town, he thought.

One of the stubbies slipped from his precarious grip and tinkled against the rocks.

'You brought some grog, did you, Reggie? That's good. I could do with a drink. It's so muggy for this time of the year, don't you think?' she said as she swayed towards him like a hula dancer. Her long red-tipped fingers slyly undid her top button, so Cooley's eyes gravitated there and stared in wonder, anticipating what would happen next. She stood right near him now and looked up at him with her large blue eyes. That cruel Cupid, the moon, made them into shadows, even more beautiful in Cooley's mind. The fire from there could be seen only as a grey light amid swirling darkness. The others were only a faint murmur of voices.

158 /

'Cat got your tongue, Cools?' Kathy Sumpter smiled. 'Come and have a talk with me.'

'I brought some beer,' Cooley stuttered.

'Good on you. Let's go and find some quiet place where we can have a yak and a drink. How's that for an idea?' she said, placing a pale hand on his dark arm.

Her eyes were a metallic blue, surrounded by long lashes. Wicked and mysterious, they batted and winked in the moonlight, pulling his soul out of his body so it danced with the sparks in her eyes, a whirling, wild, exciting dance of dervishes.

They set off along the railway line and she slipped a hand into his. Her fingers made patterns on his palm and her teeth glinted in a wicked grin. Drunk though he was, Cooley thought he had never seen a prettier hand, and so pale in his brown claw. He held her tighter.

'I've never been so drunk before,' Cooley murmured, for something to say.

'You're not so drunk, Reggie. You should see my old man on Saturday nights. Geeze, he's a real card with all his jokes and things. That's when he's not in jail, anyway.'

Cooley thought of his own father and how he would be sleeping off a Friday session, even then. He thought of tomorrow and what it would bring. Then the dark trees staring down at him and the silver moon with all her attendant stars, and the busy coiling clouds all whispered, like summer rain, for him to stay and become someone for once. A drifting ghostly white owl swooped down and called out eerily, 'Good hunting, brother.'

'Why are you so quiet? We aren't strangers, are we, Reggie?' Kathy prompted.

'I got nothin' to say.'

'I've seen you staring at me in class, Cools. Do you like me?'

He stared at her while his mind tried to urge his tongue to reply. Come on, Cool Cat. Robert Redford here. Burt Reynolds, too. Come on, boy. If them fellahs can do it on the big white screen, you can do it right here in this dark bush. Sweep her up on your horse. Listen to that orchestra play the love music.

'You're pretty,' he breathed, at last.

'Come along here, Reg. There's a nice clump of she-oaks just down off the line. We can sit and have a talk, know what I mean?'

'I reckon it's goin' to rain soon,' Cooley said, hesitating. 'It's real cloudy, but. Look! I can't even see the Southern Cross.'

'That's because the Southern Cross is in the south, not in the east, amazing though it may sound.'

They both laughed at Cooley's mistake and it seemed natural they should fold into each other's arms, still laughing.

'I'm never going to get lost with you out here, Reg. We'd never find our way home.'

'That wouldn't be so bad, ya know,' Cooley murmured, staring into her eyes.

Her soft lips engulfed his and he remembered all that he had read in the paperbacks and cheap 'love' magazines he had periodically bought furtively from the Herron River co-op and kept hidden under his mattress.

But still, when they broke apart at long last, Kathy's sly Siamese cat eyes gazed up at him and she giggled softly.

'Why, Reg Cooley. I don't believe you've ever been with a girl before in your life!'

'Well,' he began shyly.

'Come with me, Cool Cat! I'll bet you've got a hot dog there, too, for my oven,' she grinned, giggling happily as she led him into the she-oaks.

She was a true mistress of her trade, sculpturing him gently; chipping off a little shyness here, a little there, with soft words and well placed hands. Then he was all hers, even though she let him think it was the other way around.

He peeled away her white dress (which was all she wore, for in truth she had arranged this night with sly cackling Morry a week before) and looked down at her naked body, so pale and white, like a frangipani petal lying on the ground. Like the frangipani flowers his mother had sometimes entwined in her black bushy hair. Her lips smiled languidly up at him and her shadowed eyes promised all kinds of sins.

Then he too was naked and beside her on the soft, crackling pine-like needles of the she-oaks. The soft evening breeze whipped across his thin brown body and Kathy Sumpter's plump breasts that he had seen pushing out her school uniform, and her hips and thighs that had rolled in sensuous rhythm so often before his eyes.

Tonight they belonged to him.

His first woman.

He was clumsy and he needed help from a more expert Kathy. He didn't feel as he thought he should afterwards. He was too nervous really to enjoy the experience. But he was no longer a virgin.

When it was over, they lay in the scuffed-up needles. A great

160 /

shyness overcame Cooley and he sat up suddenly, reaching for his clothes.

'Where's the hurry, Cool Cat?' came Kathy's soft voice from the shadows. But she held no mysteries now.

'Better go now. I've got to feed up the animals of ole Packer tomorrow; today, I mean,' Cooley muttered.

A hand rested on his knee so he stopped still, like a kangaroo sniffing the air for danger.

'Did you like it, Cools? Did you like tonight?'

'It was orright,' he whispered.

'You want to come out more often. You can have more fun with me than with Packer's animals, eh?'

He turned and smiled down at her shyly.

'You stay here for a while longer, Cool Cat. There's still some beer left.'

'No, I've gotta go, see. Be dawn d'rectly. Dad's goin' to go off 'is 'ead when he sees me.'

'Suit yourself, Cools,' she said, shrugging her shoulders. 'I might see you another time,' she called softly after his departing figure.

He set off along what used to be the railway track towards the town. The man-made mound wound above the tangle and confusion of the bush below. He had only the moon for company.

It didn't matter tonight what the town thought of Kathy Sumpter, what the boys would do when they found out, how they would mock him. Tonight was his night and now was his Dreaming.

He knew that on Monday in the honeysuckle hideout, the two cousins would rip and tear his brief Dreamtime apart with laughter as loud as a bubbling creek, washing away all the dreams and leaving only the truth; two black crows on a dying sheep's back. Instinct told him that Morry had arranged tonight not so much out of friendship for him as out of a mischievous desire to get amusement from him. He was right. Morry had sidled up to Kathy one day at school and grinned into her ear, 'See ya after, 'ot-lips.'

'Yeah? What about Moira Bunyol or Judy Crow?'

'No, I wanna arrange somethin' for me cobber, ya know. Somethin' nice, see?'

'Who's your cobber? Lindsay Pepper? Because I wouldn't go with him in a blue fit! I reckon he's got the pox.'

'Well, 'oo gave it to 'im?'

'Not me, sport. Might have been you, eh'. You never can tell, can you, stud?'

He had grinned at the white arm draped around his shoulder

161 /

and at the hip burning into his side. He had stared into the big eyes that questioned him.

'No, 'oo we talkin' about 'ere is Reg Cooley.'

'Reg Cooley?' she had cried and started away.

'What's wrong with Cools? He's the same colour as me and Norris, any rate. Go on, ya might even like it. I tell ya what, sis. I reckon 'e never been near a girl in 'is life.'

'Do you really think he's a virgin?'

'Well,' Morry had smiled, 'unless ya count kangaroos and sheep and cows and chooks and, ya know? 'E spends every day on that farm and never comes anywhere. Come on, mama, do yaself a favour,' and he had hooted with wild joy. She had joined in, after a moments thought, and agreed.

He was little more than another of Kathy Sumpter's long list of conquests. Even as he wound his solitary way homewards, Kathy was probably heading for the fading warmth of the Herron River mob's fire to snatch another piece of joy in her young life. Was that love you felt, Cooley? I don't think so, mate.

III

He arrived home in the grey dawn when the two roosters were arguing whether it was a good day or not. He sat outside the rickety picket fence that surrounded what was Mrs Cooley's idea of a garden and opened one of the two stubbie bottles that resided in his torn brown coat pocket. He rolled himself a cigarette, not caring about his father's anger just then, and thought of the night again.

How'd that song go, Cooley? 'The loveliest night of the year'. That was about right.

He was still there when Nat Cooley came out of the front door. Cooley heard the heavy workboots scuff down the cracked path and heard his dad hawk noisily to get rid of the night's phlegm.

The boots stopped at the gate.

'Yer up early, aren't yer?'

He didn't look up but stared straight ahead with wary eyes, smoke dribbling from his thin nostrils.

'Yer've caught th' best part of the day, for once,' his father said non-committally, trying again.

'Yeah,' Cooley said sullenly, and stood up, grinding his cigarette out with a dusty boot. He slouched off, half-expecting to be followed by angry words. This time he'd argue back, maybe even fight; he didn't know. All he knew was that he didn't want anyone to spoil his thoughts, especially the man who called himself 'father' yet ignored and disliked his dark-skinned sons. But Nat just hawked again and clumped away over to the tractor, scratching his baggy behind and mumbling to himself.

Cooley made his way into the kitchen and past the kids who were screaming over something, even at that hour. He barely gave harassed Mrs Cooley a glance; even when she cried, 'Did you see Dad? He was a bit upset the way you carried on last night. Oh, shit! Now look what you've done, you little bitch! Go and play outside with Sammy, or something.'

Cooley wafted past her like a bird a thousand feet up in the air and, grabbing three pieces of toast and someone's fried egg and bacon, he disappeared into his room for a good sleep.

After that first party Cooley often went down with the other boys, although he never drank so much again. He didn't see Kathy Sumpter again, either. In class she seemed to ignore him, or she would suddenly turn and grin at him, eating him with huge eyes. Then Morry and Shaughn would giggle soundlessly and Cooley would feel like disappearing into the cracked jarrah floor. The other boys began to guess what had happened because it was impossible to keep a secret in this small blob of civilisation. They would stare at him with knowing eyes and smirking faces. Anonymous wolf-whistles followed him everywhere. If he was ever late for morning assembly, skilful planning made sure he had to stand beside or behind Kathy Sumpter, who stood quietly and glanced at him wickedly, while Cooley squirmed and looked everywhere but at her.

Afternoons were spent in the old abandoned railway shed or the tunnel that cut through the rocky brown hill, with the Quinns and Garpeys, Peppers and Peters and Bunyols. Sometimes Dan Crow would come along, too. He had left school one day and had never come again. His father didn't care and the youth looked after him whenever he was around. But Dan Crow was a wanderer and no one knew where he would be next; interstate, up in Thursday Island, in prison. He was everywhere. Right then, he was working as a storeman for Wilson's in Maidstone. The mob played cards and drank beer, keeping a sleepy eye out for the police. They told dirty jokes and laughed over something that had happened at the camp, in town or at school. They spoke about football and shearing and boxing and girls. That was their world.

These were the times Cooley felt like a man and not a dirty, skulking half-caste. He would laugh with the rest, joke with the rest, smoke with the rest, drink with the rest. Big Cooley.

Then came the picking for the first eighteen and more trouble for Cooley. He was picked for centre because he had a long, straight kick and a high mark that made up for his lack of height and strength. But the white boys were jealous, especially Ken Packer, who would otherwise have got the position.

One night, Cooley was up in the feed shed, having a quick cigarette before he got to work. He softly sang a Hank Williams song, 'Long Gone Lonesome Blues', and thought of the evening ahead with Earl Reeves' country and western night on the radio—his favourite programme of the week.

The two Packer boys walked in. He had never liked them because they were always flash and full of importance. They always spoke in a plummy accent and were full of spiteful little tricks and they were everything he would never be. But he hated them mainly because there wasn't a thing he could do about them. They were the boss's sons and the boss loved them and believed them—no matter how far-fetched their stories seemed. How many times had Cooley got into serious trouble over Ken's and Lou's lies?

Lou shut and locked the door then turned and leered at him. Cooley still sat on the bag of oats and carefully took in a drag, then slowly expelled the blue smoke through his nose. There was a dangerous silence in the shed—even the rats were still. Then Ken, leaning nonchalantly against his father's wall, said, 'You're feeling too sick to play Jingalup on Saturday, aren't you, Reg?'

Cooley looked surprised and a puzzled frown creased his lean brown face.

'Nuh. I'm okey-doke to play. Got a bit of a cold, but that's nothin'.'

Lou moved forward.

'You're not all right to play, Reg, mate. You had a little accident, see. Tonight while you were feeding up. Lucky for you me and Ken came and found you. You could have died, eh, Ken?' Then he turned to his brother. 'What'll we give him, Kenno? A broken arm?'

'No, a broken leg takes longer to heal,' said Ken, moving forward also.

Then Cooley saw what they were up to and rage whipped his body like a north-west typhoon. So they would take away the one good thing he could do, would they? They would break his body

164 /

like a stick they had no further use for? Let them try!

He butted out his smoke and leaped up the mountain of bagged food. The two boys mistook his action for cowardice and charged after him. Lou reached the top first, then gave a strangled yell as a boot in the jaw sent him falling down, to land with a thud on the brick floor, where he lay motionless.

Young Ken hesitated and Cooley sprang upon him with all the hatred of eleven years of persecution. They rolled over and over to the bottom where Ken sprang up and kicked Cooley on the side of the head. Cooley went reeling, then fell over again, hit in the eye. He staggered up and ducked Packer's wild punch. He kicked the white boy in the shin and as Ken let out a cry and hopped on one foot, Cooley's fist smashed home again and again and Ken Packer was dropped like yesterday's lunch.

For a while Cooley lay against the wall, then stumbled out.

'Bugger the bloody animals. Bugger Packer too, same time,' he grunted.

He had a shower over in the old shearer's quarters. It didn't help get rid of his black eye, but its soft, wet fingers got rid of the rage that flamed inside him. He felt dull and his head rang from Ken's foot and fist. Calm again, he thought he should go back and see if the brothers were as hurt as he was.

'No, fuck 'em,' he snarled. 'Fuck the whole lot of white bastards,' he said.

You wait, Cooley. You ought to be Bruce Lee. You're too too good for those Packer boys. Even old Packer himself you could flog with your kung fu, boy! Cooley smiled and dreamed and dried his bony body.

But out of the dark shearer's quarters, out of the darkness of the night and into the light and facing the eyes of the family who disliked him as much as he did them, he was just shuffling Cooley the coon again.

Everyone stared at him, Mum Cooley with a cold, expressionless gaze as though her stepson wasn't there. For all the care she took of him, he might as well not have been. Cooley often wished for the dark face and soft brown eyes and long bushy black hair, soft against his skin, of his real mother. But tonight Cooley was the man. Hadn't he taken on two blokes and flattened them alone? Just wait till Ben heard about this. Cooley the big bloke—Lionel Rose was nothing to him.

'Why you late, you little bugger? I bet you been smoking again. And what happened to your bloody eye?' growled his father.

He shuffled his feet and licked his lips and thought: Can't tell Dad, else he'd belt me for laying into the boss's sons. Who's going to believe me against them white blokes?

So he looked up and lied, 'Oh, I never seen this pole when I was feedin' up.'

He was too upset to listen to Earl Reeve but there was a good movie on TV; lots of murders and some beaut car chases. Cooley tried to dream about being the big gangster, shooting every single Packer there was. But, every now and then, he would glance fearfully at the phone as he thought of Packer ringing up and saying, 'Your damn son killed my two boys.'

Then he thought of the belting he would get. He suddenly remembered he hadn't fed up yet and decided to do it when he was supposed to go to bed. But he didn't: he was warm in bed and it was cold and dark outside. So the morning of another day appeared, grey and emotionless, cold and still.

Cooley set off for school, armed with a stick. Maybe the Packers would be waiting for him. That was just their style, to hide behind a bend then come charging out of nowhere. There was no sign of them, however, along the track, and for once he was pleased when he came in sight of the school. As he entered the playground, Shaughn called, 'Look at Cooley the caveman. What you doin' with that nulla-nulla, buddy?'

'He's goin' to ram it up his arse for a thrill,' murmured Ned Grey and his mates cackled in appreciation of his wit.

Cooley wandered over to Morry and Shaughn, keeping a wary eye out for the Packers.

'You seen the Packers t'day, Morry?'

'They never come yet, bud. What you so anxious to see those pricks for?'

Cooley spat on the ground and glanced around, then whispered into the boy's ear, 'I got a feelin' I might of killed them last night.'

Morry doubled over, hooting in laughter at the best joke he had heard for ages. He rolled on the ground coughing and spluttering and gasping. It nearly killed him and Shaughn had to pound his back. Then he started off again.

'Ooooohh! Cooley, you should see your face!' then he stood up and feigned terror as he cringed away. 'D-don't kill me, big Cool Cat. I—I never meant none of it, true. Oohh, boss, p-please spare me. 'Ave mercy on m-my black soul. Ooooh, Mummy, this Cooley gunna kill me d'rectly.'

It was the best joke and all that day, whenever Morry looked at

166 /

Cooley, the small youth's face would crumple into joy. Even Shaughn laughed until the joke wore off for him. But Cooley was worried, so worried that he was caned twice during the day for not paying attention. During football training he caused the coach, Jimmy Conner, to say, 'Geeze, Reg, if you don't pick your game up you'll be out of the team. Jingalup's a good team and we want to win this season.'

He kicked his way home after practice, not bothering to keep an eye out for the Packers—he was sure they were dead.

He went around the house and on to the sheds. Just as he got there he noticed Packer's shining new Mercedes, then he saw the big man himself and the hairs on the back of his head tingled as though he had just seen a featherfoot.

'You, Reggie! Come here!' the boss shouted. Cooley, wiping an arm across his nose, shuffled forward, head down. 'Get in, you. By geeze, boy, you've had it now!'

'Aw, what 'ave I done, boss?' cringed the boy, although he already knew. What happens to murderers, boy? Are they hanged, or what?

'You don't know what you've done, eh?' snarled Packer, and grabbed a handful of the boy's long brown hair, giving it a vicious tug. 'You cold-blooded bastard, you'll see, you half-ape,' he cried and jerked his foot on the accelerator.

They reached home too quickly for Cooley, who was as dead inside as a jarrah with dieback. He was hauled out of the seat and dragged up the garden path that beckoned like a crooked finger. Come inside to my web, you juicy fly. I'll suck all the life out of you. His coat was nearly choking him.

Packer burst in through the cottage door without knocking and pushed Cooley into the room. Cooley's dad, in his singlet and braces, stood up in surprise from the table, while the other Cooleys stopped eating and stared. Nat scratched his stomach nervously.

'G'day, Mr Packer. What's wrong?'

'This bugger is wrong,' shouted Packer, which started the baby crying, so Mrs Cooley took it outside. 'You know what he's done? Put Lou-boy in hospital and nearly blinded Ken.'

'Well,' growled Cooley, feeling a little better to discover that no one was dead. 'What did they do to me? Kiss me?'

'You shut up!' snarled his father.

Packer went on. 'Do you know why that animal attacked my boys? Crazily attacked them? Because they caught him smoking in the feed shed and he was afraid they would tell.'

167 /

'Hey, that's bullshit, anyway. Listen, they was ...' Cooley began, then received a slap on his face from his Dad that sent him reeling back into the corner and left a purple mark on his cheek. He saw Packer smiling in triumph and hated him as only he could hate. In that moment he could have killed the big man, but the time for dreaming was over.

'Smoking in the hay shed so a spark could send the whole thing up in smoke,' Packer continued. 'Then after all that, he didn't even feed the stock last night.'

Nat Cooley reached for his thick leather belt.

'You're damn lucky I don't have him sent to a reform school. A bit of discipline, that's what the vicious ungrateful little bastard needs.'

Cooley's old man purred softly as he ran the belt through his fingers. 'You lazy little shit. I ought to skin you.'

Cooley looked at the stranger who wasn't his father. This was not the man who had given him pony rides and piggyback rides, laughing with him and explaining things to him, the man who had been teaching him how to work with rawhide when his mother had died. This was a drunk, old, balding man, going ugly in his old age, as an old boomer becomes nasty when he's toothless and grey. This was a man who pushed his kid around because he was a constant reminder of a bygone folly.

Cooley clenched his fist and his Dad growled, 'Threaten me, would yer? By the Christ I'm sick of you, you little prick.'

The belt lashed out and stung Cooley's back. All he could do was cover his head and turn away from his tormentor while he backed into the corner. His thin trousers and frayed coat gave no protection from his father's frenzy, and the belt left red welts on his brown skin and bit into his bare legs. But Cooley kept the tears back, even when one stroke lashed into his mouth with the viciousness of a scorpion's sting, splitting and numbing his lips so blood ran in a thin river down his bruised face. He would cry when there was no one around to laugh and jeer. He got enough of that just being himself. He sensed Packer, Linda, Rebecca, Sammy, all watching him in his shame and pain, and he hated them all as much as he had ever hated anyone.

I'll get even, Pig Packer. One day Cooley will hold the aces and I'll make you cringe, cunt!

Nat Cooley kept going until the sweat ran into his eyes and his beer-pot quivered and Cooley lay crouched on the floor. The man's arm hung loosely by his side. It was the worst of the many hidings he had given Cooley and he hoped Mr Packer was impressed at the way he disciplined his son.

'Get to bed and let that be a lesson you'll not forget.'

It was. Cooley was too sick to go to school the next day and he wasn't able to play in the football team that week. When Cooley told Morry and Shaughn and showed them the bruises, the two cousins were full of plans, which they half-believed were possible, for beating old man Cooley and Packer into fertiliser. But Cooley snarled while his eyes flashed like knife blades.

'No, boy, you leave those bastards to me.'

Morry felt fear touch him and was glad he wasn't Packer or Nat Cooley, sleeping off a drunken spree one balmy summer night.

Ken came back to school a week later, with his eye all black and yellow. He kept away from Cooley and the half-caste sensed King, Mizen and Grey staring at him during class. But they didn't have the courage to attack old Cooley—cousin of Dave Sands or Ron Richards, maybe! When Morry saw Packer's face, even he was surprised.

The days went by faster now; there was a lot for Cooley to do. He read that big Ben was best player in the game against Victoria. The term exams were coming up, too, although this didn't worry the three Aborigines. It just meant they had more time to read comics or mess around under the guise of study. Also, Cooley was a rising star in the football team—all he had to cling onto now. In football he had a chance to prove himself, just as Ben had done.

Cooley often thought of Ben. His older brother was a bigger version of him, with long yellow hair. Ben had learned early to stick up for himself and had gained a name as a tough, whipcord fighter. Everyone respected Big Ben Cooley, and he had been afraid of no one or anything. The trouble was that he had fought Cooley's fights, too; now he was gone and Cooley was alone.

Ben believed in truth, while Reg lived in dreams. This had always been so. Cooley wished he could be like Ben. Like last year when Ben had leapt off the tractor and yelled at Packer, 'Listen, you big shit! You wanna do the ploughin' your way, then ya can bloody well do it yaself, ya fat-arsed prick. Christ knows then we'd all be 'appy 'cos I can 'ave a rest an' you can bugger up ya paddocks and really 'ave somethin' to complain about, ya stupid bastard!'

Then he had loped off, leaving Packer, redder in the face than usual, gaping after him. Cooley had laughed because he had been safe beside Big Ben. He wasn't laughing now, only hating, and he was alone. The football scout had come down and watched Ben play against Maidstone, then asked him to come to Perth. The big half-caste had played several trial games, come down to say good-bye, and left.

IV

So life rolled over Cooley, Quinn and Garpey, and they grew older while they did nothing. One day it was Cooley's birthday, but no one remembered or cared, so it didn't really matter. Soon it would be the end of another year.

Then things happened—too fast for Cooley, who liked to take things slowly.

Cooley had fed up early for once and was eating a hot meal with the rest of the family in the warm living room. Sammy was wolfing down his meal so he could get seconds, Linda and Rebecca—dirty little grubs—were arguing in high, trembling voices and Mrs Cooley, hair awry and eyes weary, was trying to feed baby Johnny who was crying, as usual. Nat sat drinking beer and reading the paper. Cooley, wishing he hadn't come in early, had finished his meal and was getting up for more.

'Leave some for me, Reg. You had enough, anyway,' Sammy whined.

'Yes, Reg. Don't be greedy,' reprimanded his stepmother, staring through him as always.

Then there was a knock on the flaking three-ply front door.

'Get that, will you, Reg?' asked Mrs Cooley, and Cooley growled angrily as he saw Sammy spring up and scrape out the bowl. Those spuds had been good, too. He slouched over to the door and opened it, expecting Packer. His jaw dropped when the two police-men from Maidstone came in. His brain worked overtime as he tried to think of something he might have done. The rest of the Cooley family fell silent and started in surprise, then Nat stood up, brushing his mouth.

'G'day. What youse blokes want?'

The biggest policeman, with a bass voice, said, 'Is your name Nathaniel John Cooley?'

'Yeah, of course it is.' Nat said. 'You know that already, sarge.' He smiled, uncertainly.

The policeman stepped forward and placed a hand on Nat's heavy shoulder, saying solemnly, 'We are enquiring into a rob-bery, conducted with violence, on the night of the fifth at Johnson's garage. We have reason to believe you may be able to help us in our enquiries. We have a warrant to search the premises.'

'Well' blustered Nat in surprise and confusion, 'I dunno what's goin' on, sarge. Course I'll 'elp if I can. But what are you searching for 'ere? I suppose you can search the place. I dunno!' And he turned to his wife for comfort.

Even as he was talking, the other policemen had moved into the bedroom and now emerged carrying a heavy black box.

'Looks like this is it, sarge,' he said.

Cooley surveyed the room with quick eyes. Did he detect a look of fear in his dad's grey, glazed eyes, wide open in shock?

'Aaah, cripes! What's goin' on 'ere?' cried Cooley senior.

'Packer saw you come home at midnight, just after Johnson rang to tell us he'd been robbed,' jumped in the young policeman.

Nat shuffled his dusty boots.

'Yeah, well I heard the bull bellowing,' he said. 'Went out to see why. But what's that got to do with Johnson and the robbery? And what's that box? I never seen it before.'

'It's no good, Cooley. Just you come along with us,' growled the sergeant.

'Oh, Nat! Nat! What's happening?' cried his wife, and the children started bawling. Only Cooley, sucking his bottom lip, stared at his stepmother in a perturbed way. She seemed to be acting—how?—falsely, maybe? Then the three men were going outside. Nat turned his head and cried, 'Get Mr Packer, Vi. He'll help get me out of this mess. I'm innocent, Vi, believe me!'

'I wouldn't believe you if you was God 'imself,' thought Cooley, and gave a grim smile.

But Mrs Cooley ran to the door and cried out, into the darkness that had swallowed up her husband. Then she turned to Cooley, her thin face flushed and wild-looking. 'Put the children to bed, Reg. I must go and see Mr Packer at once.'

Cooley put the children to bed and for once there were no pillow fights and noise. The three little white faces stared up at him sadly and silently, too young to understand, but knowing that a calamity such as they had never dreamed of in their worst nightmares had befallen the family.

'Reggie,' whispered little Linda, 'Would you read us a story, please?'

So Cooley, because he was full of good hot food and his Dad had gone, read to them in his deep, halting voice. Then he went out to his small room near the wash-house and joined in the wild laughter of the wind.

'Eeeee, I 'ope you get an 'undred bloody years, you old bastard,' Cooley said to the spider in the corner of the dusty ceiling.

But this is not all that happened. The next afternoon Mrs Cooley asked him to go down to the Packers' and find out what had happened to Nat, since she hadn't been able to get into court that morning. He was also instructed to borrow some tea, milk and butter.

He went outside, whistling happily. Cooley, you've changed, now the old man's gone. He drove the ute down the five-kilometre track that wound among the green trees and stubby bushes, then past the young crop just starting to peep out of the brown soil.

He skidded into the drive, in front of the big house with the blue-sheened wattles around it. He stepped jauntily up the stone steps and along the wide verandah. *He* didn't care if his father went to jail. He knocked on the heavy jarrah door and Packer opened it. Cooley lost all his bravado and became himself again.

'G'day, Mr Packer. Mum wants to borrow some tea, milk and butter for our breakfast tomorrow and to know about Dad,' said he, staring at his feet, keeping all his secrets to himself.

'Come down to the kitchen, then. It's getting cold,' grunted Packer, turning his back and stalking ahead.

It was warm in the kitchen. Cooley sniffed and wiped his nose on his coat sleeve. Then he noticed the girl at the sink and stared at her.

He didn't think he had ever seen a girl like her, not even Kathy Sumpter, with her brazen blue eyes and voluptuous red lips and hips that suggested songs of love. This girl had henna-red hair that fell to her slim waist and shy turquoise eyes that washed over him with the gentleness of a spring shower. Her hands that deftly washed the dishes were small, but her fingers were long and slender. Her nose was perfect and her lips (with just the faintest touch of light orange lipstick) were lifted in a faint perpetual smile, as though life was one long joke. Small brown sunspots caressed her dimpled cheeks and the end of her nose to add character to her face.

She completely distracted him so he was unprepared when Packer came hustling back from the storeroom carrying a box with the provisions and beckoned him outside onto the cold verandah.

The big man was dictatorial.

'Now you listen, Cooley, and listen well! Your father didn't go to

172 /

court today, he's going tomorrow and it seems a pretty clearcut case against him. I saw him and there are several other reliable witnesses to testify against him. Is that clear? Do you understand?' Cooley nodded and listened to the breeze and watched the wind whip up little ruffles on the water of the pool. 'There's going to be some changes, now.' Packer was warming up. 'I want the chores done properly now. No more buggering around with those niggers from the camp. If any come onto this farm I'll have them for trespassing, OK?' Cooley nooded his windswept head and wished the fool would hurry up and finish his speech so he could go. It really was going to rain, he thought.

Packer continued, 'You thought you were hot potatoes with your big brother. Just don't forget I'm the one who pays you—if I feel like it. Next year you can work full-time, if you're any good. At least we can keep you out of trouble. I may pay you sixty dollars a week if you're any good. If you're not, you can clear off out of it for all I care. I won't want you around like a bad penny. I'm doing you a favour and giving you a chance, like your father would want me to do.' He paused and strutted a bit on the verandah, then hitched his trousers up and glared back at Cooley. 'So no more backchat. No more cheek and pull your digit out, smartarse, all right? Understand?'

'Mmmm,' Cooley murmured.

'What!'

'Yeah,' he murmured again.

'Yeah—Mr Packer!'

'Yeah, Mr Packer, that's as clear as water.'

'Good. Take this to your mum.'

Cooley glanced up as he left and saw the girl's face through the window, watching him with her strange calm eyes. As soon as she noticed him looking at her, she went back to her work.

All the way back to the Cooleys' house he didn't see the swaying trees and bushes and shrieking black cockatoos, or the flat ploughed red-brown paddocks pricked with green. All he saw was the smallish, slim girl with the soft eyes and quiet smile. And the long silky auburn hair tied in two plaits. He told himself that she would have nothing to do with a half-caste—but still, he could dream.

He got to school early next day and, when Morry and Shaughn came, they all had a smoke under the honeysuckle canopy of their castle.

'You comin' down to the bridge t'night Reg? I'm takin' Sarah

Pepper,' grinned the woolly-headed Shaughn.

'Why you always gettin' sluts, Shaughn? Must be that face.' laughed Morry.

Cooley lay back in the dirt. Today was a good day for him. His dad had gone, he'd met a wonderful girl and big Ben had scored four goals against VFL whom Western Australia had beaten.

Cooley's boss now. You can keep your black girls. You can keep your sluts. Old Cool Cat's got a real white lady, Cooley dreamed.

'Hey, what ya reckon, Cools? Old Black Mac 'ad an 'eart attack and now we're gettin' a new teacher,' said Morry.

Black Mac leaving! This truly was a day for rejoicing.

The next day, the principal called Cooley out and took him into his office.

'Your father has been sentenced to three years in jail, Cooley. This is a great sorrow for your mother, of course, but I intend to try and not let it affect your schooling. What I propose to do is see how your examinations go at the end of this year. That will decide whether you go on to the Maidstone high school next year. It would please your family and teachers very much if you succeed, of course. But only you can make the effort, Cooley.'

The half-caste listened with closed ears, returned to class and continued to read his comic.

Cooley didn't go down to the bridge with the rest that afternoon. Instead, he checked his rabbit traps up on the hill, then went down by the river that swept past Packer's mansion.

Here he saw the girl and in a moment of bravado he loped up to her. But when he got to her side, all his confidence and dreams vanished.

'G'day,' he said shyly and squatted down beside her. She glanced up at him equally shyly, then stared in horror at the three dead, limp bundles of bloodied fur.

'Oh, did you have to kill those beautiful rabbits?' she burst out, running a hand over the little bodies. Cooley was surprised out of his shyness.

'Uh? But, shit, they're only rabbits an' us fellahs gotta eat some'ow. That bastard Packer don't give us no meat, y'know,' he said, then could have bitten his tongue off. This girl was probably a relative of Pig Packer's and now she'd go off and tell him what Cooley had said. Now she'd never be his friend.

But the girl seemed to sense his thoughts because she smiled at him, saying, 'Don't worry. I'm only the maid there. You see, my mum died a while ago. Now I live with Uncle Reeney at the Two

Mile and work as a maid for the Packers.'

'That's tough luck, ya Mum dyin',' said Cooley. 'My mum died too, once.'

'We all have to die one day, I suppose. But thank you for your condolences.' Her voice was so soft and her eyes so friendly. She gave a smile that brightened up her whole face and emphasised her high cheekbones. She truly was a goddess in the boy's eyes. 'Let's not get morbid while the sun is out and it's such a glorious day. What's your name?'

'Aw, Cooley. Reg Cooley,' Cooley said, lying down beside her. He watched the movement of her hands and the movement of her body as she breathed, just as he would lie for hours and watch a bird building its nest or a wallaby with its young.

'That's a funny name.'

'Aaah, us blokes gotta keep our cool,' the boy returned, and joined in her muted laughter. It was the first time he had laughed for ages.

'My name's Rachel Layne,' came the soft voice. 'What does your father do? Is he a workman, or something?'

Cooley lost his smile.

''E's in jail.'

'Oh, I *am* sorry,' began the girl, but stopped short as Cooley's bony brown fist hit the green grassy bank.

'I wish the bastard had got fuckin' life instead of three pissy years. Still, when 'e comes out I'll be nineteen, then won't I make 'im sing for what 'e done to me. I'll give it to 'im good,' Cooley said, lips pulled back from his teeth, like a rabid dog.

Rachel stared at the boy and her turquoise eyes were full of wonder at the hate in his thin body. She felt like reaching out and touching him and drawing him into her soul. She too, was lonely here in this land of strangers, with only her Uncle Reeney as a friend. She sensed that Cooley could be different if treated kindly, and she was nothing but kind. She had never done a cruel thing in her life, perhaps because she preferred the company of books and paints to people. But she couldn't understand Cooley's hate, branded on him by his father's belt and white man's abuse.

Cooley stood up, shy again. He wished he hadn't become angry just then, when everything was going perfectly. Now who'd want to know a vicious little bugger like you, Cooley? All this talk of getting even, I don't know. You must be Al Capone, here.

Suddenly he froze into stillness and the girl, looking up at him, thought how handsome this strange boy was. At that moment some of Ben's regal looks, the same as a long time ago old Nat Cooley had had, showed briefly upon the boy's bitter face, and his amber eyes became as soft as his mother's brown ones had been. He moved his hand, indicating silence and then the girl heard the trilling notes of the bird.

'Cuckoo,' Cooley murmured. 'You only 'ear it in winter. Pretty sound, eh?' He smiled faintly.

He helped the girl up and she sensed his wiry strength. His yellow-brown eyes were warm now and he flashed her an even, white-toothed smile.

'S'pose you come 'ere tomorrow, Rachel. Might be I'll 'ave one present for ya.' Then he slipped away as silently as he had come into the green bush. For a moment the girl's clear gaze followed him, then she set off for the farmhouse.

Cooley thought, 'If she loves rabbits I'll catch her a few, then.' He made his way up to the sheds and proceeded to make two wire cages. For the best part of two hours he toiled at his task. After making the cages he quickly fed up, then heaved half a bag of oats onto the back of the ute and roared back into the rocky red hills. He came to his favourite warren, lying in a pool of white sand between two ravines and, in the dying light, his slanted cat's eyes searched the sand around the burrows. He found what he was looking for; tracks that said a rabbit was living there but hadn't come out yet. So he put the cages down and scattered oats in a trail up to them and their wooden floors inside. The trap was designed with a funnel-type entrance that let the rabbit in, but that ensured it couldn't get out. He stood up and surveyed the orange-purple sunset as the sun died again. His sunset—his land, and when all the white men were dead and mouldering, his spirit would live on. All the other dark, silent spirits that mingled with the mists or smoke from campfires, and whose voices echoed with the wind or didgeridoo—they would return and it would be their land again.

So, all in the space of twenty-four hours, Cooley had lost someone he hated and found somebody whose peaceful love puzzled him as much as his hate puzzled her. Cooley wasn't to know that this girl was to change his entire life.

He drove the ute back to the house, then collected the chicken eggs and chopped some wood without even being asked, so his stepmother gave him an extremely rare smile.

'Why, thank you, Reg. You *are* being a help since Dad's gone.'

Cooley shrugged and took his tea into his room, leaving her to

176 /

stand and stare after him. Old habits die hard, and he wanted to be where no one could disturb him. He lay on his back and thoughtfully chewed a piece of mutton bone from the stew. It began to drizzle again. His world was filled with the whispering rain that settled on the roof with a murmur and scratched the window pane gently. Just the rain and his dreams.

'Rachel Layne,' he mouthed and thought for a second. 'Missus Rachel Cooley,' he murmured and chuckled like the water running down the rusty pipe by the door. He repeated the words to see how they felt in his mouth, then began to dream and let his stew go cold.

The last event that changed Cooley's life was the arrival of the new teacher, Mr Roper. He was short and solid and brown, with greenish-brown eyes that shone like an eagle's under a jutting brow. He had thin lips and a crewcut and he was worse than Black Mac could ever have been. It was bad luck he and Cooley got off on the wrong foot.

Cooley arrived late, thinking there was no hurry now Black Mac had gone, and blundered into the strangely silent class. Morry and Shaughn were up the back, but Shaughn was sullen and Morry was without his lazy smile. All this should have warned Cooley, but he was in the middle of a Rachel Layne daydream, so didn't take it all in. When Mr Roper looked up at last, his eyes narrowed. Another Aboriginal—that made three boys and two girls. All troublemakers, obviously. He studied this late arrival with obvious distaste. He saw a long, curly tangled mop of brown hair falling like a crazy waterfall surrounding a lean face and resting on thin shoulders. Cooley's eyes were almost yellow instead of brown, and the whites a brownish colour. He had a thin, aquiline nose, slightly hooked, above thin lips. His chin jutted out stubbornly and he had high bony cheekbones. His body was in a permanent stooping slouch and his hands, thin and bony like the rest of him, were thrust into his faded blue trouser pockets. A thoroughly unpleasant sight, decided the teacher.

'Why are you late, boy?'

Cooley, to be the big man in front of the class, shrugged.

'Dunno.'

'What's your name?'

'Reg Cooley.' He grinned and winked at Marcia Quinn, who stared back blankly.

The teacher was on his feet so suddenly that Cooley reared backwards. He was prodded in the chest with a heavy blunt finger.

'Take your hands out of your pockets, stand up straight, and address me as "sir". And *never ever* come late to my class again, do you understand? You will come back here on Saturday, with your friends Garpey and Quinn. In fact, you may find yourself coming back the Saturday after as well!'

Cooley's jaw dropped. Saturday? What about football?

'Hey, but ...'

'Don't argue, Cooley, unless you want six of the best,' snapped Mr Roper. 'Get to your seat, this minute!'

For a moment Cooley hesitated, then he shuffled down the aisle. He would play anyway, and see what the man did. But Morry muttered as he sat down, 'This bloke's worse 'an Black Mac, Cools. 'E caned Shaughn and drew blood, look. We can't play either.'

Roper was satisfied; put Aborigines in their place the first day and you got results. He looked at the three Aboriginal boys. Big dark Shaughn sat sulking, with his head in his arms. His cousin, Morry Quinn, who was supposed to be a rebel and who fought at the slightest opportunity, had a face that was almost a semicircle from his round, receding forehead to his small snub nose and round chin. His hair, as black as an Apache warrior's, fell halfway down his back. His large black eyes hid behind long black lashes so he could look as innocent and demure as a young virgin. But he was the main troublemaker. Then Cooley. He was a body with no soul, no pride. Give him a good kick and he crumpled, afraid of the white man.

Roper set the class some maths. Most of them began working, but Cooley decided he would rather read his comic, since he felt in a rebellious mood. It was a good story—about Australians in Crete—and the first Cooley knew of Roper's presence was Shaughn giving him a warning punch. The comic was whisked away from him and he stared up into Roper's triumphant face. Said the teacher, 'Well, Cooley—commando, eh? *The digger.* Fancy becoming a soldier, do you? Defend Queen and country with your life and all that sort of thing? Mmmm?'

There was laughter at that, then Mr Roper beckoned to Judy Crow. 'Burn this rubbish in the stove, Miss Crow.' He turned back to a sullen Cooley and said ever so softly, 'Have you done the work I took great pains to print on the blackboard?'

Cooley shrugged, then swore loudly as Roper grabbed an ample handful of hair, pulled him painfully to his feet and sent him stumbling down the aisle. He cracked his shin on one of the desks and swore again, more softly than before because he finally realised here was a force to be reckoned with.

Roper turned to Morry, who returned his gaze intently and coldly, never wavering for an instant.

'You can join him, Quinn. I don't like my pupils eating in class.'

'Hey, what?' Morry's dark face crumpled in bewilderment. 'I was chewin' me tongue, sir, that's all!'

'Just get down there with your friend. It's obvious I'll have to keep my eye on you three.'

Morry stood up slowly, dignified, and sauntered idly down to Cooley, hands in pockets. A member of a dying race, refusing to give in to the white people who thought they owned this land—and owned this soul and mind, to thrust *their* ideas into.

They were both caned in front of the class with sisters and girlfriends watching. The dust rose off the patched seat of Cooley's old trousers and the thin whip-like cane stung into his flesh, drawing pain and blood. The same happened to Morry.

Then Morry sauntered back to his seat, his dark face showing no emotion: no shame at having been caned in front of the girls. His hands were in his pockets and his head held high, showing everyone, showing the white teacher, that no one could defeat Morry Quinn.

Cooley tried to act the same as Morry, but couldn't. White man had defeated *him* on the day he was born.

He had no identity and belonged to no tribe. One day he would skulk down by the railway line in East Perth or Midland or scrabble around in some rubbish tip or be found on the outskirts of some country town—an outcast in his own country.

He wasn't the only one. Some became famous at sport, but the famous one would be beaten or fade away into obscurity and those who clutched at him or her would have to find someone new. The white men would nod wisely and say, 'There you go; I told you these Abos couldn't stick anything out. They haven't got the willpower, see.' And the forgotten half-caste would grow old and die, clinging, to the end, to his time of fame in the white man's world. A forgotten member of a forgotten people.

Forgotten people? No, the white man's lust that had spawned this tribe then ignored it could never be forgotten. There would always be a drunk old man, begging for a few bob, angry, loud old women fighting outside a pub, thin little children playing in the dust, a frightened young boy in court. There would always be these people to remind the arrogant white man, who strode the land, that here were his half-brothers and cousins.

So Roper met some of these people and treated them as most other white people treated them—with contempt.

After school. Cooley made his way through the dripping quiet bush. For a white person, there were burnt slimy logs to trip over, hidden red rocks to stub toes on, prickle bushes to scratch the face. But Cooley's lithe brown form slipped silently through his bush. Tall green old trees with scratched scraggly bodies rustled to him from the grey drizzle and Cooley grew wet and cold. But he didn't mind. Away over a hill, a kookaburra laughed. The green moss on the knobbly rocks caressed his big flat feet, while his boots danced a jig around his neck. Greeneyes flitted in amongst the moaning, olive-coloured leaves and whistled to him. Parrots fled, shrieking over the hills at his approach. Cooley blended into the swirling shadows of the bush and the black cockatoos' cry echoed in his mind. Back, back to a thousand years ago when a wild, short full-blood had also fled silently into his sanctuary. Cooley's slouch and sullenness were gone, and a rare glint shone in his yellow, evasive eyes. Cooley was home. The wind that sang for him told him this, the leaves that brushed gently against his face told him; and Cooley was free, alone, a man again.

When he was here he could forget all about the troubles that fell upon his sloping shoulders. He could forget Packer with his red face and contemptuous blue eyes, he could forget his lying, sneering brood. He could cease worrying about the insults heaped upon him by the white boys in class, or by his family at home. He could forget the teachers with their canes and detentions and more subtle insults. Now he was Yagan. Now he was Pigeon. Now he was king of the universe.

He reached the rabbit traps and saw that he had caught a black one and two brown ones. For the first time he looked properly at the creatures—not just at a skin and something to eat, but the softness and the fear; the big warm brown eyes and long silky ears, and he was ashamed of killing his kin. Hunted by white man, they were hunted by half-caste Cooley too.

He put them all in one cage and began the long walk down to the river. The cage balanced on his shoulder and bit into his skin. The rain probed him with cold fingers and the wind whipped his hair into his eyes, stinging him. But he didn't care; he was doing all this for Rachel.

When he reached the river, he sheltered near a huge old white gum, whose mottled grey trunk kept away most of the rain. His curls were all gone and his hair hung like rats' tails down his rat-like face. He thought for a moment that she wouldn't come. Rachel wasn't Kathy Sumpter, after all. She had only been teasing him yesterday with gentle looks and soft words, the cruellest insults of all.

Then she came. She still looked beautiful, even in this cold, colourless environment, and Cooley felt a tug at his heart.

Rachel Layne smiled in happiness and turned friendly eyes up at him. 'Oh! Aren't they gorgeous? You've got a black one, too.'

He smiled at her happiness, then they started for the big house, Cooley carrying the cage. Rachel prattled on about what she had done that day, working in the kitchen and around the house. Cooley told her about the new teacher and the trouble he had had.

They stopped underneath the wattle grove and Rachel looked up at him with her gentle eyes. She murmured, 'Poor old Reggie.' Then her arms were around his neck and her mouth was warm on his cold face. She skipped back, lifted up the cage and walked off. Then she turned and smiled. 'I hope that makes you feel better, Reg. See you, maybe. Thank you for the rabbits.'

Then she was gone.

For a long while Cooley was transfixed with wonder. A girl had kissed him. A *white* girl had kissed him! Not Kathy Sumpter, but a real white lady. Cooley was really happy for the first time in his life. He could have floated over hills, he could have climbed Mt Kosciusko on his hands, he could have swum the entire length of the Indian Ocean. He wouldn't have cared. Cooley was in love.

The next day, at school, Cooley told Morry and Shaughn, while they shared a cigarette and a yarn before school. 'Hey, I gotta girlfriend. 'Er name's Rachel Layne.'

'No-one called Rachel Layne 'ere, koordah. Bet you bullshittin',' said Shaughn.

'Naw. She don't go to school. She works as a maid at Packers, see.'

'What you say 'er name was, Cool Cat? Rachel Layne? I bet she has been, too, by them Packers. Ole Ken'll 'ave sunk the bluey, no worries there,' Morry grinned.

'If 'e 'as, I'll kill 'im,' Cooley growled.

'Heeeeeeey, boy, you must be a solid man, or what? You Romeo or 'oo, Cools? Big 'andsome Cooley,' Morry laughed, and Shaughn joined in.

'Look 'ere at Casanova Cooley!'

'Cool Cat wanta look out 'is own woman, Kathy Sumpter, don't find out about this Rachel Layne. She'll make you koomph!'

'She'll go right up your 'ole, budda,' cried Shaughn gleefully.

'Aaah, Kathy Sumpter was just one girl, ya know? I'm talkin' about love 'ere. I caught 'er some rabbits and she kissed me properly. Besides, that Kathy Sumpter, she ignores me since that night, you know that. But me and Rachel is different, see?' Cooley answered, and a dreamy smile spread over his lean face.

Morry turned to Shaughn.

'Oh, Rachel, I love you true. You know I'm mardong for ya, girl. You just send me to pieces,' he said and Shaughn took up the joke with his assumed American Negro accent,

'Oh, hoooney! It's ex—sta—ceee! Oh, Cool Cat. Oooh, you big tomcat, do that to me one more time, baby.'

''Cos I truly love you, girl, Rachel,' cried Morry, slinging an arm around Shaughn's broad shoulders.

'Oh, Cooley, I love you, too. Shall we get married? Give me a kiss, honey, Cooley?' returned Shaughn.

Just as it appeared the two would actually kiss, Morry pulled back in surprise, saying, 'But 'ow? 'Ow shall I kiss you? I only did 'ave one kiss before, and now I forgot 'ow.'

Then the two cousins clung to each other laughing, while Cooley stamped off in annoyance. Everything was a joke to Morry. Nothing was serious to this little Nyoongah. One day he might marry, or he might die. He didn't care one way or the other. But Cooley did.

V

That Saturday, while the rest of the class went over to play Rocky Gully or watch their mates and boyfriends, the three Aborigines sat in the large empty classroom doing maths, watched over by Mr Roper, who sat like a stone up front. The sun shone through the windows and mocked them, as it was a beautiful day for once. A day for walking in the bush, searching for the wild bees' honey, or rabbits, or baby foxes in the caves of the hills. This was a day for enjoyment, not for doing something they could only half-comprehend, anyway—if that. The trees threw green shadows onto the dusty chipped floor. Outside, cheeky parrots whistled to the world and magpies argued in sweet melodies, while little birds of every kind joined in and sometimes peeped at the three miserable forms hunched over desks. This is worse than getting caned, thought the three boys. But at last the dreary day was over and they were free to run as quickly as they could from the flat, black playground.

On Sunday afternoon Cooley drove the old ute down to the Packers' mansion, to borrow some flour and sugar. He parked beneath the wavering blue-leaved wattles and ran onto the verandah. He would have been in a bad mood if it hadn't been for the thought of seeing Rachel. Thick black clouds heaved themselves over the gentle hills. Sudden bursts of fierce squalls sent the trees moaning and shivering and the bedraggled sheep into tight, wet groups. Lightning leaped over the sky and licked at the edges of clouds. On such a day he would rather sit and watch TV, or just sit, than run errands for his stepmother.

He pounded on the door and waited, then pounded again, not caring if he annoyed Packer, but wanting to get home as quickly as he could.

The heavy jarrah door was opened cautiously and the girl stood there, her soft body wrapped in a towel and her hair wet from the shower, her eyes apprehensive until she saw who it was.

'Oh, goodness! Come in, Reg. It's terrible outside, isn't it? Such a change from yesterday.'

'Yeah, it's bloody murder out there. That wind nearly had me off the road two times,' Cooley returned and moved inside, shaking the drips off him.

Once inside though, away from the wild frivolity of the wind and the rain, close to her near-unclothed body that smelt of lavender and orange flowers and sweet things in his nostrils, he became shy again and his eyes darted everywhere but at her serene face.

'You see, um ... looks like I disturbed ya shower, ay? I ... um, gotta see Mr Packer, see. About some flour and sugar. Make a damper, see, cos we're clean out of bread,' he dithered and tried not to look at her, so thinly concealed behind the thin towel.

'They've gone up to Perth to visit Mrs Packer and should be down tomorrow. I'll give you some flour and sugar, though.'

'What? You all alone 'ere? Don't ya ever get lonely?' Cooley said, surprised, glancing into her face and keeping his gaze there.

'No. Sometimes I like to be alone.' Rachel smiled at him, then turned. 'I'll just go and get dressed, if you would like to put the kettle on for some tea.'

Cooley stoked up the old stove until it was roaring, then put the huge blackened kettle on top of it. He found some bread and made up a little feast of bread and jam for the girl he loved.

When she came in she looked even more glorious than the first time he had seen her. She wore a pair of silk patchwork slacks and a silky blouse that hugged her body as tightly as any lover. Her feet were bare and pale and white and delicate like her hands, like baby mice or a butterfly, or petals on the prettiest flower in the bush.

'Why, Reggie! Jam sandwiches as well? You'll make someone a good wife, one day,' she smiled.

'Well, ya look a bit skinny. We gotta fatten ya up.'

'Goodness, Reg, *you* can talk about being skinny.' She placed a hand on his arm. 'Thank you, anyway, Mr Cooley.'

'S'orright,' he muttered, while his eyes flew everywhere like birds in a cage. They alighted on Packer's pipe that nestled in its rack on the wall, looking smug and content in all its affluence. A cheeky grin split his hatchet face.

'Wait 'ere, Rachel. Be back, d'rectly.'

The girl sat sipping her tea and wondering about this strange boy, then stared in amazement at the apparition in front of her before laughing.

For Cooley was transformed. He wore one of Packer's best suits upon his ragged shoulders, a silk tie around his scrawny neck and Packer's Sunday hat upon his unruly head, with Packer's pipe in his cheeky mouth.

If there was one thing he had inherited from his mother's people, it was the trick of mimicking, anything from kangaroos and emus to publicans and station owners. So, for a good while, Cooley had Rachel in stitches while he mimed to perfection his worst enemy. He had him buy his two sons, by mistake, at the pig sale. That was a good one. He had him caught by old Dean Garpey, with Dean's old lady. He copied exactly every habit old Packer had, from rubbing a nervous finger across his big bulbous nose, when he was excited, to scratching his rear after making sure no one was looking.

The girl was thoroughly entertained. Tears streamed from her eyes and she shook with laughter while she clapped her hands. This was better than watching TV or reading a book or painting a picture. At last Cooley ran out of ideas. When he sat down she looked at him and started laughing again. Cooley joined in her laughter until they both forgot what they were laughing at. They were just happy in each other's company.

'Aah, it's good to laugh, I reckon,' Cooley said.

He put away the clothes, but decided to light up Packer's pipe, just to see what it was like. So he smoked and they talked of the day's happenings. Then, at length, he had to go. It was growing dark and Mum Cooley and the kids were getting hungry, most likely.

His fingers, shy as bandicoots, touched her thick, still damp auburn hair and he murmured, 'See ya soon, Rachel,' while his eyes, softened now, glanced fully into hers. She saw his soul for a brief second before the whirling, howling night swallowed him up and whipped away her farewell. When she went back inside and saw the two cups, she, who had spent so much of her life in solitary joy, felt lonely for the brown boy's coarse words and gravelly laugh and cheeky grin.

In the days that followed she often caught glimpses of him as he walked to school, surrounded by the smaller, rowdier, white children of his family or as he trudged off alone on Saturday mornings to the football oval—or in Kelly's old orange bus if it was an away game. Then in the afternoons coming home, shuffling despondently along, muddy and bruised, with his head down if Herron River had lost. Or leaping into the grey sky, a bird for a moment, taking almost incredible marks, kicking imaginary goals and dodging unseen opponents in boundless joy if they had won. She would watch him as she hung out the washing or cleaned out a room, seeing him from the window. She would share his joy and sadness at these times and so became a part of him.

She would watch him feeding up Packer's stock as he effortlessly hurled bags of oats and bran around and the big square bales of hay. One day, she thought, he would be a strong man, and handsome, too.

One Sunday she awoke to a warm and pale blue day, with a soft wind ruffling the surface of the world. It was a truly glorious day and she decided to go on a picnic, since Sunday was her day off.

She busied herself around the kitchen preparing salads and sandwiches and meat. She was almost ready when Packer came in, having moved a mob of sheep closer to the sheds in preparation for carting to the sheep sales in Midland on Tuesday.

'Aah, going on a picnic, Rachel?' he smiled.

'Yes, Mr Packer. I thought I might see a piece of the country.'

'See what's cooking on the other side of the mountain, eh? Yes, well, you certainly picked a nice day for it. A very nice day,' the man bumbled as he wandered around the kitchen getting some breakfast together. 'Do you want the boys to go with you to keep you company? They should be finished yarding the sheep soon. You know you could get lost out there.'

'Oh no, it's all right, Mr Packer. I thought I might invite Reg to come. He knows the country inside out, I hear,' she said as she arranged the basket, so didn't see the look that spread over the man's red face.

He put his cup down abruptly and stared at the girl in consternation. Then he rumbled, like thunder before a storm.

'Reg? Reg Cooley is the only Reg *I* know. If you mean to go out with him, alone, into the bush ...' He let the sentence lie there like a death adder, full of buried threats.

'Mr Packer, Reg has been very kind to me. He gave me those rabbits for pets and he has never been nasty to me. I should like to repay his kindness now. Besides, I'm almost eighteen and can surely choose my own friends,' Rachel said gently. She smiled at the glowering man, who tried again.

'That's as may be, but his family and friends are a bunch of thieves and liars, a regular thieves' kitchen, indeed. You don't know his brother, but he's a common lout who was always arguing and fighting. He worked for me until I kicked him out. Of course you might have heard about his father, and blood runs with blood, *I* always say! Then his mates, like those beer-swilling Peters boys and Quinn and Garpey. Not to mention Lindsay Pepper, who's as many—faced as Rubik's cube. And anyhow, he's black—or brown—and you're a white woman.'

During this speech, Packer had moved around the room. Now he sat down again and took a sip of his tea. 'It's your decision, of course, but with no family to look after you I feel a bit responsible for you.' He smiled up at her, certain of victory.

'Thank you, Mr Packer. I'll go and get Reg now. The day will soon be over,' she said quietly, and left him sitting there, dumbfounded.

She made her way up to the shabby old house right at the top of the hill. As she passed the sheepyards, where there was a commotion of noise from sheep and dogs, and swearing, she got a coo-ee from Ken and a leer from fat, dark Lou.

'Where *you* going, sugar plum?' Ken shouted.

'Could you be Little Red Riding Hood, by any chance? Because I'm the big bad wolf,' cried Lou, and let out a loud wolf howl.

She ignored them and made her way to the clearing where the shearer's quarters and the milking shed were.

Up above, the sun seemed to drift from cloud to cloud like a butterfly, never stopping, because to stop would cause pain. It was going to be a wonderful day.

Mrs Cooley opened the decrepit door to Rachel's hesitant knock. Her hair was lank and untidy and the mumbling baby, Johnny, clung to her thin hip and stared at the girl while snot dribbled from his nose. The woman's faded eyes looked the fresh young figure of the girl up and down.

'Yes?' came her exasperated voice.

'I'm Rachel. From down at Mr Packer's. I was wondering if Reg was at home?'

'Oh. Yes, he is. Come in.'

Rachel edged her way into the room nervously. Like most quiet people, she didn't like being the star attraction. This was a dining room and living room combined, crowded with chairs and tables and a second-rate lounge suite and the television set. There were children all over the chairs and floor, it seemed, who stared at her out of predominantly blue eyes in an atmosphere that had gone suddenly quiet. She clutched her basket closer to her, nervous in this environment. She could sense the dislike in this house.

'It's a bit messy, now. You'll find Reg in his room out back of the verandah. Just go through the kitchen,' the woman said in her tired voice.

'Thank you,' Rachel breathed.

'What? Oh, yes. You're welcome,' the woman said unsmilingly, then she was gone.

The two sons of Lucy Fluter had been given their own room out in the back garden. Nat had built it when he first came there, so the two could have some privacy and the rest of the family could ignore the two black sons. It was merely a corrugated iron room about six metres by three metres, with two beds, two chests of drawers, a cupboard and an old armchair rescued from the dump on one of Ben's foraging missions. But it was their own piece of land and no one was allowed in there without their permission. Even Nat, when Ben grew up, kept away. Ben had jokingly called the room 'Cooley's Camp', which was indicated by a rough sign tacked on the door. Everyone needs a home to hide in, like a tortoise.

From inside, Charlie Pride sang songs of prison and cheated love and the wind played with a loose piece of iron on the roof, making a rough tune. A tuneless voice sang with Charlie.

She knocked softly on the door and was greeted with a sullen growl, so alien to Cooley's usual voice that she wondered if it was really he.

'*Now* what ya fuckin' want? Look, I cooked the bloody dinner last night, and gutted them rabbits. Can't ya do anything, ya stupid buggers? I might as well—' then the door opened and he stopped in mid-sentence, staring at her with eyes that melted from agate hardness to soft confusion and shyness. He stood there in a pair of faded dirty levis and nothing else. The sun ran hands as gentle as a woman's over his thin chest.

'Oh,' he said at last. 'I didn't know it was you. I ... you know ... um ...' he faded away, then grinned in embarrassment as he busied himself with the agile rolling of a cigarette while she stood there trying to think of something to say.

'Nice day,' he said at length, lighting up.

'Yes. I thought it would be a good idea if we went on a picnic. Shall we do that?'

She watched his profile anxiously as he stared out away over the hills to some land that only he knew, then he turned to her with the warmest smile he had given her yet.

'Picnic, eh? Ya know ... ya know, I never been on a picnic before.'

'Well,' she smiled back, 'there's always a first time for everything. If you don't like it, you can leave it.'

'Well, 'ang on. I'll put some clothes on. Come off the verandah, anyway. I aren't ignorant.'

She followed him into the room and gazed around at the yellowed clippings of football and boxing stars, the few naked white women and the big poster of Elvis Presley. They all lent the room an individuality and a warmth that the rest of the house lacked. One of the beds was lonely in its cleanliness, empty, with the blankets neatly folded at the end. The other was a mess of dirty grey-yellow sheets and thin grey blankets and lumpy pillows. A Sunday paper lay open at the sports pages and a cheap paperback lay spreadeagled on the floor near an ashtray full of cigarette butts.

Cooley went away armed with soap and a towel and she heard water gurgling in the wash-house next door. He came back as clean as he could be after a quick wash. He selected one of his few clean shirts and his old familiar brown coat.

'Righto. Let's go, then. Where ya wanta go for ya picnic?'

'Oh, some place nice.'

'Up to Watson's pool be all right. Gilgies and marron up there too. Might be we'll find a fox's place. But, like, it's your picnic, eh?'

'Watson's pool sounds wonderful.'

'Come on, then.'

She never forgot the joys of that day. It seemed to her that in the serenity of the bush the boy changed completely. His body relaxed and his eyes lit up and a tiny smile played on his brown lips. He no longer seemed clumsy, but glided along like an animal of the bush, noiseless and at home. Every hundred metres or so, he would stop and tell her what a sound was, or a sight meant.

'The place in those rushes is where yesterday a kangaroo made his home. Those marks means that a possum lived in this tree, probably in that dead branch halfway up. Those tracks are a fox's imprint, different from a dog's because of the claws. That sound is a rabbit thumping a warning to his brothers that strangers are about. That bird is a black cockatoo that the mob down here called munadj the name for police too; because once the policeman's uniform of dark blue was the same as the cockatoo's coat of feathers, some fellahs said. When you see cockatoos wheeling and crying, it may rain soon. That's a wallaby trail—different shit from a kangaroo, see? Up there in the tree is an eagle nest, not a crow's nest, which looks the same. See that bush there? That's what white people call a zamia palm. The nuts are poisonous, but if you prepare them in a special way, by soaking them in running water and things, you can eat them. Tastes like a tomato a bit, yeah. You ever eaten red-gum blood that oozes out and dries in shiny lumps on the sides of the trees? Even blackboys, you can eat the middle-of-the-bush leaves; just take hold of the centre spikes and pull them out and chew the greeny-yellow bottoms. See, they're delicious, taste like young almonds. In the dead blackboys you find bardi grubs that are all right, too. Sometimes you see a quondong tree and the red fruit is good tucker too, but I don't think there are any around here because it's the wrong country.'

On and on he went. Sometimes it seemed to the girl that Cooley forgot she was there until he turned and smiled gently at her.

'You need never be afraid of this place, sis. There's food and shelter all over for them 'oo know where to look.'

Go on, old Headmaster Cooley. This is *your* school. Never mind the building in the town where you forget tomorrow what you learned today. Come on, Professor Cooley, you teach these white people about your land.

Then he began telling her about his real land. Once, when they were resting, he looked up from rolling a cigarette and said, 'You know, soon I'm leavin' 'ere. My mother's land, and 'er people's land, ya know, well, that white bloke 'oo owned the station, 'e's given it to them now. Why, they got an emu farm goin' there, and a watermelon farm and all kinds of things there. You watch. As soon as I can buy a car. As soon as Ben comes 'ome, we're takin' off—'im and me. You won't see me for dust, girl.'

The pride in his voice transformed him. He wasn't Cooley the shuffling, snuffling, yellow Abo any more; he was Cooley riding a stock horse behind his herd of cattle upon the land of his ancestors.

'If I go up there soon, I could even go through the law. I wouldn't mind that, ya know. There was one white bloke there before and 'e shacked up with the leader's daughter there. Well, I suppose ya might call that old bloke the chief, I dunno. But 'e went through the law, scars and all. I seen 'em one time.'

The girl listened and feared she was losing him to this wild brown woman, the spirit of the bush. She touched him gently on the faded knee of his jeans, and his smile down at her reassured her.

'Come on, Rachel. We nearly there at the pool now. 'Ave some gilgies with our tucker, what ya reckon? Ya never 'ad gilgies before, eh?'

The pool was a small part of paradise. It was a roughly circular patch of water about ten metres in diameter in a hollow of the hills. A small clump of old gnarled paperbark trees, looking as if they had been there since the earth's creation, guarded the dark pool's secrets carefully. Covering the ground around the pool were clumps of wild couch grass and bushes that had stunted, fleshy leaves with a salty taste. The paperbarks looked like beggars in their ragged, scruffy coats, but they held their heads up in pride. An even older body of a huge dead white gum dipped into the still waters.

Once Watson's pool would have had a more musical name that sang softly from brown lips. How many stories had rippled across this small green pool like the webbed feet of silent departing ducks stirring up the water? How many campfires lay buried beneath the sticky warm black mud? How many dark young couples had lain together on the grassy bank, stared up at their stars and shared their dreams? Had these old paperbarks heard stories about the coming of the first white man, the ghosts of the returned dead? Then the orange flames rose high in wrath and shadowed faces gazed up into the sky fearfully, but the stars held no joys now. Had stories of the white man's cruel laws and uncivilised ways reached even here? Had the pool's own people been chased and raped and diseased and destroyed for ever, so only the stars and the moon and their reflections were left? Perhaps they had been friendly, awed by the arrival of the spirits of family, the *djanga* or *wetjela*. No one would ever know, not now.

One day one of the walking dead men, bringing the stench of his kind ever inland, had stumbled upon this piece of beauty and in arrogance had named it after himself—Watson's Pool. Now the stories were as dead as the gilgies or marron that the kingfishers had killed and eaten and whose dried orange claws were left strewn around the muddy, track-marked edges. But the pool itself would never die, because it was fed by an indestructible underground spring and would stay green and glorious until the end of time.

Cooley busied himself collecting sticks and old hunks of wood to make a fire in the lee of the grey, fallen giant's trunk. As soon as the fire was flickering softly he smiled at the girl.

'Get ya some bush tucker now, eh?'

He went down to the side of the pool with the billy and filled it with water. A series of small dark holes clustered in the mud. He thrust a long yellow finger down one and in a moment, whipped it out. A green-black crustacean clung desperately to him, and he flung it up the bank. The girl squealed, half in fright and half in joy, and he turned a grinning face to her.

'Catch 'im now, before 'e gets back into the water. Grab 'im by the 'ead, so 'e don't bite ya, see?'

He laughed at her gingerly-made attempts and her squeals, so she laughed too and finally got the prawn-like creature into the billy, where it thrashed around.

He made his way right around the pool, selecting holes, until they had about twelve gilgies fighting and squirming in the billy.

'Doesn't that hurt your finger?' she asked.

'Not much,' he smiled. 'I just think of the feed we'll 'ave d'rectly.'

What a feed it was. While the gilgies bubbled away in death and the meat Rachel had packed sizzled on the piece of tin Cooley had found as they walked through the bush, he told her more stories about his mother and brother. He didn't talk about his father. He told her about the country of his birth, of the sprawling station house with the wide verandahs and the frangipani and hibiscus trees in the big green garden and the purple flowered sharp-thorned bougainvillea that covered the verandah and the out-houses, of his raggle-taggle cousins and the games they had play-ed on the plain of spinifex grass and mulga and boab trees, or down at the waterhole where lilies covered the surface in coloured glory, as sweet as a nubile young woman—and where sometimes a crocodile lurked like an evil lover, ready to grab someone in a hug of death.

She, in turn, told of her life in the city, in a flat suburban land of houses and lawns and foreign trees and noise; a place where there were more cars than birds and more people than trees and no dreams at all.

She told of the private school she had gone to until her mother died, where all the girls wore the same boring fashionless uniforms and were taught to be 'ladies'. There had been no boys at all in her life, only when the school had an occasional social. She didn't tell how, after one of these socials, an older boy had torn away the only true thing she owned and left her broken open like an oyster. That was her secret.

So the hours drifted past like the clouds in the sky, and the morning became afternoon.

The boy glanced up at the sun peeping shyly from a cloud; his eyes peeped shyly at hers from behind his untidy brown fringe.

'Come on then, Rachel. I'll find ya some foxes now, if ya like,' he murmured from behind his cigarette.

'Could you, Reg? I've never seen a wild fox,' she cried happily.

They left the basket by the pool and headed up the softly undulating hills. Near the top was a jumbled pile of red-black ironstone to which the lithe youth glided, stopping occasionally to sniff the air. At last he beckoned with a crooked finger and, turning, pursed his lips towards a jagged hole. The earth was trodden flat and the bones of small animals lay round. Even she could smell the musky scent now.

'This fox isn't too clever, 'avin' a place 'ere. Not too many people come out this way, but, so I s'pose she thought she'd be safe enough,' he said. Then he whispered, 'Can you 'ear them?'

By concentrating her hearing she could just make out a faint whimpering and snuffling.

'Come on,' he said eagerly, and bent to enter.

'Oh, Reg, it might be dangerous.'

He grinned from the darkness of the opening and shook his head.

'Tracks tellin' a story 'ere. Ole Mum Fox gone for a walk and never come 'ome yet, see? There's no danger.'

Inside was a terrible smell and the walls felt too close, while the air seemed too heavy. But, in the corner, their little eyes glaring green in the light of Cooley's lighter and their little white fangs bared as their lips turned back in snarls, lay three baby foxes. It was the greatest joy of that joyful day for the city-bred girl to share for just a moment the primitive habitat of that wildest of animals and stare at her young. Was the mother old or young? Was that her first litter? How many would fall beneath the farmer's gun before the year was over?

She stretched out a hand to touch one, but the boy's hand rested on hers and he shook his head again.

'No, Rachel, ya can't touch 'im. Ya see, if ya do, the mother will leave 'im alone and 'e'll starve to death. More better if we go now, else our scent'll scare the mother away.'

'We'll leave them in peace,' the girl agreed.

They set off down the hill towards the pool and unobtrusively she slipped a hand into his. He turned and stared at her with troubled eyes.

'I like you, Reg. You're so kind to me. I don't care what anyone says, you're my best friend. No matter who says bad things against you, you're my best and true friend.'

''Oo says what?' he murmured, while his eyes darted away from her clear turquoise gaze like snakes in long grass. Then they glanced back again while he rested a hand on her shoulder.

'Mr Packer says I shouldn't go out with you. He says I might be hurt by you.'

'Ya told Packer you was seein' me t'day?' he questioned, surprised.

'I've got nothing to hide, Reg, and neither have you. Mr Packer doesn't own us.'

'Well, but, ya shouldn't of told the old prick. 'E can make things bad for us, ya know. 'E could make up a story and get me sent to reform school. That's what 'e said 'e'll do, any rate. Why, 'e could even send you away. That might kill me, you gettin' sent away,' he added.

'He can sack me, though he won't because I'm too useful and don't cost him much. But he can't send me away. I live here now, with Uncle Reeney. No matter what he does, he can't hurt us, Reg. I like you so much, Reggie Cooley, that words can't say.'

His eyes flickered at her a moment, then he turned away.

'Better get 'ome,' he mumbled. 'Got school tomorrow.'

It was a quiet walk home. Darkness slowly came down and purple clouds gathered at the edge of the world, ready for tomorrow. Cooley wished today could last a thousand years, but tomorrow was quickly coming with all its mysteries.

At the Cooleys' gate they parted.

'See ya when I see ya.'

'Not if I see you first,' she countered, and they smiled at the old joke. 'Thank you for the best day I've ever had, Reggie. It was marvellous.'

'It *was* a good day, eh?' he said shyly, and ran a hand tentatively over her face. 'See ya.'

She reached up and wrapped her arms around his skinny waist, then her moist red lips smothered his brown ones. Tongue met tongue in a proper kiss, while she sucked his soul dry.

At last they parted and she gave a wicked smile. 'See you, Cool Cat Cooley,' then she was skipping off down the hill towards the Packers'. Cooley turned and walked up the cracked garden path.

His quick eyes caught a glimpse of the curtain being lowered and when he opened the door he saw his stepmother's worried face and Sam's cheeky grin and knowing eyes. As he made his way through the kitchen, he could hear Sam's voice and the giggling of the two girls from where they sprawled in front of the TV set. But when he got to his room he lay on the bed and dreamed, amidst the untidy sheets and dirty blankets, about him and Rachel getting married: in a proper church, with a priest and organ and all. And Rachel in a white gown and veil, with himself ... He would be dressed in a purple velvet jacket, with a lilac silk shirt and black trousers, and a pair of R. & M. Williams elastic-sided boots, the very best in footwear. Ben as his best man would be dressed the same, and what a pair Lucy Fluter's boys would make.

VI

When Rachel opened the door of the kitchen, the three Packer men stared at her with smouldering eyes and said nothing. The only sound was the clatter as they ate their tea.

'Good picnic, was it?' old Packer grunted at last.

She turned from where she had been putting away the picnic things and smiled at the glowering trio.

'Yes, Mr Packer.'

'I was thinking, Rachel, that you need a bit more time off. To make a few friends and get to know people in the district. After all, I was thinking today, you came to work here as soon as you arrived at Reeney's, after your unfortunate experience. Go to the .

Katanning drive-in and the Maidstone disco. Let your hair down and make a few mates in your new home. Lou and Ken will be happy to introduce you to a few of their friends.'

'Why, thank you for the offer, Mr Packer, but I already have a friend in Reg.'

'Shit! With friends like Cooley, who needs enemies?' sneered Lou with typical lack of originality, and Ken, from the side, added, 'I'd rather be friends with Idi Amin than Reg Cooley, any day of the week.'

'You two get off and do your studies,' Mr Packer ordered, then, when the two boys had gone, he turned to the fidgeting girl. 'As for you, Rachel, you'd better go to bed and get some sleep or you won't be fit for work tomorrow. But just think over what I've said. Young Cooley's no good and if you get too friendly with him you're only going to choke off all the decent young blokes in the district who would be glad to take out a pretty girl like you. Off you go.'

She went out to her small room and lay on her cold bed pondering and absently fondling her pillow.

She showered and admired her young body, a gift for only one man, she thought. Who that one man was she didn't quite know yet. Then, warm and clean, she went to bed, holding her fluffy white pillow to her white body. In her dreams the pillow became Cooley's wiry yellow body.

So Rachel Layne taught Cooley love and Mr Roper taught him maths and another month went by. Cooley went down to the bridge with the usual gang on Saturday night. Morry had a couple of stitches under his eye from a punch in football that day. The person who gave it to him had a suspected broken rib and lay in the Maidstone hospital determined never to pick a fight with an Aboriginal again. Morry cuddled Judy Crow and bragged. Dan Crow told how his cousin had discovered some paintings in a cave down at Mandurah and had his picture in the paper. Aborigines weren't only getting their names in the paper for violence, Land Rights and football.

They played poker with a dirty, creased pack of cards. A red fire flickered shadows on the trees and the stonework of the bridge uprights and the dark shining faces of the boys and girls.

'There's a good fillum on tomorrow night at the hall,' said Danny Crow, who knew such things. 'One picture about Indians. With Charles Bronson as an Apache, too. Then one Bruce Lee picture.'

'Aw, I'll be in on that. Bruce Lee? 'E's a muritj bloke, orright.'

'Yeah, I know. I taught 'im 'ow to fight.'

'Fuck off, Lindsay. You taught 'im shit, budda!'

Cooley looked at their hybrid faces and strange thoughts churned in his mind. What were these people? Were they Aborigines? With clothes and boots, cigarettes and cars, radios and money? Greed and hate and jealousy? And a strange mongrel language, product of their mongrel breeding?

Once upon a time there had been a naked man on a red hill. Strong and healthy, with his spears and family and dogs—with his laws and religion. Then another man had come, white and weak and diseased, with his beer and smokes and clothes and hatreds. He said to the first man, 'Come with me and I'll teach you things you've never seen the likes of.'

So the Aboriginal had followed—now he died of white man's pox and drowned in cheap wine and suffocated in prejudices and his laws were trampled by white man's laws. They cried as all they had was turned to dust when they listened to the white man's lies. And the white man laughed and jeered at their plight and their efforts to mimic their masters.

But Cooley was happy. He thought he was all right now. He had a girlfriend, his mum didn't boss him around so much and he hadn't seen Packer for days. The kids at school left him alone now. And Herron River, for the first time, was doing well in the football carnival. But Cooley couldn't see that a different type of trouble was catching up to him.

It all began that night, when he was feeding up. He had just stoned two rats that writhed in death on the chaff-strewn brick floor when he heard a rustle by the door and spun around. He was expecting one of the Packers, but relaxed into a grin when he saw Rachel.

'G'day. I'm just feedin' up. Like to help me?'

'Why, yes,' said the girl, then looked in horror at the two dead rats.

'Oh, Reg!' she said reproachfully. 'Why did you kill those poor things?'

Cooley stared at her. 'Rats?' he said, puzzled. 'Hell, you love everything, eh? Rabbits, rats. Geeze, I dunno.'

Rachel looked up with her soft eyes. The love he felt for her chipped away a little more of the hate he'd built up against the world.

'I just hate anything dying. I don't see why other things should give their lives for man's greed and anger. Don't you think so,

Reg?' her gentle voice whispered.

'Well, ya right, Rachel. Do I care if the rats eat out Packer's oats? It's 'is bloody farm, any rate,' he smiled at her.

The girl's arms encircled his thin waist and her red lips reached up and met his brown ones.

'I love you, Reg Cooley,' she whispered, and her voice was so different to Shaughn and Morry's rough imitation that those two might as well never have been alive. There were only Rachel and Reg in a world of softness and love.

And love, to Cooley, was a waterfall, loud and powerful and forever. So loud it made the rocks shake and mountains tremble, so a man could not talk but only stare at the dancing rainbows in the mists that swayed over the wild, white water. And love was like a mountain of flowers, of red and pink and mauve and blue, standing supremely alone in a vast, harsh, dry red desert. And love was like the shape of swans flying into the sunrise of a cool morning, quiet and slow and rhythmic. Like the swan that gently crossed the sun's warm red heart for an instant, then faded into the greyness of dawn, Cooley allowed himself to float into the pools of the girl's soft green-blue eyes and their souls met.

This was not Kathy Sumpter with her eyes as blue as the sunstruck skies, as bright as the midsummer sun. This was not the girl who manoeuvred her body with the expertise of a machine, like a champion woodcutter with his axe or a jockey with a racehorse. That was Kathy Sumpter and her body. Rachel did not have Kathy's red-painted lips and purple-painted eyes, her powdered cheeks and the scent of cheap perfume to send a boy mad. Being with Rachel was not rocking and rolling among darkened trees with a wild moon cartwheeling through the jagged clouds, making a boy wild and crazy as well—for a whole night.

This girl was as shy as he was. Her small dainty hands fluttered and hovered like hummingbirds and delved into the flowers of youth to get some sweet honey. Her mouth tasted like mint. The petals of her clothes were folded away to reveal a flower the beauty of which had never been seen before. So soft and white like the most delicate rose, like jasmine, like a lily of the field. This was a girl whose eyes were coloured like the hearts of oceans, whose mind and soul and love was as deep as the oceans and just as secret.

Cooley's heart felt like bursting. The girl's pale fingers wiped away the last shards of hate and mistrust from his slanted, light eyes and her soft murmurs of passion wiped away his tension and hate so that the fortress he had built himself came crashing down and he stepped from the ruins like a prince freed from some evil spell.

The Nyoongahs down south said the swan was the soul of the dead and whenever a swan was born, another ancestor was reborn.

That day, Cooley was a swan. He would soar above the sun. He would dive to the deepest, darkest bottom of the ocean and learn all the secrets there. The whole universe was his, such was his joy. The girl's hands, as fragile and white as eggshells, had moulded him into a new being, a peaceful gentle being.

The girl wrapped long legs around his bony body, not like a spider catching another fly, but like a cool snowflake settling onto the brown earth as it prepared for winter.

Their bodies crushed the hay beneath the scattered clothes, so the sweet scent of the straw was their perfume. And so they loved while daylight died a graceful death and purple misty clouds spread over the sky like a blanket on a bed or a flag on a coffin. All the world's troubles were forgotten for a short while and the only world they knew was the warm feed shed and themselves.

Afterwards they lay in the straw.

'That wasn't ya first time, eh?' Cooley said softly.

'No.' She turned her head to give her strange serene smile. 'Does it matter?'

'Not to me. any rate. I s'pose ... um ... I s'pose ya me girlfriend now, eh?'

'Would you like me to be?'

'Well, would you like me to be ya boyfriend, but? Ya know what most people would say, don't ya?'

'No. What would they say?'

'They'd run ya down somethin' wicked.'

'We'll just have to stick together then, won't we?' she said and she leaned over and kissed him again, so he cuddled her for a second.

'We'd better get up before some of the Packers come. Wouldn't they spew if they caught us like this?' Cooley chuckled.

'No hurry. They've all gone off to Perth again. Mrs Packer doesn't spend much time here, does she?'

'Naw. Too busy, she reckons. Well, we got time for a smoke, then. Packer's animals can bloody wait t'night. It's our night t'night, ay?' he smiled, and ran a hand down her body. 'Ya so soft, girl,' he said in wonder.

'Here's a question, Reg. What would you rather be? A white man or an Aboriginal?'

Cooley smiled at her. 'What would you like me to be?'

'What *you* would like to be!' returned the girl, then they both laughed.

'I dunno,' muttered Cooley, suddenly serious. That was the thing about the half-castes—people imagined they had a choice. Some choice, since neither culture wanted them. Then Cooley put the question out of his mind and, jumping up, rolled them both a smoke and they dressed and began feeding up.

'I don't know how you can smoke these foul contraptions,' said the girl. 'Have you ever smoked marijuana?'

'I get in enough shit without 'avin' drug charges on me, too. Coupla blokes just out of Maidstone grow it, if ya want to buy some. Go into the Railway Hotel and ask for Les.'

'Goodness, whoever am I mixed up with here? You're a regular book on all the district's underworld activities, aren't you?' she giggled, and hugged him.

'Yeah,' he smiled down at her. 'I'll die a gangster's death, me. Real violent, same way as Baby-Face Nelson. Bugs Moran, that's me,' he grinned, surrounded by squealing pigs and with the remnants of the moon shining down casting sharp shadows on his face.

A shiver ran up her spine and she shook herself.

'Brrrr! A goose walked over my grave.'

'You cold?' he said, full of concern. ''Ere ya go. Wear my coat while I walk ya down to the 'ouse, orright?'

So he walked her home. At the door, as he was leaving, Cooley said, 'Hey, Rachel. Like to come and see me play footy on Saturday? We're playin' Mobrup for the grand final.'

'Why of course I will, Reg. It should be fun,' returned the girl.

That was when the trouble began.

Saturday loomed cold and wet, with grey clouds racing over the jagged horizon and cutting their soft stomachs open so the rain fell out. In the little tin shed that shook like an epileptic and clattered away to itself, the boys changed and froze, no matter how hard they stamped their feet. Jimmy Conner gave them some tips and a little speech about wearing the school's colours with pride—and a promise that if they won he'd shout them all to a party, with beer and a barbecue and all. This brought the biggest cheer from the ragamuffin boys, then they ran out onto the playing field and into the rain. The creaking old grandstand echoed to encouraging yells from the people who had come to watch.

The Mobrup team was undefeated; so was the Herron River side, and the game promised to be good. There was a line of cars and trucks huddled along the boundary, miserable in the rain. Men crowded into the bar so steam rose from drying clothes. It was important to supporters of both sides that their team won. There were many heated arguments, words spilling among the spilt beer, and everyone on the field had his personal supporters in the bar.

Even Cooley had someone to watch him today, for the first time. He could see her lonely figure standing under a drooping river gum; two slender white bodies together. Cooley had received a huge partner, bigger even than Wally King. But Rachel was watching today, so he leapt high into the air and won the first knock. He sent a long torpedo kick out towards Morry Quinn on the flank, and he scored a goal.

Wally King, Shaughn Garpey and Rick Mizen were excellent rovers, seeming to be in three places at once and the other players had it all over the Mobrup team, who had grown soft as the undisputed champions. They couldn't quite believe, even when it became obvious, that they were losing to Herron River.

Cooley seemed to kick a little further, mark a little higher and play harder now that he had someone cheering for him. He played so well that Jimmy Conner said at half-time, 'You're playing well, Reg. A good game, mate. Why you're as good as Ben ever was, no bullshit. I was thinking of changing you into Wal's place, because you drew such a big 'un, but she'll be apples, no worries.'

Cooley, shy of all the praise, wandered away. He glanced over towards the tree and saw Rachel waving to him. He waved back and was loping over to see her when the siren went for the start of the third quarter.

It was raining consistently now, coming down in a grey deluge, and play was sluggish. The ball was hard to mark because it was slippery and wet, but Cooley still took some good marks and kicked well. However, the torrents of water hid the game from the umpire and the Mobrup team started getting their own back on the cocky, jubilant Herron River side. Cooley was shoved in the back and went skidding through the mud on his face. Then, as he struggled to rise he got a boot in the ribs that winded him and a knee in the fleshy part of his thigh that nearly made him faint and sent a searing pain through him. As he was carried off in agony, supported by Morry and Jimmy Conner, he heard Micky Jackson say to Ken Packer, 'Look, he's so muddy he looks like a full boong now,' and their laughter followed him off the playing field.

They don't care how well you play, Cooley. There you went, thinking you were Stephen Michael or Maurice Rioli or the Krakouer brothers. But you'll always be a boong to them.

Then Rachel was by his side, staring worriedly into his pain-ridden face. 'Oh, Reg? Are you all right?'

Big Cooley, the man, speaking. 'Yeah. A little kick don't 'urt old Cools,' he wheezed.

He couldn't hear Jackson and Packer laughing now and was glad Rachel had come. The girl leaned over and kissed his wet, muddy face, then hurried off, calling, 'You take care, Reggie!'

He was taken into the tin shed and Jimmy Conner sat him up, head between knees. The young coach grinned.

'Who was that gave you the kiss of life, Reg?'

'Me girlfriend, Mr Conner,' Cooley smiled back. He was happy today, despite his injury. He'd had complete control of the game and had scored three goals and a point himself. Then, to cap it all, everyone had seen his girlfriend.

He went to have a shower then, and didn't see the thoughtful look in the man's green eyes. Jimmy had gone to school with Ben Cooley and lived only for football and girls himself. But the girl was white and Jimmy could see trouble looming, because they obviously loved each other.

VII

The next day was Sunday and Rachel was going to see her old uncle. She and Cooley wandered up the path to town from the Cooleys' house. It was a lazy blue day, with the remnants of yesterday's storm lying in tattered wastes across the sky.

Last night, there had been a party at Jimmy Conner's place, just as he had promised. But Cooley hadn't stayed long. He wasn't much of a socialiser at the best of times and he still felt sick from the blows he had received in the game that day. Besides, being in a crowd of semi-drunk white boys hadn't seemed like Cooley's idea of fun.

He had walked home and sneaked around the back of Packer's house and knocked on Rachel's window. Then they had gone for a walk to the sheds. They had talked and made love and talked some more.

So today he was relaxed and happy.

He showed her the long, low school, with the hedge and wooden verandah all the way around. One side was walled with weatherboards so the kids could eat their lunches in a dry place. The school was a ship of learning, sinking in the bitumen sea of the playground.

Cooley showed her the caning room and put on an act as though he had been cut. He got plenty of practice during the week. He mimicked all the teachers, so Rachel laughed and hugged him.

They wandered on through the empty town, past the two or three drab town houses with the wet white tin roofs, muddy derelict gardens and lopsided picket fences which huddled around the sprawling hotel with 'Orlando Wines' and 'Swan Lager' painted on the brick wall. The garage, swimming in yellow mud, with the grass-grown mechanics' ramp out back, with blue and red drums lying, strangling, in the hold of the wild oats. They wandered over to where the old hall stood alone, except for the trees and the main football oval. It was made of creaking wood, grey and moss-covered, held up by sprawling stilts, as though the weight of the building threatened to collapse any day. The tin roof was rusty and flapped noisily whenever there was a meeting on, or leaked during picture shows and church services, having no respect for human dignity. The old building knew so much; the arguments that had echoed around its walls, the sermons and services held within it, weddings, christenings and funerals, the picture shows it had seen. Only the hall knew what Lou Packer and Isobelle Clark had done under the building last night. Only the Hall knew where the three Crows, Dan, Judy and old Pete, slept while they waited for their house the government had promised them. They had been promised it three months before and still they slept under the hall, where it was dry.

The hall was far more than just a building. It was a social centre and a symbol of some sort of community spirit, much like a tribal meeting house.

Cooley saw Rachel off on the old, dented, orange-yellow school bus when Mr Packer went back to his farm after the morning session at the hotel. Then he set off more or less where his feet took him. He reached the dark old store, with tattered sale price notices sticky-taped to the window and a few rusted, battered cans sitting despondently on the dusty, barren window shelf. It started to rain, just a fine drizzle at first, and Cooley sheltered under the store's awning. He leaned against the wooden wall and waited for the rain to stop.

He noticed the mob of white boys come laughing and kicking

down the street, then fall silent and nudge each other when they caught sight of him. Once Cooley would have run off like a stray dog, at the sight of all those boys, but lately he had been left alone and his wariness had ebbed. So he stayed where he was, rolling a smoke, his biggest problem at the moment being that he was running low on tobacco.

Only when they surrounded him and stared silently at him did he realise his danger. Big Wally King, with his shock of hair and huge brown, almost red arms, matted with black hairs, stood in front of him. He smiled down with his wide mouth, but his pig-like eyes stared out, unsmilingly, from under his jutting moronic brow. 'How are yuh, Reg, mate?'

Cooley finished rolling his fag, then lit it and, taking a draw, gazed around the group. Besides King, there were little brown Rick Mizen and the white-haired Austrian Fritz Bauer, thin Micky Jackson with the wiry black hair and laughing grey eyes, the Packer brothers and Ned Grey, Stewie James who walked in a permanent stoop as though his lantern jaw was too heavy for him.

Eight blokes, Cooley, and those Garpeys and Quinns are all away down at the camp. Take it easy, boy.

'How are yuh, Reg?' repeated Wally.

'Good,' muttered Cooley.

'Got us a weed, Reg?' grinned Micky Jackson.

'Ahh, naw. I'm down to me last dregs, see.' Cooley was cautious. He could smell beer on Mick Jackson's breath and recognised the direction they had come from. The football party must have gone on all night and just finished that day. It had probably been a wild affair.

'What? Not going to give yuh old mate a smoke?' the white boy pressed.

No answer from Cooley, who shuffled his feet and wished he could fly. But his feet stayed firmly on the ground and the white boys still surrounded him. He looked up.

'Ah, look, youse blokes. I done nuthin' to you,' he whined. 'Why don't ya leave me alone?'

Wally King looked at the others.

'Our old mate here thinks we're hassling him. The star of yesterday's match and all. Isn't that what Jimbo reckoned?'

'Aaah, c'mon, Cools. We're just having a little talk. You too good to talk to us white blokes?' said Stewie James.

'Just because you can kick a footy around you think you're king of the bush, is that it, Cools?' said Rick Mizen.

'King Billy, more like,' smiled Ned Grey coldly.

Again no answer from Cooley, who was frightened now. He looked up and down the street for a friendly dark face. There was no one.

'What's your Dad doing, Reg?' grinned Micky Jackson.

'Time,' replied Fritz Bauer, and there was laughter.

'C'n I go now, youse fellahs?' Cooley pleaded.

'Sure, mate,' said Wally King, not moving.

Cooley rubbed a hand across his nose.

'Ya ... um ... ya in me way.'

'Am I?' grinned King.

'Yeah.'

'Aaaaah,' sighed the giant.

A chill ran up Cooley's spine and stayed there. He moved forwards, but a bump from King nearly sent him to the dirt.

Said the giant, 'Geeze, I dunno. Won't lend his mates smokes. Won't talk to us, pushes into me. It's almost as though old Cools wants a fight. And we being nice to him and all. You just can't change a tiger's stripes, can yuh?'

They all moved closer to him and Ricky Mizen wrapped a limp arm around Cooley's scrawny neck. He leaned close and whispered, 'How's your chick goin', Reg? She's real spunky, eh? I'll bet you make her grunt, you old tomcat. Kathy told us all about how good a root you do, know what I mean?' he grinned.

Cooley recoiled, snarling.

'You leave Rachel alone, ya white cunts!'

'Yes. That's just what you're going to do, Cooley,' said Lou coldly, speaking for the first time. 'You see, Ken likes her and he's taking over now. You go back to those gins where you belong.'

'Yeah, Cooley. You'll give her the pox and spoil it for all of us. So you can fuck off now,' answered his brother.

Cooley flattened himself against the weatherboard wall, his eyes turning to yellow slits of rage. So they would try to take the only thing that meant anything to him and spread her around on their filthy tongues and destroy her peaceful smile forever, would they?

All the white boys saw was a thin, weedy half-caste.

Then he sprang like a dingo, brown and sleek, into a mob of white sheep, all the more menacing in his silence. His boot connected with the Austrian, right in the stomach, and sent him sprawling to the dirt. A hard fist between Grey's eyes made him spin crazily into the wall and fall, stunned, onto the verandah.

204 /

Then King's huge hands grabbed Cooley's thin frame and hurled him back into the wall, where he stood shaking his head, dazed. He was in no condition to fight the six remaining boys who closed in on him, but he remembered something his brother had said, 'You face up to those white blokes, Reg, and keep standing up, else they'll wipe you into the dirt they think you are.'

Fight 'em, Cooley, fight 'em. Stand up for Rachel and Ben and Lucy Fluter and you, boy. Kill 'em, Cooley!

He kicked Mizen in the crutch and the boy dropped as though he'd been shot. His hard, bony fist shot out and connected with James's jaw.

Like a willy-willy he was everywhere, but the odds were still four to one.

First big Wally King punched him in the stomach and he felt like chucking up, then Jackson hit him twice in the face and Cooley collapsed. Now the Packers put their boots in. They kicked him in the face, head, chest, back and, finally, a few times in the groin, nearly making him black out. They kicked him as though he were the football that could have taken him to fame and pride and other forgotten, or not yet known words, one day. They staggered off, those brave victors, and left him lying, a small curled-up ball in the blood and mud.

He managed to crawl away before the people came out of the hall after church. He got out of town, then lay down in the green-brown arms of the bush. He coughed and spat out blood and wiped the blood away from his blackened eyes, while over the trees Sally O'Brien's organ boomed out melodiously and the priest shook hands with the congregation as they departed.

The pain of his wounds and the memory of his humiliation brought tears to his eyes. Several teeth were loose, he was sure he had a broken rib and his groin felt swollen to twice normal size. He ached all over.

One day soon I'll kill you bastards, he thought. You could do it, Cools. Make a bomb and blow the whole fucking lot into such small pieces the remains wouldn't fit into a matchbox.

He staggered home. The birds crooned in the leaves for their conquered brother. Branches touched him gently on the face and arms, but he had no feelings of love to return to them. There was a great killing rage in his heart.

When he got to the stumpy clearing, where most of the trees had been cut down, he hesitated in the shadow-dappled area at the edge of the bush. He decided to circle his house and get in his window, then no one would ask about his battered face and body. He lurched like a drunken man around the outskirts of the ragged bush. He reached the front side of the house, then his slinking form froze into the stillness of a stump.

Packer's Mercedes was parked there and the huge man was smiling down at his stepmother; his stepmother, whom he hardly recognised with her powdered face and lipsticked mouth and lank hair combed and tidy. Even while he looked, the man stooped and kissed the woman on her pale face.

Red rage shook Cooley's thin form. His eyes glowed like a lion's, tawny in anger. Oh, now he could see their little game! No wonder Mum Cooley hadn't been so worried about her breadwinner going away. Now everything became clear. It had been Packer's evidence that had condemned his dad!

Geeze, Cooley! You should of been that detective bloke, Boney. Don't you see? They must of planned it together. When his dad went out to see about the bull after his wife urged him to, she rang up Packer who drove into the garage, faked the robbery and planted the evidence to get rid of his dad.

Got out of his big, soft, double bed and fucked everything up. He owned vast tracts of land and two cars—both fine ones, no rubbish—lots of money in the bank and respect from the entire district. Now he had Cooley's stepmother as well, and that went just a little too close to the boy's heart.

For, although Cooley's dad had belted him, he had once been good to him. Besides, Cooley always associated his dad, Ben and himself as all together with Lucy Fluter in a time where dreams were true in the Dreamtime of the earth. His stepmother had always bullied him and treated him with contempt; now she was kissing, laughing, smiling at the man he hated most of all. Suppose he got rid of his wife and they got married, where would Cooley be? In the biggest problem he ever came across. It could never happen. Never!

His eyes were like the coming of a summer storm. Like the bursting of a rain-swollen river, hate and rage and violence flowed forth and swept away Rachel's love like the bloated bodies of sheep caught in the flood or the immaculate lines of Packer's fences flattened by the storm.

In his eyes shone a bright yellow light as dangerous as broken bottles. All the hurt he had felt on this day sent his mind reeling as he watched Packer place his arm around the woman and guide her along the path.

206 /

He was his old hating self, with a sneering snarl on his thin lips. What to do, Cooley? Then he remembered what he had said to himself once, when Packer had yelled at him for being lazy. 'One day I'm going to put a bullet through that bastard's head.'

Well, why not, Cooley? You got the gun, you got the guts. Hey, you'll be main actor, Cooley. You'll be Number One.

He sneaked through the tall greenness of the wild oats that sought to dissuade him with soft gentle whispers. The birds in the old grapevine whistled, 'Look out, Cooley, and have some sense.' But he was a volcano with bubbling red and yellow larva in his brain. He crawled along the tumbledown stone wall surrounding the back garden that was rife with weeds. All the children were over at Kelly's, he remembered. Only Mum Cooley and Packer were there—with the angry, thin brown snake edging through the mess of the untidy garden, ready to strike with the deadliness of a king brown.

You've had it, Packer. You've boiled your billy.

He climbed in through the window of his room. Out back, near the laundry, cold and ignored. That was Cooley. But not now. Cooley, the big man, avenging his dad, or really, avenging himself, his tribe.

He sat on his lumpy, springless bed then reached under it and carefully took out the gun. It was Ben's and only two years old, but Cooley had become acquainted with it and knew its every movement. How tight to hold it, where exactly to aim it if you wanted a direct hit. The shiny red wood had grown into him like a third arm.

Cooley adjusted the telescopic sights with reverence and a strange smile appeared on his deadpan face, while his slanted eyes glowed with a burnished yellow light. From a box he took a handful of golden slugs. It was Ben's gun; Ben had taught him how to use it. Ben would take part in this killing as much as Cooley would. Thus the Fluter boys would hold their own. An eye for an eye. That was the law from long ago, as ageless as the purple jagged ironstone mountains the boy could just remember. That was the law that kept people's pride aglow, like the fire that never went out.

As Cooley slipped out of the window he heard the deep bass laughter of his enemy and his rage poured over and spread through his battered, shaking body. Only one thought was in his head and he mouthed like the hissing of a snake, like the tiny sounds of a lion about to spring on his unsuspecting prey.

Just you wait there, Packer, laughing and drinking tea and kissing and rooting. Just you wait there, Mum Cooley, and watch your lover die. Just you wait there, all you white arseholes who hurt me and turned me into dirt. I'll show you a thing or two.

He slithered out of that house, along the bush to the cattle yards. He climbed up the slippery wooden wall of the milking shed. Thrown on the tin roof was a pile of bags and Cooley settled himself down. He was about three hundred metres from the homestead and the gun could bowl over a boomer from a mile away. He wouldn't miss.

Thunder rolled like the droning of a didgeridoo and clouds twisted and wreathed in a sky corroboreee. This was the time for his coming-of-man ceremonies. Now he would be a man, with man scars across his thin yellow chest and his foreskin ripped off with a sharp rock and his mother and uncles and old Bandogera shouting and chanting for him from the grey swirling sky.

Rain, like dust, touched his face with the gentleness of tears.

The old faded door of the home opened and Cooley took a slug from his pocket and put it in the breech. The bolt slammed home and Cooley raised the gun.

Packer was by his car and stooping to kiss his dishevelled lover when the shot rang out across the cold air, splitting the stillness. Packer fell, a fountain of dark red blood spraying from the side of his head, and Mrs Cooley screamed and screamed. The screams penetrated Cooley's hot mind and, instead of rage and triumph, he felt terror, stark and vicious like a slap on the face. Cooley slipped off the shed and ran for the bush. They would discover that the gun and he were both missing. Then the police would come and shoot him.

Oh, Cooley, you're in the shit now, boy. Those white fellahs are going to kill you. Run, Cooley, run. Think, Cooley, think!

But Cooley, never a great thinker, couldn't think at all now—his brain was frozen in fear. He just ran. Past the sheds, past the Packers' house, over the stone crossing that cut across the creek, and into the bush. He kept on running until he came to a little old rotten wooden cattle crate. Once, years ago, he and Ben had found it and quietly made a cubby out of it, pinching wood and tools from the Packers' shed and making a two-storey hidey-hole only the two brothers knew about. It was their castle, their retreat and the only territory Cooley could call his own, as a kangaroo will call a blackboy bush his own where he can sleep away the hot bright days, as a possum can call a hole in a tree his own.

So Cooley came back to it.

His boots were wet from the puddles he'd stepped into. His thin trousers and coat were wet and the wind that sliced between the cracks of the slapdash walls froze him. His long curls were gone and the wet rattails of his hair fell in his eyes. Poor Cooley.

He got right up in the darkest corner where the top floor still stood. It was dry and dark, if not warm. Cooley's wild eyes kept a sharp lookout and his thin hands kept a firm grip of the gun.

What, Cooley? You a relation to the Governor brothers, or Musquito, or who? Cooley, here come the white men, creeping, creeping. Ready to pull you under and wipe you out. Old Nigger Cooley, you're nothing to them. You killed the richest man in the district, just like flicking your fingers. And what about Rachel, boy? You see her when you killed them rats and rabbits. Now you killed a man. She'll go right off you, Cooley.

Everyone was against him and Cooley was afraid.

Mrs Cooley had not wasted any time. Still in serious shock, she had covered the dead man with a blanket, then rung the Maidstone police. For once the police had been fast in coming out. The big sergeant had said, as he looked up from the body, 'A three-o. Who's got a three-o around here, Mrs Cooley?'

'Why, Reg has one,' answered the woman, 'but he never uses it. He prefers his snares.'

'Where is Reg, Mrs Cooley?'

'I haven't seen him all day.'

'What was Mr Packer doing up here?'

'Why, he was just visiting, you know. Checking that we had sufficient food, you know.'

'Yairs,' the man said laconically, then, 'Well, do you know where Reg keeps the rifle?'

Mrs Cooley led the police into the little room out back and she bent to look under the scruffy bed. When she stood up, her face was a mask of pale, dumb shock.

'It's missing. It's not there,' she whispered. Then she screamed, 'It was him. I *know* it was him—the little yellow mongrel!'

The police car roared off down through the town and into the reserve. It stopped outside the Quinns' shack. A bigger quieter replica of Morry, with white in his black hair, stared placidly at the policemen and still kept puffing at his old black pipe.

'Good-day, Charlie. We need you for a tracking job.'

Charlie still stayed hunched in his greatcoat and grunted, "Oo ya trackin'?"

Inside the house, Morry, in the act of cutting up a stolen sheep, stood listening.

'Reggie Cooley. He done Packer in with his three-o and is still wandering about. He might have a go at anyone, you know.'

'Aaaw, yeah. Rightio,' Charlie said, and stood up. He got into the back of the car and settled back with his thoughts and his pipe. He was the best tracker this side of Carnarvon. Cooley would be found in no time.

As soon as the police car had zoomed out of the muddy reserve, Morry took off over to the Garpeys'. Shaughn was having a sleep, but when Morry shook him awake and told him in shocked tones what had happened, Shaughn knew where Cooley would be. He had followed Cooley once to the cubby house, curious to see where the skinny youth went when he vanished sometimes. So he would be gone for days and no one would know where he went, no matter how many times his Dad belted him or the teachers caned him. But Shaughn never told Cooley he knew, let alone anyone else. The big solemn Nyoongah knew the need for a secret refuge.

While the police and Charlie were scouting around the Cooley house looking for Cooley's tracks, the two cousins ran full pelt for the old cattle crate. They came around behind it and Morry called, 'Hey, Cool Cat. It's me and Shaughn 'ere, buddah.'

Cooley faced the door, gun raised, then lowered it when the two came in and squatted down.

Morry stared at the boy in awe.

'Shit, Reg. Waffor ya go shootin' Packer for? Dad's trackin' and there's three munadj with guns.'

Cooley spat and shivered.

'What 'appened to ya face, Cools? What's been goin' on t'day, koordah?' Shaughn asked, puzzlement in his dark eyes.

'You blokes gotta 'elp me. I gotta 'ide somewhere. You could borrow Norris's car, ay, and get me the fuck out of 'ere. I could go back to me own mob, up north.'

Morry shrank back from the figure crouched in the corner. He thought he knew this boy after eleven years. But when it came right down to it, he was as strange to southern Morry as the red land of his birth.

'No, Cools. We can't 'elp ya. You gotta give up,' he whispered, and there was fear on his dark round face where before there had always been laughter. Shaughn gazed blankly into the yellow eyes of the demon who had been born this cruel day.

For a long moment Cooley stared at the two boys, seeing them properly for the first time. He suddenly realised they had fought for him only because they had liked the physical act of fighting, not because of friendship. They hadn't laughed with him, but at him—like all the white boys. Now, when he really needed their help, he might as well have been a white man. He would get no help from these two.

He ducked his head and said in a weary voice, 'You two better go, then.'

Morry reached out a tentative hand to touch him on the shoulder, but Cooley shrugged away and stared out at the bush. The two crawled out and away, and Cooley was alone with just the singing wind playing on its wild flute. Alone as he had always been, now he had time to think about it.

Cooley waited. Like a human bloodhound, Charlie Quinn came closer and closer. The big sergeant looked at the rifle he held and hoped he wouldn't have to use it. This district was a peaceful one and the policeman was worried. He hoped he was handling this situation properly.

Aah, heck, he thought. It's just a kid out there. Most probably as soon as he sees our uniforms he'll give up.

It began to rain again but they were in the bush now and Charlie's sharp eyes picked up bruised grass and broken branches. Then they saw the crate.

The rain fairly swept down in grey slashing waves, hurling itself with the dedication of a kamikaze pilot onto the mildewed wood of the crate. The wind moaned through the cracks like the devil's dogs howling to a red moon on a black hill. It bit into Cooley savagely; it swirled the treetops around in a mad dance against the purple sky. Up above, the thunder roared and rumbled like an awakening bear. Even the weather was against him.

As he peered out the cracks at the grey rain and the thrashing trees, he thought of all those westerns he had read. What did all those blokes do to the bad fellahs, Cooley? Lynch 'em! Is that what they'll do to you?

Suddenly he saw a form coming towards him out of the mists of the rain and the swaying trees. He aimed and fired.

The sergeant shouted as Kenneally went down, shot in the shoulder.

'Hit the dirt, men! He's in there!' Then he muttered to himself,

'Shit. Perhaps I should of waited until the boys from Perth came down.'

Kenneally crawled back, pain written all over his young face. The sergeant gave the constable's rifle to Charlie, then stood up and shouted again, 'Settle down, Reg. Don't be a bloody fool now. Give up.'

But the wind tore away his words. All Cooley saw was a policeman yelling at him and he fired again. The bullet grazed the officer's cheek and he threw himself onto the ground. He motioned Charlie around the back way.

'If you have to shoot, Charlie, only wing him. He's just a kid, after all.'

Charlie nooded silently and crawled away through the dense curly jungle of the bush until he was nestled up against the crate. Through a jagged hole he could see Cooley, his rifle still aimed at the police.

'Reg Cooley,' he called softly.

The boy swung around, startled, and fear showed in his slitted amber eyes. As he raised the gun to fire Charlie stood up too and, raising his rifle, pulled the trigger. He meant to shoot above the boys head or in the shoulder, but he slipped on the long wet grass.

A hole appeared in Cooley's forehead and blood flowed into his eyes before he dropped dead. Quick and clean was Cooley's death.

They took Cooley back to town and the people stared as his body was taken into the hotel, where a doctor from Maidstone was waiting. Cooley, the dreamer. Cooley, the hate-filled and hated half-caste, Cooley, the dead boy.

After the inquest he was buried in the small cemetry out of town. Only the preacher, the sergeant, Rachel Layne, Shaughn Garpey and Morry Quinn were there. And Mrs Cooley for appearance's sake.

Not a big funeral.

Poor Cooley who was going to be a big, strong man who would beat up all his enemies, a farmer with his own land, a famous footballer.

Silly Cooley, born a half-caste, die a half-caste. That's life, boy.

Now the Cooleys have moved on. The Packer boys left school to run the farm and Rachel Layne hangs around with Ken Packer. You can't love a dead boy, and it can't hurt him now. Morry and Shaughn go down to the bridge with the other Nyoongahs, and no one notices the empty seat in the classroom. Maybe next year, in the football season, people will ask, 'Where's Cooley?' but it's unlikely.

So everyone has forgotten Cooley. Even big Ben, who got married over east and didn't come home after all. Grass grows between the stones on Cooley's grave, and a wildflower or two. Here lies not a Polly Farmer, Lionel Rose or Namatjira; only a small-town half-caste who tried to raise himself out of the dirt and who was kicked back down again. Only a half-caste, whose restless spirit couldn't let him laugh and live like his mates Morry Quinn or Shaughn Garpey—people who didn't care what happened day by day, as long as they ate, fought, smoked, had a girl or two—people who didn't mind living in the nothing town as nothings.

Only a half-caste who had been pushed around and beaten, humiliated, made to eat dust from the dust of his degraded life. Who, on his first day at school, as a six-year-old, had been pushed around the circle of grinning white boys. They had kicked open his new case and broken all his new things, then rolled him in the dirt that was to become his life. They had bloodied his mouth and nose and blackened his eye. That had been Cooley's introduction to the white man's institution of learning and his first taste of white man's law.

He had even been treated with suspicion down at the Aboriginal camp, by the old rusted railway. They had talked to him, but the shutters had gone down behind their dark eyes and the boy had never learned their secrets.

He had leaped high for the mark on cold grey days, sent long, graceful kicks up high in the air and listened to the shouts from the crowd as his thin, long fingers plucked the ball from the sky. He had dreamed of the day when big Cooley, Number One, main actor, ran out on the field in the state football team.

Only a half-caste who had lived in a world of football and dreams. Who had hated with all his heart, who had had his soul eaten out by white man's ways, but who had been killed by a black man.

Only half-caste Cooley lies here.

GLOSSARY

BANDOGERA	(norwest) bush turkey
BAROI/BARDEE	a grub somewhat like the desert witchetty grub, only smaller
BOYA	money
BOONDIES	rocks or stones
BUDJARRIE	pregnant
BUNJI	'to bunji around' is to go from person to person, conning them and so forth. A bunji (man or woman) makes love to anyone.
GABBA	wine; literally 'blood'
GILGIES/MARRONS	fresh water crayfish resembling the eastern state 'yabbie'
GUNYAH	bush hut
KOODGEEDA	(norwest) snake
KOOMPH	urine; urinate
KOORDAH/COODA	brother, friend
KWON	posterior
MARDONG	when someone really loves you and wants to go with you
MONAYCH/MUNADJ	police; literally 'the man with chains'
MOONY	sexual intercourse
MOORITCH/MURITCH	good — nice or pretty
NULLA-NULLA	Aboriginal weapon resembling a club

214 /

NUMMERY/GNUMMERAI	narcotic bush hence cigarette
NYOONGAH	originally the Bibbulmun people of the south-west but nowadays any part-Aboriginal person
ORGA, YORGA, OR YOK	women
TUPPY	vagina
TCHOO/TCHOO-CHOO	expression indicating shame or embarrassment
UNNA	'isn't that so' or 'is that the truth?'
WADGULA/WETGALA	white people
WINYAN/WINYARN	not altogether there in the head
WONGI	really the people from Kalgoorlie way, but any full-blood Aboriginal
WOODARCHI	evil spirits, small hairy men with red eyes, some say, or else a featherfoot
YARRAMAN	(norwest) horse
YORRN	an expression of sorrow